The Reticent Executioner

John Fullerton

GW00390835

S✲CCIONES

ISBN: 9781099713835

Cover design & typesetting by Socciones Editoria Digitale
www.socciones.co.uk

"We bear within us a reticent executioner, an unrealised criminal. And those who lack the boldness to acknowledge their homicidal tendencies murder in dreams, people their nightmares with corpses. Before an absolute tribunal, only the angels would be acquitted. For there has never been a human being who has not - at least unconsciously - desired the death of another human being."

E.M. Cioran, *A Short History of Decay*,
translated from the French by Richard Howard, Penguin, 2006.

1

Kramer lowered himself gratefully into the front passenger seat and pulled the door shut. He was warm and dry and the little car snug and scented by the woman at the wheel.

She looked not at him but straight ahead. 'Belt.'

Kramer did as he was bid, fumbled for the strap, pulled it across himself, snapped it in place. As they rolled out into the streets, he relaxed, lulled by the thud and scrape of windscreen wipers. His mind drifted free. He was mere lens, both passive observer and sound recorder; as the wipers juddered back and forth, the city's slick black streets swam in and out of focus, revealing ranks of redbrick terraces braced at attention.

Cocooned in the unmarked hatchback, Kramer floated between two worlds - that of his office with its comings-and-goings, slamming doors, shrieking telephones, loud laughter and louder profanities, glimmering blue computer screens - and their destination across the Thames in north Lambeth, located by a succession of police codes and acronyms crackling over the radio, all of which, taken together, unscrambled, amounted to a body, freshly killed, dumped in a doorway like so much fly-tipped waste. In the interregnum, with the Skoda hybrid butting through sluggish traffic, a delicious sense of illicit liberty enveloped him. Kramer's mobile beeped. He ignored it. It beeped again. Again he ignored it. The driver's cell buzzed, but she ignored it, too. Kramer spoke no word, gave his companion not a glance, though he was acutely conscious of her, her deft use of gearstick inches from his right thigh, her right hand light on the wheel, the rings on her fingers, the pink nail varnish, her pointy knees. No, no, he wouldn't look. Mustn't.

Once under Vauxhall railway bridge, they swept into the right hand lane and into the South Lambeth Road. Kramer tensed, took possession of himself, his interlude of rest at an end, blood strumming in his ears with a peculiar blend of excitement and dread that preceded all his murder inquiries. At the lights, just after Vauxhall Park, Detective Sergeant Nicole Arden swung left into Fentiman Road. Kramer scanned the industrial montage of crime detection: black and yellow police tape, uniformed officers in high visibility vests redirecting pissed off drivers, police motorbikes, the forensics van, a brace of scientific officers in white noddy suits and rubber boots, one tall, one short. He recognised the crime scene manager, baby-cheeked Roth, mountainous under his rain slick. Kramer absorbed the gaggle of gawkers braving the shitty weather - mostly builders in steel-tipped work boots and yellow safety helmets along with a handful of local residents huddled under shared umbrellas.

'A'right, boss?'

Kramer did not respond. He'd not said a word so far today, and in little over ten minutes it would be 8 a.m. Far too early for craic. He freed himself; his right hand released the safety belt, his left opened the car door before the Skoda had come to a halt. He was out, squarely on his feet, pulling up the collar of his pea jacket, adjusting his scarf and squinting over the car roof through squalls of rain at the forensics tent.

The tall noddy suit was Morrison, his shorter, squarer companion Brady. They staggered from van to tent, weighed down by large white cases. Rain needled Kramer's cheeks and scalp.

Arden glanced back. 'I'll get on with the neighbours.' She crossed the street at a half-run, so light on her small feet she seemed to float as if literally trotting on water, tugging her coat around herself and not waiting for a response.

Kramer turned on his heel, breathed in the metallic stink of what passed in London as fresh air, absorbed the images of the sodden park opposite the houses, its phalanx of glistening black spearpoints atop the iron railings, the lordly London plane trees, the squat and unprepossessing Anglican church on the corner, now disused and humbled by neglect like a dead armadillo gently decomposing, its flanks plastered with tattered red-and-white Party posters overlaid with black, spray-painted roundels pierced by giant capital As. Kramer was mildly amused. He summoned up an image of lads - black, Asian, chavs and jakeys and neds of one sort or another - out after curfew in skinny jeans, black hoodies, masked, with their paint cans, constantly looking over their shoulders. They were as plucky as their actions were Quixotic. Not everyone was so daring. Most surviving Anarchists along with Socialists and Greens were already behind the razor wire in Kent and Devon. Was it worth the risk of getting shot or banged up indefinitely? Decidedly not. For a moment Kramer imagined himself out there at night, loping through the rain, dodging armed patrols and daubing walls. It would be an act of resistance, admittedly, but a futile one. If someone was determined to risk life and liberty, and had the balls for it, then such an act of defiance should surely be effective. It would be necessary to strike the head of the snake, do real damage, not toy with it. He looked past the Sicilian deli and Portuguese caff (what had happened to the families of the Sicilians and the Portuguese, or that of Kramer's former dentist, a young and thoroughly professional Neapolitan?) and down the length of Fentiman Road itself, around four hundred metres in length, punctuated by speed bumps and two pedestrian crossings, extending in a more or less straight line as far south as Oval and ending in a church spire, a spiteful middle finger in red jabbed up at the low cloud.

Fentiman Road was a bog standard south London street, standard in that shoddily built late Victorian terraced houses worth well over a million apiece were interspersed with monster blocks of social housing thrown up by the post-war welfare state in gaps helpfully excavated by a Luftwaffe generous with its high explosives and incendiaries. The grand, self-important stucco homes at the Oval end, some them early Georgian, were worth twice as much at least - whereas most social housing had long since been sold off to private landlords or taken over by so-called housing associations. These days a grotty two-bed ex-council flat even here, in south London, could easily fetch half a million - far, far beyond Kramer's means.

Someone had told him - or perhaps it was something he'd overheard in the canteen - that Lambeth's professional criminal fraternity had decamped to the suburbs and commuted into the city centre to 'work'. Fentiman Road was part of territory newly captured, cleansed of *sans culottes* and colonised by the well-heeled: the divorce lawyers, the bankers, the City traders, the Harley Street medical practitioners, the architects, chartered accountants, public relations types and senior management executives. People like us. People who didn't get their hands dirty. People who didn't make anything useful. People who were overwhelmingly white and overwhelmingly Party supporters. The evidence was in the number and type of motors: Kramer identified BMWs, Volvo estates and Mercs. The quiet, dilapidated pubs where a punter could have bought a clean semi-automatic or any mind-altering substance known to mankind along with his pint just a few years previously had been refurbished as 'gastropubs' whose blinkered, braying, privately-educated clientele included hedge fund managers, commodity brokers and interior designers. Doubtless most of these recent settlers had their main residences in the English countryside,

3

and their crimes were far grander than a mere shooter and spliff. Fentiman Road was for their weekday pieds-à-terre. Kramer knew several Members of Parliament and peers lodged in Fentiman Road while the Commons and Lords were in session. He'd seen their plainclothes police protection officers slumped in waiting Range Rovers. It was a matter of convenience: Fentiman Road lay just within the Division Bell so that the oh-so-very honourable members of the Commons and Lords could be summoned to a vote the Party would always win.

Kramer pulled a black flat cap from his jacket pocket and jamming it down on his badly cropped hair, he followed DS Arden across the road.

*

He bent, pulled on blue plastic overshoes and gloves and pushed his way into the tent. He wiped the rain from his face with one sleeve, watched the technicians work, moving around them softly, silently, on the balls of his feet, keeping out of their way. He waited for the photographer to finish, then moved in closer. He was methodical as he was patient and possessive; this was his work, after all, his vocation. Kramer formed a mental grid map over the crime scene, noting details from the outside in. At 12 o'clock in his outer circle a key protruded from the Yale lock of 191's front door. He set about defamiliarising the objects before him, stripping them of their labels and seeing them anew, or trying to; the doormat was no longer merely a mat but a forest of closely woven fibres, the black tiles were no longer tiles but a slippery surface, slightly reflective, that had been scrubbed clean very recently, within hours or days preceding the killing. The door was no door but an ocean of gloss white besmirched by a swarm of sticky red ovals with tails, like tadpoles.

Kramer's face showed no emotion, but a slight tic appeared in the corner of his mouth. He put up a hand and touched it as if brushing away a fly.

The victim was crouched, knees bent, legs drawn up tidily, almost as if in death she was apologetic at having left her remains leaking on the black tiled doorstep; her weight was on her right side and what he could see of her face seemed ageless, smoothed out by loss of life, like a child asleep, just as her killer had left her. Her bottle blonde head, hair matted with her own blood, rested on the step. Once, no doubt, this woman had been a child herself like any other, laughing, loved and loving, entirely innocent. Only the previous day she had been a celebrity, rich, powerful and, according to her own lights, a highly successful career politician.

She wore what seemed to be an expensive cream and pink suit and blouse, tights. Chanel, possibly. The shoes lay to one side as if she'd casually kicked them off. The big mat - Kramer recognised the kind made by both guests of His Majesty and the blind and sold at John Lewis in Oxford Street - was drenched in her blood. Some of it had splattered the white front door up to waist height - those flotillas of oval tadpoles large and small.

With a rustle of his forensics suit, Morrison stood upright, nodded to Kramer. His tone was brisk, properly and self-protectingly distanced from the event itself and the emotions it might evoke. 'Right. You can see for yourself: single shot to the head. Seems she was forced to the ground, or struck so that she fell, then the weapon was held against her left temple. He probably held her still with his free hand. The bullet entered the left temple and emerged from the right temple. Straight through, more or less. If it had been a soft nose or hollow point the effect would have been very different. It's consistent with the blood patterning. Looks at this stage like a .38 or 9mm. If the latter, whoever pulled the trigger also retrieved the cartridge case. Weapon not found as yet. Probably happened very quickly. A couple of seconds.'

The misshapen slug lay in Morrison's gloved palm like a pulled molar for Kramer's delectation.

Kramer broke his silence. 'Shooter was left handed?'

'Difficult to say.'

'Try.'

Morrison didn't enjoy working with Kramer and Kramer knew perfectly well why - he wasn't prepared to wait until forensics were finished before making his own assessment of the crime scene; he always barged in.

'Yup. Probably.'

'And the killer held the muzzle against her left temple to muffle the sound?'

'Seems likely. Some of the noise would have been contained by the alcove anyway. If you ever feel the need to shoot someone in public, this is a pretty good place to choose to do it.' Morrison wiped his face with his forearm. It wasn't the rain. His exertions in the suit were making him sweat. Either that, or Kramer's questions.

'You said 'he'. Could the shooter have been a woman?'

'No reason why not.'

5

'But?'

'Male or female, the shooter was strong - strong enough or tall enough to force the victim to her knees quickly before executing her. There are no signs of a struggle.'

'Because she was taken by surprise, or because she knew her attacker?' Kramer didn't look at Morrison. His gaze was on the murder victim and he was addressing himself as much as he was Morrison and the corpse.

'That's your department, Kramer. Better wait for the Home Office pathologist. He's on his way.'

'Was she coming out of the house or going in?'

Morrison shrugged.

'Time of death?'

'From the state of the victim and the blood I'd suggest this morning, sometime after five. I can't be more precise. Sunrise was 7.10 and given that the weather was poor it would still have been pretty gloomy even then, notwithstanding the street lights.'

'Boss.'

Arden had stuck her head into the tent.

'We've a witness. Next door.'

Kramer turned.

Arden's large, dark eyes absorbed the scene; the body, the blood, the shoes. 'Resident in 189 heard a woman cry out, and heard some kind of a detonation. She thought it was car backfiring or a door being slammed. Looking out of her first floor bay window, she saw a tall, dark haired Caucasian walk quickly away along the pavement towards the corner of Fentiman Road and South Lambeth Road. The witness stated it was around 6.30 a.m. She swears he came from next door at 191.'

'Londoners do walk quickly in the rain. Age?'

'She's not sure. Mid 30s, she thinks.'

'Appearance?'

'Dark jacket. Slim build. It was pretty dark.'

'Where was he headed?'

'She says he went into the park in the direction of Vauxhall Tube.'

'The park was already open?'

'Apparently.'

'Please check. Had she seen him before?'

Arden forced herself to look away and she turned to Kramer. 'She says not.'

'Did she see his face?'

'Only in profile and at a downward angle. The witness called it in, by the way.'

'Find someone to take her in, give her a cup of tea and get a statement. Make sure she's not left alone. Get a WPC to keep her company. Don't rush it, let her take her time with the details. We'll need a police artist. Then organise a lift home. I want her DNA, prints and please test both hands for residue. We'll need all Transport Police CCTV videos from around the Underground and bus stations.'

'Boss - '

'*What?*' Kramer was down on his haunches, inspecting the step and the bottom section of the door.

Kramer stood then and so did Arden, facing each other. At a crime scene, the shabby little man with a bent nose was an elemental force, and God help anyone who got in his way or questioned his methods. For Kramer's part, he believed he knew what Arden was thinking: no-one is a suspect without probable cause, but then to Kramer the witness was just that. Who would voluntarily take it upon themselves to call the police in this day and age - an age of mass surveillance, detention without trial and secret trials - unless he or she had something to hide? It might be unfair and it might be counter-intuitive, but in this case it was Kramer who decided who was and who was not a suspect. Probable cause be damned.

Arden seemed to know he knew what she was thinking, and she side-stepped the issue - there was little point in trying to argue because she would lose, and Kramer knew Arden never did like losing.

'We know who she is. The victim, yeah. I recognised her at once and the neighbours confirm it. She's Party, something of a celebrity and on television a lot. Famous she is, yeah. Former fashion model and businesswoman. Ran her own agency and made a fortune when she sold it on. Now a Party spokesperson as well as a junior minister in the government. The new breed of ultra-patriots, so the papers say.'

Kramer squeezed his eyes shut and opened them again.

The media would be all over this. Flies on shit.

'Mostert. Chelsea Mostert. You must have seen her on the box.'

'I don't have tv. The name sounds Dutch.'

Arden's expression reassembled itself into one of disbelief. How could anyone possibly survive the week without a daily anaesthetic shot of consciousness-numbing, sleep-inducing television with its nightly farrago of so-called news? 'Well, maybe her family was Dutch originally, but she's definitely English. Born in Hampshire, childhood spent in Australia where her parents still live. Dad's a businessman, mum a former midwife. Private day school in London for four years, took a year out as a Party intern, then Oxford on a scholarship. I've googled her on my phone. She has her own website. She's a junior minister at Work and Pensions. Was. Sorry. Cutting benefits of the disabled and unemployed was her thing, aside from media work for the Party. Thirty-six, if you can believe that. I'd say she was well on the wrong side of 40. '

Arden was groping her way out of the tent.

'One thing, Detective-Sergeant - '

'Yes?'

'Whose house is this? Is it hers?'

The rain hammered on the tent and they had to raise their voices.

Arden shrugged. 'No idea.'

'Find out. I want two uniformed officers out back to watch the rear door and windows. Two out front. The shooter might still be in there. You're armed?'

'Yes, sure. Aren't you?' She knew he wasn't.

'Take two officers with you. Don't go in there alone. I'll get Morrison and Brady to go over it once we know it's clear. And bag that key in the lock. I want prints.'

Kramer knew perfectly well, all too well, who and what Mostert was, what she had been. She had indeed been a Party stalwart and television celebrity, the youthful, self-made, up-and-coming Party apparatchik with a growing reputation for ruthlessness. Her Party colleagues thought she could be a future prime minister; she had the telegenic looks, she had brains and she was utterly unscrupulous, willing to brand and re-brand herself every which way. A loathsome creature, to be sure. Perfect for the role. The pool of potential suspects was therefore big, very big - huge in fact, sufficiently numerous to embrace several hundred thousand people, perhaps more. Plenty folk loathed her guts, even if they were too scared to express how they felt and even less inclined to do anything about it.

'Anything else while I'm here?'

'Push the cordon out and close the street. All of it. Side roads, too. Everyone on foot heading to work, motorists, too. Males especially - heading towards Oval or to Vauxhall Station. I want their names, addresses. Put together a brief questionnaire. We'll test them later.'

An involuntary grunt escaped from Kramer; the collision was in his gut, a pang of apprehension and excitement. His passion for hunting the killer had locked horns with Kramer's instinct for self-preservation. A lesser man might have recoiled, but not these two Kramers, simultaneously investigator and perpetrator. He almost allowed himself a smile but thought better of it.

2

Arden held her peace, let the male chatter wash around her.

Ere he comes. Gawd, just look at im. What a bleedin shambles.

Spent the night under Waterloo Bridge by the look.

Snorts and sniggers all round with one notable exception.

Why doesn't get a decent aircut and shave?

Know what they say, doncha?

No, mate, we don't. But you're going to tell us.

E's not a Party member. I ave that on good authority, like. Amazin he got as far as DI without a Party card, yeah? Fuckin unbelievable. Must ave friends, know wot I mean?

Think he's a closet Trot, do ya?

Never packs a gun neiver. Keeps his piece in his office drawer. Unloaded.

Not one for regulations, then.

Law unto himself is Kramer.

Dunno how he gets away with it, really I don't.

Where's is bike?

Keeps it in a lock-up down the road.

Kramer's not English, yeah.

Yid?

Who the fuck knows.

Kraut, more like. Shoulda deported him along with the rest of them Eurotrash.

Fuckin immi-grunt. Probly one of them Poles.

Why haven't they given him the sack, then?'

Connections, mate, connections. Friends in high places. Has to be, yeah.

Arden stared down at her cappuccino, teeth clenched. This was too much. 'Because he's bloody good at what he does, you morons, that's why.' She regretted her sally in Kramer's defence the moment the words were out of her mouth. She would pay for her declaration of loyalty, for allowing herself to be so easily provoked.

Aha! Still carrying the torch for your beloved Kramer, are you, love? What is it he does, then, your guvnor, that's so bleedin wonderful?

Ooh, good in the sack, is he, DS Arden? Do tell.

Don't leave anything out, darlin. We want the full and unabridged X-rated version, straight from the back seat of your poxy Skoda.

Bit cramped isn't it, darlin? For a straight shag, I mean.

Thought he was married.

Yeah? Anyone seen er?

Kids?

Daughter, so I heard.

Looks like a scabby paedo if you ask me.

Arden's cheeks burned. She couldn't help herself. 'Fuck off, you wankers.'

Laughter.

They slumped on stools, elbows on the counter, shrouded in wet dog reek, four men and Arden, all plainclothes, all Serious Crimes or Homicide, all short of sleep, two badly hungover, and all concealed carry as per the new State of Emergency regulations. Three sucked on cigarettes. One chewed gum. They faced out through the plate glass window, mugs of tea and coffee in front of them, entertained by the parade of latecomers at Scotland Yard, formerly New Scotland Yard, while delaying their own entry to the rear of the stone-fronted, neo-classical Curtis Green Building until the last possible moment; to Arden they were overgrown kids playing truant. Now and then one or the other would lean forward and use his hand to clear the vapour from the glass. It was still raining.

Now they'd got their rise out of her, the aimless tide of drivel resumed. For the most part they spoke randomly as if to the world at large beyond

11

the misted-up window.

- And I said to her, if you want a cat, you'll have to keep it someplace else, I'm not having no animal in my flat. You can forget it. I hate the bloody things, I hate the way they smell and all the cleaning up. Who the fuck's going to do that, I ask you? All that fuckin fur. Cats ain't loyal and they ain't cheap, neither. Fuckit, no way.

- She's alright, she is. Built, and when I say built, I mean *built*. Not thick neither.

- Bit of alright, yeah. I like a bird with 'two and two is four', like.

- Arsenal, of course. I mean I know it's not a good season but always have, always will. I was born a Gunner, yeah?

- She can't get enough of it, mate. What's worse, daft cow insists on telling me the latest, follows me around with the latest episode. She seems to think it's real, that they're family. No, really she does. She cries when one of em is killed off, even what's-is-name, the nig-nog. I just switch off, know what I mean. Really don't have time for that shit, yeah.

Arden watched as Kramer, out in the street, played hopscotch over giant puddles in a futile effort to keep his feet dry; she noticed he still wore his bicycle clips. He'd been off on his own somewhere, but where? He gave no sign that he'd noticed them watching him.

*

Arden had never known Kramer to fail. His pursuit of suspects was relentless. She wasn't quite sure how he managed it, but from his behaviour - observed during the past eleven months as his junior partner - he was impatient of standard operating procedures and uninterested in the detail of forensic science. In fact, he distrusted evidence. He seemed to regard it as an impediment thrown his way just to trip him up and slow him down. He preferred to delegate all that humdrum legwork to her, and that was just fine; it was a great way for Arden to gain more experience and responsibility. His success seemed to boil down to stubbornness, a dogged refusal to accept anything less than capture and conviction, coupled by indifference towards the opinions of others, colleagues and superiors both, even if that opinion - especially if that opinion - was negative or clashed with his own. He was a dreamer, too, often lost in his own invincible, iron-clad thoughts.

Kramer had remarkable insight into character; where that came from she had no idea for he didn't seem to like people much and he wasn't in the least sociable. He was a loner with an eye for the faults of others. Arden decided that for some peculiar reason Kramer had made it his life's quest to solve murders and he seemed to do so by a curious trick of imagination, of intuitive osmosis, a sensing of how the crime played out, and, above all, by grasping the nature of the perpetrator for whom he seemed to have as much sympathy, or at least understanding, as he did for the victim.

Whatever it was, this instinct of his wasn't rational and it was beyond normal. Yet it worked, at least most of the time it did.

He wasn't interested in impressing the top floor, that was for sure, and he was genuinely uninterested in public acclaim; his attitude towards the mainstream media was one of ill-concealed contempt. She'd never known him to give an interview.

'Don't you want to talk to them?'

'Should I?'

'Don't you think so?'

'Would it help?'

'I don't know. I don't suppose so.'

This brief exchange had happened months ago during another case, but it had stuck in Arden's memory. It was notable not so much for Kramer's lack of interest, but his deadpan expression. At the end he had simply turned away as if she'd been wasting his time by suggesting he talk to the media.

The odd thing, too, was that even his successes seemed only to disappoint; once he had a convicted killer behind bars he seemed to plunge into dejection - until the next case came up. Success was always an anticlimax. With him it was a mania; he was always wanting the same thing, and getting it, and it was never enough or maybe it was the wrong thing. Somehow, fulfilling Kramer's desire to solve a murder was almost worse than failure. Detection work was his addiction, and like all addictions it was not something he could admit to. It was unmentionable. Yet he craved every fix he could get. It was the wanting that mattered, somehow, not the getting. All things considered, he was a peculiar bastard, a freak - though Arden would never say so.

Months earlier Arden had decided she couldn't make him out at all, but that didn't stop her trying.

The officers sitting on either side of her in the coffee shop had a soubriquet for Kramer, a nickname she thought inappropriate, after a vengeful character from their favourite reading matter: the Marvel comic books. It was the character known as The Punisher. Yet Kramer wasn't that way - at least, she'd seen nothing to suggest he was.

Aside from work, nothing else seemed to matter to Kramer except his daughter and his wife, apparently in that order, though he kept both relationships closely under wraps. He wouldn't speak of them. Nobody she knew had seen either of them. When Arden had broached the issue of family at one point early on in their professional association - a tentative effort to establish rapport with her weird, shambolic, monosyllabic and obsessive chief - Kramer's retort was as sharp as it was final: 'I don't do personal.' That was that. Arden had been warned off. She didn't try again.

Gradually she learned to respect the man, even revere him, though she was careful not to show it. She could never say she liked him; that would be going too far. She didn't know enough of the man to *dislike* him. But he was no racist. He didn't treat her as a woman but simply as a colleague; he had never made any reference, direct or indirect, to her being black or to her sexual inclinations. She appreciated that. His eyes didn't linger in all the wrong places; he never knowingly touched her, not even accidentally on the arm. He said nothing about her hair or her clothes or her legs (not like some), and he treated her as a fellow detective, as an equal. He didn't try it on with half-baked compliments, either. There were no stupid jokes about lesbians; he didn't patronise her about her driving skills and he let her get on with her job with minimal interference. If he wanted something done, he asked. Nicely, for the most part. He never invited her out for a drink or questioned her about her lovers, he didn't make jokes about black men and how big they were and, superficially at least, he seemed entirely indifferent to the existence of other people, Arden included. Human beings only seemed to matter to him in a functional sense, or when they were newly dead murder victims to be mined for information on the mortuary slab. And yet she suspected he had a soft spot for her, a protective and perhaps even a brotherly affection. Was she imagining it? Perhaps his very indifference - his lack of male neediness was another way of looking at it - was a form of reassurance. She felt safe; he was no threat. She had no idea why she thought that. Wishful thinking? Maybe.

Not that she fancied men at all, especially not male police officers.

It helped that Kramer wasn't handsome. He was very nearly ugly, but not quite. Arden had no idea how old he was; she thought he could have been

14

anywhere between 35 and 55. He had the eyes of an owl, staring and penetrating, yet without depth; their flatness seemed dangerous, they never seemed to blink and that alone was disconcerting. His nose was skewed and the bridge was flat; whether he was born that way, or whether it was the result of a sports injury or street fight, she had no idea.

There was something birdlike about him, not entirely human, that was both unsettled and unsettling; he seemed unceasingly alert, watchful, about to fling himself forward off his perch, to take flight in an instant. His was a face that looked as if it had been thrown together from spare parts found lying about a scrapyard: he was a mutt, a mongrel off the street, not a Cruft's pedigreed pure-bred, a common brown house sparrow and no robin redbreast.

In fact, come to think of it, what she really *did* like about Kramer had nothing to do with his appearance, but the blank space at the centre of the man, the empty quarter she couldn't navigate because there were no intelligible signs, no natural, recognisable features, no spoor or tracks. It was this missing element that she appreciated, this *absence* of personality. Kramer reminded her of one of those ancient maps where the baffled cartographer has simply written across unexplored territory: here be dragons.

There was perhaps some kind of dragon buried deep in Kramer; she imagined it must be scaly, fierce, fiery, with fangs and claws, and she prayed she would never have to face it.

'DS Arden…a moment?'

Something brushed her shoulder, settled on her arm.

Arden drew back at once. 'Sir?'

Detective Superintendent Malaparte had no inhibitions about touching Arden, or standing too close. He did both now, in the corridor. There was no escaping his immense belly, his soft, plump hands and his sickly cologne. It stank like insect spray, only the insect himself was wearing it.

Yuk.

'A word? My office?'

As if she had a choice.

He closed the door and went around his desk and sat down, steepling his fingers.

'Sit.'

Arden complied, reluctant, cautious, back straight, knees clenched, hands in her lap.

Malaparte was a man who smiled all the time. He had floated to the top of the Metropolitan Police Service or 'Met' on that buoyant smile; it was a smile that scoffed or ingratiated, a smirk of complicity or contempt. Arden imagined that Malaparte would smile even as he kicked the shit out of a suspect in the sound-proof basement cells nine floors down. It was said that Malaparte liked to participate in the more active interrogations, especially at night. Arden believed it. Once she had seen him well after midnight as he burst from the lift on the ground floor, sleeves rolled up, collar undone, shirt black with sweat, stinking of booze, jacket draped over one arm, looking mightily pleased with himself, as if he'd just scored a winning goal. There were flecks of what looked like dried blood on his collar and his cheek. The grin was in place, only more maniacal. He had been taken aback to see her.

It was also said he was one of the founders of the Party, and as a consequence had plenty of powerful patrons at Westminster. He was one of the Untouchables.

'How are you getting along with DI Kramer? Quite the oddball, isn't he?'

'Fine. Sir.'

'He wanted you for the Mostert shooting.'

'Sir?'

'Kramer said it was about time you had your own team, and a few homicides of your own under your belt. Said you were more than capable and that promotion was long overdue. He was pretty persuasive. He asked me to hand you the case, put you in charge. Surprised?'

'No. I mean yes.'

'Unfortunately, this is very high-profile. The Home Secretary asked for Kramer by name, I kid you not. I'm sorry. I knew you'd understand.' Malaparte raised his big hands, palm upwards. He was still smiling. What did he think he was doing? Trying to turn her against Kramer, to stir up resentment? The sick fuck. 'Regardless of his many shortcomings as a police officer and as a human being, Kramer is the best we have. He might not be fully house trained and somewhat unorthodox, but hey, he has the experience, the track record. His orders from me are to clear this up fast. We want results, DS Arden, and quickly. Yet we can't afford to take risks with this one. So it's a case of horses for courses, all right? Kramer's a

16

winner and I got to have an arrest by the end of this week. You do see?'

She nodded several times, her face stiff with dislike.

Why was he telling her all this? Why the laboured explanation? It could only be because Malaparte was trying to turn her against Kramer. If so, it was very much in character.

'You like working with him?'

'Pretty much. Yes.' She couldn't help the edge of defiance in her tone.

'Why?'

'He trusts me to do my job.'

'Is that right?'

'We make a good team.'

'He's lucky to have you.'

Arden hesitated, uncertain how to react to flattery, especially from Malaparte.

'If I were you, DS Arden, I'd be very careful.'

'Careful, sir?'

'Kramer's no white knight. He has a past, and it's not one most people would be proud to call their own.'

'I'm not sure I understand. Sir.'

'The number of officers with a criminal record is far bigger than you realise. It's around 30 percent in the Met. That ever occur to you?'

'No, sir.' What the hell was this?

'What would you say if I told you that Kramer once stole police evidence? That what he stole was a controlled substance?'

'I don't know what I'd say. I would find it hard to believe.'

'Did you know he had a breakdown at one point? They said it was stress.'

'No, I didn't know.'

'Does Kramer own a tie?'

'Sir?' She spat the word out, more insult than respect.

'Do us all a favour, DS Arden. Get Kramer to wear a tie, if you can, and encourage him to clean himself up. He can get rid of that leather jacket, too, and those cords. Jesus, the lining hangs down in strips. Fuckin' hobo. Sorry.' Malaparte shook his head. 'But I'm sure he'll listen to you. The Mostert murder is too big to have him looking like a tramp on the front page of *The Sun, GMT* or on *Newsnight*, right? He won't take it from me, but maybe a woman can get through to him, yeah? In fact, it's probably best if *you* handle the media. Let's keep him away from the cameras, shall we?'

Arden had a sinking feeling about the tie. Kramer listened to no-one. He made the rules, no-one else. He was no team player unless it was his team, and he would be delighted to be officially off the hook when it came to briefing the media.

'I'll do what I can, sir.'

You sexist bastard.

'Good. Good. That's the spirit. Now you're here, you might as well brief me on the latest.'

So that was it. Malaparte wanted his own nark on Kramer's team - and who better than Nicole Arden?

'Well. Sir. We've interviewed the neighbours, we have officers at the nearby Underground stations and Vauxhall bus station. Transport Police are giving us a hand on the trains. We're checking all the videos. We have distributed an artist's impression of a man walking away from the crime scene. We're doing a house-to-house out to half a mile. There's the family, of course - the deceased's brother is flying in as we speak. And we'll start interviewing Mostert's associates tomorrow. We're going back to the house with the technicians now.'

'Associates?'

'Ministers, MPs, Party members, office staff, constituency workers, her media contacts.'

'Tread lightly, DS Arden, for your own sake.'

Such concern for the detective-sergeant's well-being. 'Of course. Sir.'

'Leave the tricky ones to your boss, okay? Let him carry the can.'

Patronising prick.

'Ballistics?'

'An upgraded replica, 9 mil., but we haven't found it yet.'

'Ah, so not a professional shooter, then. Not a political assassination.

That's a big relief. An amateur with pliers and a file. That's why he didn't double-tap his victim. He had only one shot and had to take it at close range. He knew her, it's personal, someone close with a grudge. That's good. Very good. It'll be a lot easier to find the bastard. Am I right?'

Arden knew better than to challenge the Detective Superintendent's many instant judgements. 'Kramer says he's keeping an open mind. I mean, about the weapon.'

'Is he indeed? And Mostert's husband?'

'Boyfriend. They broke up. She was selling the house where they'd lived together for the past three years when she was shot. They'd had the cleaners in a few days ago and she'd come to inspect...'

Malaparte cut her short. 'He's also Party, you know, a big cheese. National chairman, no less.'

'Kramer will do the interview.'

'Do me a favour, Nicole. Keep me up to date, okay? Pop in now and then. Once a day, at least. Don't hesitate to call me on my mobile, day or night, if there's a break in the investigation. The Minister wants to be kept informed. This is very sensitive.' Malaparte clambered to got his feet, shot his cuffs, brushed imaginary dust off his expensive-looking suit jacket. Threw a big toothy grin at Arden. He was being chummy, or trying to be.

'One thing more. Kramer would be wise not to break too many eggs and so would you.'

Arden went to the door quickly, before he could get around his desk and intercept her, opened it and walked into the corridor. She was hot, her skin burned with suppressed anger. She hated it when Malaparte called her by her first name. He had no right. The dickhead wanted her to inform on Kramer and thought that if he waved the big Party stick at her, she would. The smug look on his bully's face told her he took it for granted she would comply if she wanted that promotion.

The hell she would. Malaparte could stuff his promotion where the sun never did shine.

3

Kramer had picked Chelsea Mostert from a large cast of possible candidates.

For the five months before her death - ever since the Party had been elected on 23 percent of those eligible to vote - he had sifted through the possibles. He thought about little else, weighing up his options. He worked tirelessly at the issue. He stayed up into the small hours with his online research, using an encrypted browser that also hid his metadata. He began with the overall picture. After a couple of months, he drew up a shortlist of fifteen candidates, gradually whittling it down to three. Then, little by little, having selected Mostert just days after their first meeting in February, he took the decision to go ahead. Once he had the who, he narrowed the focus in ever decreasing circles, right down to the tiniest detail: the what, the where, the when, the how.

He realised that what he was doing was running his own private murder inquiry, but this time backwards, in reverse and culminating in violent death.

At first it was as if he lived with her and she with him. She coloured everything around him red, red for aggression, red for danger, red for blood; she affected his perception of the world, the way a lover would, someone emotionally close, someone who shares a man's bed and his secrets. She became his filter, the lens through which he perceived the exterior reality, however imperfectly. He felt they shared everything, that all he had to do was stretch out a hand to touch her, say a word and she'd respond.

He wore out shoe leather tramping around her neighbourhood, regardless of the dreich March weather. Sometimes he cycled, but mostly he walked.

Kramer viewed Mostert's televised speeches and interventions in the Commons. Not just once or twice, but over and over. She became his obsession, but not an obsession of desire, of want, but rather the reverse.

That awesome smile, utterly fake. The stupid, vacuous phrases uttered as if she was in possession of the great mysteries of the universe. Sometimes the bonhomie cracked wide open like an ugly wound in the form of sneering put-downs certainly not planned by her speech-writer - then she inadvertently revealed her wolfish side, the forest predator waiting in ambush. Mostert had a considerable temper, Kramer decided, but for the most part she kept control of herself, at least in public. He pre-recorded her appearances on the 9 p.m. news, on the state broadcaster's *Panorama*, on *Newsnight*. In the mornings, she would sometimes be on the *Today* Program, huskily explaining the urgent, national security reasons for deportations (for their own safety), mass arrests-without-trial (for the safety of society), the banning orders, the registration of all foreign workers and issue of labour permits, justifying her own animus for people of colour and Muslims especially, pouring scorn on the 'wets' who mourned the abrogation of European Union human rights legislation, rationalising the cuts to welfare as 'living within our means' and dismissing rapidly expanding child poverty as lies of a subversive and unpatriotic opposition composed of 'foreign Trots'.

Opposition? What opposition? There was none, not really, not since imposition of the Emergency. The Labour Party had split three ways and imploded. It was no more. The Greens and Socialist Party had been banned, its leaders detained, Ireland was re-united and Scotland - Scotland was tearing itself apart with Westminster's underhand help.

Anyway, all that was a long way off and not Kramer's immediate concern; what did strike him was that Mostert's media interviewers never once in Kramer's hearing interrupted her tirades and they never, ever, raised a serious challenge. The journalists were deferential. Kramer understood perfectly; keeping their jobs and pensions depended on acquiescence - directly or indirectly, they were, after all, working for the multinationals and media barons (with offshore bank accounts) that donated so generously to Party coffers.

Was Kramer fixated by Chelsea Mostert? Of course he was in so far as she was a target; he admitted as much to himself. The plain truth of it was Kramer's loathing of the woman. He stuck her images up on the bathroom mirror and wardrobe door, and they gradually spread to the walls - her face, large and small, monochrome or in colour, torn from newspapers and magazines, from the glossy make-believe world of *Marie Claire* to the meretricious *OK Magazine* (she wore a bikini in the latter). He enjoyed spending his limited leisure cutting her pictures out with scissors and pasting them up.

Kramer was not immune to her beauty, but not in the way most males might obsess over an Alpha female. Was she attractive? In a repulsive way, sure she was. Very. The way love for someone turns sour, goes bad, becomes its opposite; they weren't so different, love and hate, and Kramer was of the view that of the two emotions, hatred could be the stronger. In this instance, the disgust was so strong it was irresistible - it drew him to her and drove him away simultaneously. That broad, sunny, innocent smile that disarmed the severest critic, the deep, caressing voice that won over innumerable English television viewers (especially popular on Youtube was her description of Muslim refugees as cockroaches), and dulled the ability of listeners and viewers alike to distinguish right from wrong. The hair, so natural, so blonde, so wild, so Malibu, so American *Vogue*. So feckin' healthy. How could someone so brimming with life, so young, beautiful, feminine, wealthy, fecund - yes, fecund - be so inhumane, so lacking in compassion, in empathy, in ideals? That healthy, outdoorsy, tanned skin of a surfer, the long limbs, the freckles, the pout, the full breasts, those blue eyes, oh, Lord, yes - and yet the image of the perfect Aryan seemed to Kramer to be vacant, a composite of beauty, a pastiche of a glamorous human being without a soul.

To the beautiful falls the right of command.

He sat or stood looking at her image for hours at a time, replaying her voice and video. He came to conclusion that the photographs, regardless of angle and light, didn't add up to her face at all. They were a mask, all of them, scrupulously painted, lit, shadowed, sculpted, commodified, touched-up, photoshopped, professionally marketed. The real Chelsea Mostert - if she existed - was nowhere to be found in that face; she was elsewhere, playing away from home, no matter how long or how often he tried to catch a glimpse of the real woman off guard. Perhaps she really didn't exist. It was this fabrication that fascinated him, aroused him and simultaneously disgusted him. Any desire would have been shameful, demeaning. Kramer imagined that it must be like falling for, and fucking, one of those inflatable sex dolls.

As objects of aversion and desire went, this one wasn't even real.

*

It was Malaparte who helped bring them face to face. All it took was a nudge from Kramer. It wasn't hard; if there was one thing that Malaparte could be certain to respond to, it was anyone who flattered his vanity, his gargantuan ego so hungry for validation. Malaparte had only one genuine topic of conversation: himself. Kramer knew Malaparte looked up to his subordinate and hated Kramer for it; the solution was for Kramer to be especially submissive and respectful to a senior officer steeped in self-loathing. Kramer would grovel if need be to get what he wanted, but in the event it proved to be easy.

Kramer had chosen the Christmas office bash on December 19 the previous year to set his baited hook. Malaparte, the senior officer present and someone rumoured to lead a Mostert Party faction within the Metropolitan Police, had been tipsy, slurring his words, staggering a little, trying and failing to touch up any female officers careless enough to come within range of his simian groping. For his part, Kramer was cold sober and wished he was anywhere but there.

Malaparte finally noticed him and lurched over.

They drank together, basked in feigned mutual admiration, the very best of pals, and Kramer steered Malaparte's endless monologue on himself to politics. Carefully slurring his speech, Kramer mentioned something he'd seen in the newspapers that morning about immigration from the Middle East and the several 'holding camps' on the outskirts of Brighton, Dover and Hastings.

'Join the Party, Kramer. C'mon, son. Do yourself a big favour. Join us. We're the future, and you should be part of it. We need people like you to make Britain strong again.'

It was time for Kramer to flirt a little, to let his boss know he could be seduced.

'May I be frank, chief? I can see the Party needs successful people like you, Detective Superintendent, but I'm nobody. I'm just a cop, one of thousands. I'm nae possible use to anyone. In any case, I know nothing of politics. Honestly. It's never interested me. I don't believe I've voted for twenty years. I wouldn't know how. I need guidance.'

A barefaced lie, but Kramer's apparent naivety worked. Kramer liked people to know he detested politicians of every stripe, and that to this rather simple-minded and poorly educated copper the evils of the contemporary world could be summed up by mentioning his four pet hates to anyone who would give him the time of day: the internal combustion engine, the telephone, television and the Internet.

Malaparte laughed, threw an arm across Kramer's shoulders, leant on him, made him stagger. They were like a couple bound together in a three-legged race. Kramer ignored Malaparte's sickly aftershave, tried not to look at the thick black hair on the back of Malaparte's hands.

'You underestimate yourself, lad. You do yourself a disservice. Actually, you're already a legend. Your reputation extends far and wide, but you knew that, eh?' He waved his free arm about as if illustrating the vast reach of Kramer's reputation, one that Malaparte resented. 'You should capitalise on your achievements. Don't give me all that false modesty. Its crap and you know it. Trust me. Let me help you to help yourself. After all, if it wasn't for me, you wouldn't be where you are now. As a Party member, your future would be assured. You would be protected and appreciated. So let brother Malaparte work his magic, okay? You are English born, aren't you?'

'Of course. Dorchester county hospital as it was then.'

Trust Malaparte?

'Good. I thought so, though I've detected a touch of Irish in your voice from time to time. You're not Irish by any chance?'

No dogs, no blacks, no Irish. No Scots, either.

Wrong again, Malaparte.

'You're very kind, sir. Maybe you could introduce me to some of your Party colleagues so I can get an idea of what to expect if and when I do join.'

'Splendid. Why didn't I think of that? You *should* meet the right people. Quite right to test the water first. There's bound to be something coming up in the New Year that would suit. I'll let you know. That's a promise.' Malaparte thumped Kramer on the back. 'I know they'll be chuffed to meet my top investigator.' Malaparte winked. He had adopted the terminology of the permanent political class, the drawl of a private education. 'Splendid' and 'actually' were but two examples. Like the late Tory prime ministers Heath and Thatcher, Malaparte had reinvented himself, adopting the tone and mannerisms of his social superiors and burying his own class origins. Here, resting in peace, lay the elisions, glottal stops, dropped aitches of Malaparte's undistinguished past. Hackney and Newham were out. Kensington and received English were in. It went with the rank, with the executive pay grade, the new Porsche SUV and Malaparte's newly acquired W1 post code.

It went with the *power*.

Malaparte whispered breathily in Kramer's ear. 'See, every mouse wants to be rat, you know that, right, and right now *you're* a mouse just like everyone else out there on the streets, but as soon as you join the Party, the very moment you get your Party card, you'll be a rat too, oh, yes, you can take it from me, and then it's only a matter of time, Kramer, before you become like me, my lad, a *rat-catcher*.'

Kramer nodded, utterly confounded, trying not to breathe in his superior's stink of brandy and cigarettes and cologne. Inwardly he recoiled, felt himself break into a sweat. What did Malaparte mean - a rat-catcher? What nonsense was this?

So it was that Kramer did meet Mostert socially and in public. On the evening of a chill and foggy January 14 they came face to face for the first time at a Party affair held at the Tate Modern for the official birthday celebration of the Party's founder, Richard Henning - now Lord Henning of Dulwich. Enormous red, white and black banners - essentially the St George's flag tweaked by the Party with the addition of black fascicles - hung down in profusion from the walls inside and out. Mostert even made an effort to laugh, somewhat uneasily, at one of Kramer's appallingly unfunny witticisms. Kramer did not offer his name. She did not ask for it and pointedly showed no interest or pleasure in the grotty little fellow without a tie who sidled up out of nowhere, stood gaping up at her like some dozy spaniel waiting to be petted or kicked. She gave no sign of knowing who he was. He was just another nobody, and the world was full of nobodies. Mice as Malaparte would have it. Why should she want to know? Kramer was content at this lack of interest, at the barely concealed contempt. It suited his purposes very well.

Once Malaparte had moved away, he pushed his card into her hand.

At a second public encounter, three weeks later on February 5, Kramer met both Mostert and her boyfriend, Ryan, at a very grand black tie charity fund-raiser at the Natural History Museum. First editions by authors approved by the Party were being auctioned off to a host of celebrities whose literature of choice had until now never extended beyond the Beano, the funds to be distributed among England's proliferating food banks. The auctioneer himself was a media celebrity, a tall, horse-faced newsreader with impeccable far right credentials and limitless self-regard along with a taste for tweed and club ties that he no doubt hoped would camouflage his central European origins so out of favour with the Party elite.

Mostert liked to project a tender, generous side to her nature and she posed - alone, without boyfriend - in glittery Versace and scarlet Jimmy Choos with stiletto heels on the museum steps as the paparazzi gathered around her. She said something to the microphones about the need to help those unable to help themselves.

Noblesse oblige at its most gracious.

Kramer wore a lounge suit he'd had - his only suit - for twenty years, a cheap number bought off the racks at Marks & Spencer. It stank of mothballs and seemed to have shrunk, or more likely he'd expanded. The trousers were too short and he should have had it cleaned, or at least pressed. He left his shirt collar undone, his only tie - a wool Stewart of Bute tartan - was looped loosely round his neck. As he walked up the steps, a private security man with a wire in his ear blocked his path.

'Sir. Invite?'

Kramer was not in the mood for explanations. He pushed his Met warrant card in muscle boy's face, but the man tried to grab his arm and Kramer blocked and applied a wrist lock.

'Gonnae no' dae that, laddie.'

Without letting go, Kramer moved up a step so they were level (other than the considerable difference in height) and ground his heel as hard as he could on the arch of the bouncer's left foot.

'Awa ta fuck.'

His path now clear, Kramer regretted the lapse - not in manners but the outbreak of his normally submerged Glesga accent, prompted by a rare surge of temper.

In the flesh, Mostert was a surprise to most people. She was much thinner and shorter than her televised appearances suggested. Kramer thought she couldn't weigh in at more than 55 kg, maybe less.

Ryan Exeter was also a surprise; he was nerdy with narrow shoulders even his two thousand quid Italian custom-made suit couldn't hide. With thumb and forefinger he constantly fiddled with heavy, framed spectacles set above a small, pursed, disapproving mouth. Who would want to kiss *that*? Kramer couldn't help feel gratified that the boyfriend was no Ayn Rand hero, no locker room jock. Kramer couldn't imagine them in bed. He just couldn't. He had read up on Exeter's political career, such as it was. The son of a Lancashire miner, Exeter had twice failed as a Labour Party parliamentary candidate, then reinvented himself as a Far Right local councillor in Manchester, and had briefly held the post of treasurer in another extreme anti-foreigner faction in Middlesborough. These turned out to have been useful episodes, for at the outset the Party had been composed almost entirely of the remains of anti-immigrant groups, racist factions and neo-Nazi dregs as well as breakaway militants from Westminster's own lunatic fringe.

Generously funded by two aged American billionaires with links to nationalist-religious zealots in a Near East pariah state, the Party had grown quickly, expanding its membership across the board to embrace the embittered, the low paid and dispossessed. It quickly gained the support of the mainstream media. Its roots were particularly strong in the impoverished former industrial and mining towns of the north of England where people, betrayed by Labour, lacked a voice. Exeter, with impeccable working class credentials, presented himself as the answer to their embittered entreaties, describing himself as a 'national socialist' in favour of autarky, whatever that was.

'Let me refresh your glass, sir.'

Mostert's glass was almost full, Exeter's empty. Exeter looked surprised, but he let the unctuous Kramer take it. As he approached the bar, Kramer looked around. No-one was watching. He was invisible. He emptied the empty champagne flute into an ice bucket and dropped it into his jacket pocket.

'Champagne, please. Two.'

He carried them back, handed one to to Exeter. Then he raised his own. 'To the Party!' The couple smiled at him, chilly, uninterested smiles, unsure if he was taking the piss, then sipped in unison, turning away from him as he was sure they would. To them, Kramer was just some gruesome bawbag, an unshaven Weegie with tenement dirt under his bitten-down nails and a brazen manner who'd by some fluke managed to weasel his way past the doormen and Party bouncers. Definitely not One of Us. Kramer was an embarrassment and he knew it. Exeter would not want to remember him as ever having been there, except possibly with a shudder of distaste.

Mostert gave no sign of having met Kramer before, of knowing who and what he was.

Exeter held Mostert's arm, giving it a vicious tug to pull her closer as they moved away.

Kramer heard some of what they were saying.

'…creep…?'

'Oh, please… Stop. You're hurting me.'

'Who is that..little shit?'

'Never mind…some hideous detective….nobody.'

'Don't give me that crap. Jesus, how could you…'

'Stop it.'

'…a bit of rough…you bitch.'

'…silly.'

'Fuck you!'

They spoke fiercely in hoarse whispers, Exeter leaning in close to Mostert, the jessie spitting the words out and gripping her wrist; so loud were these profanities that they turned the heads of other guests, attracting attention even among the catering staff. Mostert tried to pull away but he held on, then tugged her again, viciously. Exeter didn't seem to care that he was making a scene. Did they know that he, Kramer, could hear at least some of what they were saying? Did they intend that he should overhear them? Was it part of their game at humiliating people they considered their inferiors?

Kramer hung around, keeping them in view, advancing and retreating, hugging the walls, sidling behind the pillars and the ribs of reconstructed dinosaurs. He didn't speak to anyone else during his solo *danse macabre* under the bones of a Brontosaurus. He smiled at people he didn't know, waved to no-one in particular, slapped a self-satisfied smile on his face, played the part and kept circling, circling, reversing, padding about on his toes, taking small John Wayne steps, appearing to play with his phone, poking it as if tapping out text messages. He knew his tactic would pay off eventually, and it did. At 9.35 his prey drifted away to a deserted table littered with glasses and half-empty plates and took possession. They sat down and started to unwind, perhaps thinking themselves unobserved. Exeter dropped his jacket on a vacant chair, loosened his collar, kicked off his shoes. Mostert put her feet in her boyfriend's lap, having discarded her Jimmy Choo heels. The crowd of guests had begun to thin out and several of those still left behind were clearly the worse for wear. A waiter went over to the table and refilled their glasses and Exeter apparently asked him to leave the half-full bottle of Bollinger, which he did.

Kramer saw Malaparte take his leave, surrounded by his Party acolytes, then moved closer to the couple. They were entirely absorbed in each other, laughing and then arguing. Exeter pretended to slap Mostert, who promptly kicked Exeter with her foot in a very tender place, not pretending this time, making him double over. She laughed out loud. Exeter grabbed her wrist again and twisted it and it was Mostert's turn to wince, cry out and Exeter's to laugh.

Like kids who enjoy tearing the wings off flies, there were no boundaries, no limits for these two.

Exeter was totally blootered and Mostert wasn't far behind.

Then Mostert slapped Exeter, a wide, swinging blow. It snapped his head back.

Kramer winced. Now that *would* have hurt.

Exeter put his right hand up to his face, cupped his nose in his palm, then took it away, stared at the spreading blood, surprised, put it back. He stretched himself out, pushed his head back as far as he could, still cupping his nose.

Mostert handed him a tissue. He snatched it from her and pressed it to his face.

'Bitch.'

The tissue turned red and Exeter flung it down on a plate. It was some nosebleed; Mostert handed him another, and a third and fourth, but the blood kept flowing.

*

The day was far from over.

They were back in Fentiman Road at 2.30 p.m: Kramer, Arden, Morrison and Brady, all except Kramer wearing blue gloves and shoe covers, Morrison and Brady in their white spaceman's suits, head covers and masks.

Number 191 had been declared safe. No shooter had been found lurking inside, much to Arden's disappointment.

Arden consulted her notebook. 'Okay. Mostert put down a deposit of 250 grand three years ago, and Exeter paid the mortgage. That came to 2,500 quid a month, excluding insurance. It was in both their names. It was put on the market two weeks ago. Three days ago - Thursday, April 14 - it was cleaned from top to bottom by Dusters and Mops of Lewisham. I spoke to them. The manager said they vacuumed all the floor coverings and wiped down all surfaces, including windows and doors, inside and out. They took up carpets where they could, including doormats. He said the place was very dusty, but other than that, they found nothing unusual. The furniture and curtains had already been removed. They sent two people. The manager was worried by my call. He kept assuring me the workers were legal, that they were English and very thorough. They arrived shortly after 9 a.m. and finished around 5. They were let in by Chelsea Mostert. No-one else was present. Now according to the estate agent, there are three potential buyers. The asking price is 1.6 million and the agent says they'll get it easily. He said they'd get more if they waited, but they don't want to. They insist on a quick sale.'

'Let's go in, shall we?'

Arden stepped over the pool of congealing blood and up to the door. She turned the key in the lock - the same key that Kramer had noticed that morning. They trooped in, Morrison first, Kramer last.

The body was long gone.

The hallway was carpeted in plain blue wool, good quality pile, though heavily worn in the entrance and at the foot of the stairs. There was another big sisal mat similar to the one outside. The place was very Colefax and Fowler with thick, creamy yellow paper, and a stippled cream staircase, also carpeted. To the left a door led to the sitting room with a polished hardwood floor, possibly oak. The wallpaper was pale pink. There was no furniture. Kramer admired the original fireplace. In the hallway, on the right as they came in, was a ledge that formed the top of a wooden cupboard painted dove grey with a mesh door for the storage heater. It must have served as a hall table, given that space was tight.

Arden had more. 'There's a utility room and cloakroom off the kitchen. The house was built in 1907 and since then it has been extended and enlarged several times and not always well. There used to be three chimney stacks but two have been removed. The attic has been converted to a fifth bedroom. Aside from the cloakroom on the ground floor, there are two bathrooms upstairs. Mostert and her boyfriend apparently did some of the redecorating themselves. There's a cupboard door under the stairs that leads to the old coal chute - it hasn't been refurbished or turned into a basement as yet.'

They headed along the narrow corridor to the kitchen and conservatory.

Morrison ignored Kramer and turned to Brady. 'We'll start in here.' They

30

knelt on the black-and-white tiled kitchen floor to open their cases. They looked like priests about to celebrate mass.

Kramer and Arden left them to it and headed back to the living room.

'I need a pee, boss. It's not a problem, is it?'

'Use the bathroom on the landing.'

Kramer heard Arden go up the stairs. He waited until he heard the sound of the bathroom door being shut, bolted; then he went out into the corridor again and stood on the mat, his back to the front door. No-one was watching him.

From the kitchen he heard Morrison and Brady murmuring to each other and from behind, through the glass panes in the closed front door, the intermittent thump of cars hitting the speed bumps in Fentiman Road.

Kramer's eyes were on the carpeted stairs. Five, perhaps six, generations had lived here. Children had raced up and down, feet thumping on the bare boards, their childish cries in his ears. When the house was built, the first housewife would have had four or five jobs, from cleaning other people's homes to taking in washing, to help keep her family afloat while her husband laboured in a local factory. Her daily diet would have consisted of a single chunk of stale bread with suet or bacon fat. No wonder that In 1907 her life expectancy would not have extended much beyond 36 years.

Kramer pulled on two pairs of disposable gloves. He gave himself two minutes. It shouldn't take more - his warning would be the sound of the lavatory being flushed and then the tap running. It would be more than enough.

4

'How did you find out, Mr Mostert?'

'Ryan Exeter called me. He wanted me to break the news to our parents.'

'Which you did.'

'They never approved of him and he thought I should do it because I was family.'

'I don't envy you.'

The big man in the black, heavy metal t-shirt and black jeans didn't respond. His eyes searched the window hopelessly. Kramer thought he didn't look anything like his murdered sister. He sighed deeply as if to steady himself against panic at the greyness of this very un-Australian world in which he found himself. There was nothing to see out there, just another concrete wall blackened by ceaseless rain. In any case, it would soon be dark. Between the visitor's feet lay his overnight bag.

He was still shaken up from the awful procedure of having to identify his sister's body through a window in the police mortuary. Kramer knew the place: it had a little curtain and a vase of plastic flowers and the morticians tried their best with the corpse before the curtain was drawn back. But it was always a shock for the witness; it could hardly be otherwise in a material world where death was a taboo even now, seldom discussed, seen, let alone embraced as the sole universal inevitability.

'Did Exeter sound upset when he called, shaken by it?'

'Can't say he was, to be honest. Controlled, like always. He's a cold fish. He called my mobile. I was in Frankfurt negotiating a new deal. I was in a meeting, you see - '

Kramer cut him short. 'Did he say how he knew?'

Mostert shook his head. 'I didn't ask. I assumed it was the police. Wasn't it?'

'What time did he call?'

'Around 10.30. Central European Time.'

'So 11.30 British Summer Time.'

'I guess. You call this *summer*? Fuck, I *hate* English weather.'

Malaparte. He would have wanted to be first, even with bad news, especially bad news. He knew Exeter, of course. They were on first name terms, Party comrades, *rat-catchers*.

'So you dropped everything and came at once.'

'Yeah, mate. Wouldn't you? She is - *was* - my kid sister.'

Mostert was examining the tattoo on his right forearm with immense intensity as if seeing it for the first time. It was quite ornate and looked - well, it looked to Kramer vaguely Maori, but then he would be the first to admit he knew nothing about tattoos or Maoris, though he did know the latter were indigenous New Zealanders and that was about it.

'I understand you live in Cairns. I'm told it's beautiful and hot.'

'Yeah, mate.' He broke off his examination of his arm and allowed his eyes to stray. They looked at everything except Kramer, searching in vain for some visual relief, some comforting object - only there was nothing. The interview room on the ground floor - one of a dozen identical spaces - was tiny, beige and utterly bare. There was a table, true enough, three uncomfortable upright chairs, a wastepaper bin - all of it standard issue. On the wall was possibly the only interesting item: a big Most Wanted poster with the dozen faces, mostly bearded, mostly foreign, mostly brown or black, mostly Muslim, and the big street map of inner London opposite. There was no solace to be found anywhere in Scotland Yard for civilian visitors, confined as they were to the suite of ground floor interview and meeting rooms; at least, Kramer thought, David Mostert - unlike most of the 250 staff, Kramer included - had the privilege of entering through the front glazed and oval-shaped entrance off the Victoria Embankment with its grand double height ceiling and its rank of entry points in the form of hand scanners watched over by armed guards.

Kramer threw him a lifeline. 'I understand you run your own successful business.'

'Uh-huh. We sell aquarium tanks, big buggers,' he opened his arms wide, 'and the fish that go in them. Hammerheads, Great Whites, turtles, manta rays, barracuda, pilot whales, even basking sharks, right down to Clown

Fish and sea anemones, can you believe. You name it. It's a world market. We sell to the Japanese, the Germans, the Americans, the Chinese.' He was relieved to be talking about something else, something he was proud of and the words tumbled out of him, accelerating as he talked. An escape. He smiled. He was talking with only part of his mind, though - the rest of it was elsewhere. With his sister, maybe, naked on a concrete slab under a nylon sheet and about to be sliced wide open like pig's liver with a circular saw.

He added, with obvious and justifiable pride: 'We employ 28 people in Cairns and another four in our Sydney office. We're considering listing on the London market - you know, the smallcaps.' He tapped one foot on the dirty vinyl as he spoke.

Mostert was powerfully built, someone who had worked out with weights at some point, but he was also overweight. Well over 90 kg, Kramer estimated. He had a moon-shaped face, strangely innocent, unmarked by life. His eyes were brown, not blue like Chelsea's. He had unnaturally long and thick eyelashes, so oddly feminine that they seemed out of place. He had a smoker's muddy complexion.

'Mostert sounds Dutch. Is it?'

'South African, mate. South African of Dutch origin. My ancestors were 17th century colonists and they settled in the western Cape. My grandparents left South Africa during the apartheid years - they hated the racial system - and my grandpa started the business after World War Two. Dad and I just took it to a new level.'

'David - may I call you David?'

'Sure.' He shifted uneasily on the hard chair and his eyes made another circuit of the interview room. Kramer could tell that David Mostert wanted desperately to jump to his feet and run - run out of this sterile, lifeless place, down the corridor and into the street, into the English rain. Kramer had similar urges most days.

'D'you mind if I smoke?'

'I do. Sorry. What do you make of Ryan Exeter?' Kramer was lying; he didn't mind at all; in fact, he could have done with one himself, but the idea was not to put the interviewee at his ease but rather the opposite - by aggravating Mostert's craving.

'I don't know him that well, to be honest.' His tone suggested that he didn't want to.

'But you must have your own opinion of him, your impressions.'

Mostert shrugged. 'He's not someone I'd think of first if I was looking for a mate to go fishing with, or share a few bevvies with over a game of pool. Know what I mean? I wouldn't confide in him, y'know? He's no barrel of fun is Exeter. A cold fish as I said. Don't know what Chelsea ever saw in the pommy bastard. And I don't care for his politics. Sorry.'

'But Exeter and your sister shared similar views - politically. Your sister was a junior minister in the government, a rising star, and Exeter is party boss. Party chairman.'

'Yeah. True. They were on the same side - the *winning* side.' David Mostert's tone was bitter. He pulled himself upright for a moment, then allowed himself to subside against the backrest. The chair was small, low and hard and David Mostert was tall and broad with a big gut. He wasn't comfortable. He wasn't supposed to be. Kramer had personally selected the room and its chairs for the discomfort of his visitor so he'd answer his questions more readily and not waste his time, a subliminal brand of torture.

'Why did they break up?'

'I don't know.' He paused, his eyes settling on Kramer for a moment, then they were off wandering again. 'Well, that's not true. Exeter used to beat her up, you know.'

'He *did*?' Kramer allowed himself to look surprised, even shocked.

'Yeah. Oh, yeah. Slapped her about, man. Kicked her. Pulled her hair out. She told me.' This revelation was delivered off-hand, deliberately low-key.

'Why didn't she report him?'

'It wasn't something she wanted in the media, I guess. You know, it might have damaged her image and that of the government. And the Party's.' He smiled, though without humour.

'So you were relieved when they did finally split up?'

'He wasn't good for her, that's for sure. Yeah. Course. I was relieved. You betcha.'

'And?'

Kramer took notes. Just a word here and there.

'He was *very* ambitious. He was jealous of her success. They were always fighting.'

'You mean - '

'Arguing. They were going at each other hammer and tongs right from the start, but the physical stuff was new.'

'Didn't she hit back? Your sister was no weakling. She was tough.'

'Oh, yeah, she did too. She was a wildcat or could be. I know. She was a control freak to be honest. That made it worse. So he would creep up on her without warning and then *wham...*' Mostert slammed a fist into an open hand, smiled without humour, a grim rictus of pain. 'She said he liked to use a telephone book on her because it didn't leave a mark. She said it was a trick he'd learned from the UK police.' His voice had a tremor and rose in pitch. He was fighting back tears.

'How did you keep in touch with your sister?'

'Emails. A phone call on her birthday or Christmas. Mainly emails.'

'Did she ever tell you that she felt in danger?'

'Yeah.'

'Tell me.'

'She said she was being watched, followed. This was around six months ago. Then Chelsea said she was being stalked. She was afraid to be alone at night. She was afraid when Exeter was there, and afraid when he wasn't. She wasn't lucky with men. But this was getting worse, week by week.'

'Who was it, did she say?'

'No.' He shook his head. 'It seemed to get a lot worse, though, *after* they broke up.'

'Do *you* know who it was?'

'She didn't say. I don't think she was sure, or she said she wasn't. I know who *I* think it was. Mind, I've no proof. I just don't think she wanted to face up to it. Maybe she was worried I would come and over and sort him out. I asked if she wanted me to help look after her, but she said no, it wasn't necessary. I said she could take a break, come stay with us in Cairns. She'd be safe with us, no worries. She said she was too busy with elections. I must've asked her a dozen times, at least.'

'So who do you think it was?'

'Exeter, who else?' Mostert looked directly at Kramer, the anger he'd suppressed was now written across his face. It flared in his eyes, stiffened arms and shoulders, the angle of his head and neck, as if he wanted to reach over the desk and butt Kramer with it. His throat pulsed with the rage he was trying to control.

'Why do you say that, David?'

'She said she was thinking of getting a court order - whaddya call it, an injunction - to keep Exeter away from her, at a safe distance, but she was bothered about the negative publicity and the way it might affect her political career. I said she should do it anyway. Her safety and well being were more important than a lousy political career. I never cared for it. I told her. I disliked what she stood for. I want to make that clear. Write that down. I detest the fuckin' Party, to be honest. They're a bunch of racists. She broke our parents' hearts with her politics. I'm not exaggerating. I thought my sister was making a big mistake. She could have been brilliant at other stuff. I told her. She could've gone back into business, started a new venture. I offered her a partnership in our family firm. You know, we have plenty of lowlife neo-Nazis like that in Australia and they're scum, believe you me, but at least they're not in power, not like here. I think she loved the power it brought her. I can't think of any other reason. Mum blames herself, saying she must have brought Chelsea up wrong in some way. Personally, I can't see it. I think it was love of power pure and simple. Making money wasn't enough. She wanted more. Always more.'

'I wouldn't broadcast your opinion to all and sundry while you're here, David. It wouldn't be wise.'

'I won't, mate, don't worry.'

Mostert leaned forward and spoke in a stage whisper. 'I'm a Green, you know.'

Kramer adopted a disapproving tone, and added an edge to it. 'Keep your views to yourself while you're here, Mr Mostert - for your sake.'

'OK - alright.' He sat back, surprised. 'Thanks. Sorry.'

'The Green Party is banned in England, didn't you know?'

'Bloody hell. You're not serious.'

Kramer's stern expression said he was. 'Did you keep the emails?'

Mostert nodded, smiled suddenly, triumphantly, displaying discoloured teeth. 'Printed 'em out, too. Brought 'em with me. Thought they might help you fellers.'

David Mostert bent forward and down, revealing a bald patch and white strands in his curly black hair, and retrieved a document case from his overnight bag. He opened the case on his knees, pulled out a sheaf of A4 papers stapled together. He leaned forward and put them on the edge of the table.

'She was my kid sister. I loved her despite her fucked-up views. I miss her already. Fuck the bloody politics. I should have been here for her.' For the first time, David Mostert looked directly at Kramer. There really were tears in his eyes.

He held something out to Kramer. It looked like a business card. Kramer took it. It was Malaparte's with the general number and his mobile.

'You know him? He calls himself Detective Superintendent.'

'He's my boss, Mr Mostert.'

'He said should I go to see him if I needed anything. If I wanted to know about my sister's murder.'

'Did he now?'

Kramer's mind was on the papers. He didn't touch them though he very much wanted to pick them up and read them right then. He was delighted by them, of course; he raised one hand and squeezed the destroyed bridge of his nose as if hiding his expression, though he needn't have worried - his face gave nothing away, not a hint of his satisfaction.

'She told me she had a bodyguard-come-driver, a police officer.'

'She did.'

Physically, brother and sister seemed to share nothing in common; had one or the other been adopted? Kramer decided it was not the time to ask.

'So I thought he would protect her. The English copper.'

'Only in the streets, in public and while on duty, not in their home.'

'I was told she was killed on the doorstep of their house.'

'So it would seem.'

'So where was her bodyguard?'

'Behind the wheel of his car, thirty, forty yards away, waiting for her.'

'Sleeping?'

'He'll be questioned, never fear.'

How did Mostert know about the location of the murder?

Malaparte again, via Exeter.

'She was selling that crappy old place, or trying to.'

'I heard that, too.'

'I've got a question for you, Detective Inspector.'

Kramer waited, watching Mostert's clasped hands. They were big, powerful, a boxer's hands. They could do a lot of damage. They writhed in the big man's lap, as if wrestling one another as Mostert tried to make up his mind how to express whatever it was he wanted to know.

'Is it true…is it true that my sister killed more than two thousand people? Some say ten thousand. Is it true?' He paused. 'Any of it?'

'She didn't *personally* kill anyone that we know of, Mr Mostert.'

'You know what I mean.'

Kramer's tone was brittle ice. 'I don't think I do. Maybe you should ask Malaparte.'

But he knew perfectly well, of course he did.

'It's said she cut benefit payments to the disabled, the sick and unemployed here in England, and Wales too, that at least two thousand people died as a direct result. Many were suicides. Around eight hundred. Others died of hypothermia and hunger. Hundreds of people actually starved to death right here, in London, last winter. Apparently she also cut the state pension and cancelled the automatic annual increases. They call it Austerity. A bloody lie, if you ask me. The rich helping themselves and the poor paying for it. I saw one figure of twelve thousand dead.'

'Who says?'

'Folk on social media back in Australia. She was hated, my sister. Really.'

'I think such comments are censored here, so I really wouldn't know.'

'They say she as good as murdered them. Do you believe that?'

'We're going to need a statement from you, Mr Mostert, but do yourself a big favour and leave out the politics and the social media stuff. At least while you're here. And take this as well-meant advice, too: don't mention any of this in your emails to Australia or you'll have Special Branch grilling you - and trust me, David, you wouldn't like their methods one bit and the quality of their accommodation leaves much to be desired. All communications are monitored. *Everything.* Got it?'

'All right, buddy. I get it. Thanks. But between you and me, okay. There's no-one listening to us in here, is there? No? Didn't think so. Did she really kill all those people? Because of her government's policies?'

'Mr Mostert - '

'Okay. Okay.' He threw up his hands, palms outwards. 'You'll get your statement. But I've one more question. No, two.'

Kramer took a deep breath, pursed his mouth, acting the disapproving servant of the all-powerful, omniscient state faced by an unruly and unreliable dissident of dubious emotional stability from some remote colonial backwater.

'Do you really think that you can trawl through so many suspects - all of whom had reason to hate Chelsea - and that even if you did eventually narrow it down to a dozen, and it seems most unlikely, that your government would let you prosecute? Do you? People like Exeter are above the law. He said so himself in one of his speeches. It was on the box, even in Cairns. He said the law was subject to Party policy, not the other way around. He said the English required a new kind of legal system. Jurisprudence, he called it. A new kind of jurisprudence. I remembered it because it made such a deep impression.'

There were beads of sweat on Mostert's forehead.

The fellow was heading for trouble; it was all very well to entertain such thoughts, but to express them out loud was a serious misreading of the situation; if Mostert wasn't very careful and didn't listen to Kramer's advice, he would face a welcoming committee of Australian special branch officers or whatever they called themselves on his return to Cairns. The fact that his sister had been murdered, that she was a Party apparatchik, would cut no ice with those bruisers.

'Let's do the statement, Mr Mostert.'

'You know he led the Party's campaign to restore the death penalty, too, and my sister voted for it. They both did. He built his career on bringing back capital punishment. It made him very fuckin' popular here in England. Sorry. Excuse my French.'

'Mr Mostert - '

The Australian blew out his cheeks, shook his head as if in disbelief and glared at Kramer. No, he wasn't going to listen, that much was clear; he wouldn't take the advice. He folded his arms, bulging with tattoos. His expression was one of contempt, but Kramer was used to that. Being underestimated had its advantages.

'If I get my hands on the bastard who killed my sister - '

Didn't they all say that, the male relatives anyhow - a bluster born of impotence?

Kramer adopted a brisk, official tone. 'I'll need a DNA sample, too, Mr Mostert. Just a quick swab from the inside of your cheek with a cotton bud, that's all it is. If you don't mind. It's a matter of eliminating everyone we talk to from the inquiry. You understand, I'm sure.'

Mostert nodded repeatedly, then leaned forward, elbows on his knees, and he covered his face with his hands. A shudder ran through him and despite his best efforts to suppress it, he started sobbing, his weightlifter's shoulders heaving.

*

Kramer accepted Arden's offer of a lift. It was dark and raining, the London night a haze of sodium yellow, brash shop windows and car headlights glittering in the wet. They were silent for quite a while, each alone with his or her thoughts.

'You live south of the river, don't you, sir? Southwark?'

'Don't call me 'sir'. Any station will do.'

'Sure?'

'Sure.'

'They found the gun.'

'Say again?'

'Morrison and Brady. They found the gun. It was behind the radiator in the hall, you know. Something else. They found a print on one of the glass panels of the front door. On the inside. And a second partial. Brady called me.'

'Good news.' Kramer seemed pleased.

'Ballistics have it. No prints, though.'

'Maybe Dusters and Mops or whatever they're called aren't as good as they claim to be.'

'That's not all.' Arden took her eyes momentarily off the road and glanced at her passenger, but as usual his expression gave nothing away.

'Brady found a fragment of paper tissue in the hall, down the side of the sisal mat. It seemed to have blood on it.'

'Or maybe it's not the cleaners. Maybe our killer's been careless.'

'Yeah, that's possible.'

'Did Technical say when they'd have the results?'

'I didn't have the heart to ask. Malaparte is climbing all over them, demanding everything yesterday. His usual threats and blandishments. If you don't mine my saying, just between us, mind, that man's a complete cunt. '

Kramer said nothing, but his lips twitched as if suppressing a smile.

'Another thing, boss. While we're alone. He wants me to spy for him. Malaparte, that is. He says I'm to visit him once a day in his office to report on your progress.'

'Do that. Do exactly as he says.'

'Are you serious?'

'Absolutely. You're a bloody good detective, DS Arden. Better than I am in many ways. Don't spoil it by getting on the wrong side of the wrong people.'

'You're kidding, right?'

'No, not at all. You're rational, you're consistent, you make the system work for you, you know how to handle people. You're tough, you've got the guts to see things through. Just don't let your personal sense of morality or pride get in the way of your climbing the greasy pole. Swallow your distaste for Malaparte. I know he's sexist and a bully. We all do. He won't be there forever, and neither will you.'

'I don't know what to say.'

'Don't say anything. By all means tell Malaparte what we're doing in great detail but only once we've done it. Keep it historical. Try, if you can, not to signal our punches. Don't tell him that we're off to Party headquarters at sparrow fart tomorrow. We're getting DNA samples from everyone there, but we have just one target in mind. Wonderful thing about a State of Emergency - probably the only good thing - is that we don't need a warrant and we don't need probable cause. Morrison and Brady with a couple of

42

other technicians will be there and we'll take half a dozen uniforms.'

'Ryan Exeter.'

'Of course it's possible that someone else might fall into our net as well.'

Silence again as Arden concentrated on the traffic.

'Why did you become a police officer, DS Arden?'

Arden didn't answer at once. She frowned, puzzled by the question and by Kramer's asking it. 'Well, I thought putting the bad guys away would be a good thing to do.'

'And is it? Have you enjoyed putting the bad guys away? Are you still serving the cause of justice?'

'You mean 'working together to make London safer', don't you?'

'Is that all?''

'Is this an interrogation?'

'Stop the car.'

'What, now?'

'You want to serve justice by bringing down some mafiosi capos, then look across the street. What do you see?'

'Parliament. King Richard, Coeur de Lion, all lit up.'

There were several armoured vehicles drawn up outside, the guardians of democracy.

'That's where you'll find the gangsters, DS Arden. It's their place of work and their clubhouse, all meals, drinks and expense accounts subsidised by our taxes. Along with second homes, executive class travel, tennis courts, castle moats, televisions and the rest. Or a little further down the road in the City of London you'll find their paymasters, the bankers. Shall we cuff a few and offer them free overnight accommodation?'

'Don't go all philosophical on me, chief.'

'Has it never occurred to you, DS Arden, that when it comes to justice, we're working for the bad guys?'

'It's not quite that bad, surely.'

'You're in favour of capital punishment, Detective Sergeant, are you?'

'Personally? No, I'm not. Of course I'm not. I'm against it.' She paused.

'Well, maybe I *am* in favour - for aggravated rape and sexual abuse of kids. And dealing hard drugs.'

'Okay. Fair enough. You're a tough cookie. I like that. You know, though, that when we get our next murder conviction the sentence won't be a life tariff of fifteen or twenty years. Take a look over there, to the left, on The Green. Tell me what you see.'

Just to humour him she peered out through the rain-streaked glass. 'Oh, Jesus. That can't be - ' Arden sat back violently in her seat.

'It is.' When Kramer peered out he too could see the metallic outline shiny in the wet, the gleam of the blade like an executioner's grin. Yes, it seemed to say, screw this up, Kramer, and it will quite literally be your neck I'll tickle.

'It isn't be the old fashioned kind,' Kramer said. 'Saw something official being circulated the other day about the Justice Ministry taking delivery of twelve brand-new guillotines from the United States, a new compact design. Much faster, they say. More heads a minute or somesuch. Apparently, the Americans have stockpiled thousands of them in anticipation of a general breakdown in social order. Where America leads, we follow. Great, huh?'

'Unbelievable.'

'Not really. It's the natural outcome of the new Capital Offences Act. They tried gas, and lethal injection. They worked, of course, but there was no spectacle, no theatre. What a One Party state must have is the spectacle of terror, you see. Just like the Tyburn Tree - near Marble Arch; then they could hang several people simultaneously, a way of terrorising Londoners into accepting the lawful seizure of their property, their impoverishment, without resisting.'

They said nothing for a few seconds, silenced by the monstrosity before them, then Arden spoke.

'It's got to be quick, though, right?'

'No, not really. It was supposed to be, true. And painless. But very soon after its introduction in France in the 18th century it was said that the victims remained conscious for up to seven seconds. They moved their eyes and mouths and so on.'

'Holy shit.'

'You're a straight arrow, DS Arden. You don't have doubts. You love what you do.'

She turned away from the grim object. 'You love it too, don't you?'

'Me? I relish the chase, the hunt.'

She noted his choice of words. 'Do you have doubts?'

'All the time.' He glanced at her. 'I admire you, Arden. You're going places; I see you as an assistant commissioner in ten years, maybe even commissioner, though Christ alone knows what price you'll have to pay to get there. The question is whether it's worth it and I suspect you wont know until it's already happened. By then, of course, it'll be too late.'

Arden raised her eyebrows, said nothing. There was nothing left to do but get the hell out of there, keep driving.

A few minutes later Charing Cross Underground's lights flickered through slanting rain. Arden brought the car alongside the curb as a couple of armoured personnel carriers, festooned with radio antennae and battened down against the weather, clanked and clattered past, parting the rush hour traffic and thundering along the Embankment in the direction of the City of London and St Paul's. Two more followed.

'Will this do you?'

Kramer disentangled himself from the safety belt.

'May I say something, boss?'

'I can't stop you.' Kramer didn't wait. He climbed out and Arden had to lean across the passenger seat and lower the window.

'*Guv'nor.*' She raised her voice to get him to turn back and look at her.

He bent down. 'Well?'

'Ever since I've worked with you, you've been carrying a bloody great cross on your back. I know you're in pain. I see it every damn day. Has it never occurred to you that if you shared it with someone it might help lessen the burden, whatever it is?'

'Goodnight, DS Arden. Thanks for the ride.'

5

'I don't get this guy, today especially.'

Arden leaned forward, grabbed a handful of cashew nuts from the bowl on the coffee table and started popping them rapidly in her mouth, one after the other. She was famished and she told herself nuts were good protein, not carbohydrate, so it was okay to stuff herself with them.

'Do you need to? I never did 'get' guys and I stopped trying a long time ago. I think I was about 13 when I gave boys up for good.'

'Beth, yes I do. I *do* need to understand.'

'Let it go. You've said Kramer's a good boss. He's effective. He keeps his dick in his pants. He's not sexist or racist, at least in public. He's not even stupid. Now that's rare for a male copper, you must admit. Be thankful. All you have to do is work with him, and when he's successful, bask in his reflected glory. Don't expect too much of others and you won't feel let down when they screw up or stab you in the back.'

'You're right, of course you are, but I hate a mystery. Something is different. Something has happened and I want to know what. Malaparte also had a go at me today, warning me off Kramer, saying he wasn't a white knight or some rubbish, then asking me to inform - to keep him informed on what Kramer's up to. Unbelievable.'

'If I didn't know better, I'd say you'd fallen for him. Kramer, I mean.'

'For God's sake, Beth. Be serious.' Arden threw a cashew at her. Beth caught, ate it.

'I really don't know why it is that every time I sit down to watch 'England Has Talent' that you want to talk about something serious. I like this shit.'

'I'm sorry. Really. I'll shut up. Have some nuts before I eat them all. I can't stand this show and you love it.'

'Sweetheart, it's okay. If that's all we have to fight over, then we have no worries.' Beth had been holding Arden's right hand with her left but let go of it to use the remote. The screen died. 'Let's talk. I like our talks, okay?' Beth took a modest pinch of cashews.

'Malaparte also hinted at something Kramer did, something in his past and suggested he had form, that he'd broken the law, that I'd be wise to keep my distance, not get too close.'

Beth said nothing, waiting.

'He said Kramer had stolen police evidence. Drugs, or so he said.'

'Do you believe it?'

'I don't know. I really don't.'

They sat next to one another on the big comfy sofa with its floral loose covers. Arden picked up one of its cushions and hugged it. She still wore her work clothes - a black suit with pants, cream blouse - but had kicked off her boots and dumped her Walther P99 semi-auto in its holster along with her keys, cuffs and wallet on the table. Her partner had already showered and was wrapped in a white bathrobe.

Beth Myers stood, walked away to the kitchen area and returned a moment later with a bottle of red wine, a corkscrew and two large wine glasses. Arden watched her with open appreciation; Beth was very tall and lean with a shaved head, a wide, full-lipped mouth that smiled easily and big, epicanthic eyes that Arden found irresistible without really knowing why. Beth was black African, she was Asian, she was Arab and she was Iranian and maybe some bits of her were Jewish, too, and for that reason alone Arden worried about her, especially living in a capital city slowly and deliberately being drained of its diversity.

'You're working the Mostert thing, are you?'

Arden nodded, her mouth full.

'I saw the news. A high profile murder. Terrific. What a delightful prospect, honey. Fame if not fortune at last. I have so much to look forward to: cold sheets in an empty bed, no-one to share breakfast with and when you *are* here, just long enough to clean your teeth and change your thong, a very grumpy bitch who won't answer her cell until it's all over - weeks, months from now, who knows? Wow. Can't wait.'

Irritated, Arden shook her head and massaged her scalp with her fingers.

'Okay, so what's the problem?'

47

'Kramer wasn't his normal self today. He hasn't been normal for a while. He's changed.'

'Is that all? From what you've told me, he doesn't behave as if he's ever normal, as in normal for a human and a police officer.'

'Gee, thanks for that.'

'Don't take it personal. I didn't mean you, Nicole, though even you do act a little oddly from time to time.' Beth grinned, showing very white, even teeth. 'After all, I have to put up with all your jibes about my being a shrink.'

With a masterful turn of her wrist, Beth pulled the cork.

'You're supposed to let it breathe for an hour.'

'Screw that.' Beth poured, tasted it herself, nodded and half filled both glasses.

'Now come sit down, love.' Arden patted the sofa next to her.

'I will.' But instead of sitting down, Beth strode over to a sideboard and returned, placing a candle and its holder on the coffee table, then went over to the kitchen, found a box of matches, returned again, struck one, lit the candle, snuffed the match out with thumb and forefinger. Then she doused the lights and drew the curtains across the only window in the living area. Arden watched her. It was a ritual that said all these things would be done now, not later, that it would be no use asking her for this or that, for when Beth did sit down that was it; she didn't intend to get up again for quite a while. This is for you, the ritual said, don't ask anything more of me. Except later in bed, of course.

Beth returned and took her place again.

They clinked glasses.

Beth turned to Arden. 'Now, what's really bothering you about Kramer? Tell me all.'

'Something happened at the crime scene, inside the house and it only occurred to me this evening, though it's been nagging at me ever since it happened early this afternoon without really knowing what it was. I went upstairs to use the bathroom. I left Kramer downstairs. Nothing unusual in that. When I came down he was still there, standing with his back to the front door, watching me come down the stairs. I realised something that almost stopped me half way down - he wasn't wearing overshoes. This was a crime scene, and he wasn't wearing overshoes. He didn't speak. I didn't either. When I passed him, I saw something else. He had gloves on and he put his hands in his coat pockets as if hiding them. Why would he not wear overshoes and then, when in the house, put on the gloves? I'm certain he didn't have them on when we went inside. Why, Beth? He turned and our eyes met. He looked terribly pale and his eyes were scary. They seemed wild, frantic, angry. I can't really explain it. I had the feeling - really awful sinking feeling - that he'd been planting evidence while I was upstairs. He looked - '

'What? Looked what?'

'If I didn't know better I'd say he looked like someone caught red-handed.'

'But you didn't actually see him do it, did you?'

'No. No, it's true, I didn't.'

'So it's just a suspicion.'

'It's a lot more than that.'

'Based on what?'

'Inconsistency.'

'What's the significance of the gloves and what do you call them - overshoes?'

Arden shrugged. 'We all wear them at crime scenes. Kramer uses Nitrile because, like a lot of people with allergies, he can't wear latex. Nitrile is rubber but it's stronger, less easy to break. And he always wears two pairs.'

'Always?'

'Always.'

'Why?'

'The whole point of gloves is to avoid cross-contamination of evidence. They protect the evidence and us, too. In other words, it prevents us picking up pathogens from the evidence itself - whether blood, semen or spittle. But two pairs also prevent the wearer from leaving fingerprints and contaminating evidence.'

'Also important if you happen to be a killer planting evidence.'

'Right.'

'Do you always wear two pairs?'

'Sometimes. Not always.'

'You always wear overshoes and gloves - never the one without the other?'

'Very seldom. I can't think of the last time it happened.'

'So you're saying he went to the crime scene without overshoes or gloves, then once there and on his own, put on the gloves because he intended to plant evidence? It doesn't sound conclusive to me. Sorry.'

Beth drank and so did Arden, who put her glass down and then shook her hands as if shaking something off them or drying them, a frantic gesture and the words tumbled out of her.

'It's not just a matter of the bloody gloves. Tonight I give him a lift to the Pimlico Tube, okay? All of a sudden he asks me why I joined the police. He's never shown any interest in me before now or asked me about my background. I say something stupid about justice and putting the bad guys away, and he asks me if it has ever occurred to me that we are actually *working* for the bad guys. I was confused, I tell you, because it was all so unexpected, so out of character. I didn't know whether to laugh or just ignore it. Then he tells me to stop the car. We're opposite the Houses of Parliament, all lit up, and he asks me why I don't go over and lock up the mafiosi inside. He calls them mafia capos. He says it's their workplace and social club, subsidised by the taxpayer. He says if I want, we can go further down the road to the City and lock up their bosses - the bankers. Then he points out the fucking guillotine thing they've put there. Right there - on The Green. Jesus, it gave me a fright. I knew it was there, of course, I saw the pictures in the papers like everyone else, but it didn't give me half a shock to see the real thing.'

'He was joking, right?'

'Sort of. He was being bitter or something. It scared me. *He* scared me. It was dangerous talk, Beth, even if it was a silly, childish remark, and irresponsible. It did give me the shivers. He's normally so reserved, so sensible - this was so *weird.*'

Beth and Nicole looked at each other for several seconds.

'Had he been drinking?'

'No, I don't think so. His Lucky Strike breath was no worse than usual.'

'Had something happened today to piss him off?'

'Not that I know of. Other than the murder.'

'Darling, I don't think you should take it seriously. I'm sure Kramer doesn't, so why should you? He was probably just very tired. So are you, and no wonder. You're both under pressure with the Mostert thingy. Forget it. I would. He's a smart guy - too smart not to be cynical about the way things are going. We can all of us see it, but mostly people just pretend they haven't. Or maybe he's testing you, seeing how you'd react.'

'Who? Kramer?'

'Why not?'

'Testing me? Why would he do that?'

Beth shrugged, took another sip. 'Maybe it's politics. I don't know. I haven't a clue. I never met the man. I think he might want to know how far he can trust you.'

'Trust me? Why?'

'Even if you're right, even if he did something like that - planting evidence - you can't report it. You know that. It would finish you. You'd be taking on the entire, white, male police establishment with its generations of built-in racism. You know this - I know you do. You'd lose out in every way. You'd never work as a police officer again. And it wouldn't be just you. I'd lose my job, too, just by association. You know what they're like now. Whole families vanish.'

'But if I'm right, and I think I am, and do nothing, that makes me an accessory to murder.'

'And if Kramer went down for this, we would too, Nicole. Look at us. Look at who and what we are. It would destroy us.'

'So I do nothing? Nothing at all?'

'Do you have a choice, love? Do any of us?'

*

Kramer drew a small rectangle of folded paper from his wallet. He opened it with care, placed it down on his desk - not really a desk, but an old kitchen table used for the purpose - and smoothed it out with his right hand, holding it place with his left. It was nothing more than a half page crudely ripped from a lined notebook, creased and grubby from frequent use, so much so that the writing, in pencil and capital letters, was faded to such an extent that only Kramer could make it out. There was no punctuation. The hand that had written the message would have been weak, the fingers trembling and unsure. The letters were lopsided, the lines uneven; it seemed to have been scrawled in a great rush. Kramer sat down on the kitchen chair. He read it almost every day, at odd moments, when he felt he needed reminding, both of the message and its author.

There were nine lines.

I' LL THINK OF YOU

IF THOUGHT IS STILL POSSIBLE

YOU TREATED ME AS A HUMAN BEING

YOU MADE ME SMILE

YOU GAVE ME FRIENDSHIP

YOU MUST DO WHAT YOU THINK IS RIGHT

FOR YOU

GOODBYE SON

LOVE C

Kramer folded it up again, returned it to his pocket. He was home at last - and not just home, but in his refuge, his sanctuary, his monk's cell, his cave. As rooms went it was small; there was space for a single bed, the kitchen table he used as a desk, two upright kitchen chairs, a built-in cupboard. The walls were insulated with books from floor to ceiling - a low ceiling, under the eaves - and the books were stacked flat, on their sides. They were hardbacks all, covered in leather, cloth and wood and old, mostly 19th century and early 20th, all bought second or third hand, in English, French, German, Italian, Russian. Books on wine, on zoology, geography, history, anthropology, philosophy, agriculture, fine art, cookery. There were a few novels and biographies. Among them, Kramer knew, was Eugene Sue's *Les Mysteries de Paris* - not the original 1843 edition, but the 1978 four volume reprint of by Editions Libres Halliers as well as a battered copy of *Biographia Literaria* by Samuel Taylor Coleridge.

They had all belonged to Clara and from time to time Kramer would read a passage at random in a belated and haphazard effort to educate himself, though of course he realised it was far too late.

'You must take them, Kramer,' she had told him. 'I don't want those bastards getting their filthy paws on them when they turf me out.'

The same was true of the worn kelims and threadbare Caucasian rugs underfoot; they had been Clara's too. They were not gifts; Kramer had paid for them, and generously, because it was the only way she would accept his money.

There was no window, only a skylight dulled with dirt, high up and out of reach and which admitted a column of wan light. Now - close to midnight - a faint sepulchral shaft washed the table in sepia, innumerable motes of dust caught dancing in its beam every time Kramer moved, though on a good summer day it could, very occasionally, be sufficiently bright and sharp for Kramer to be able to read without putting on the table lamp. The place stank of old books and of dust, though Kramer no longer noticed it.

On occasion the light would strike the spines of the books, or some of them, and their old, faded titles in gold or silver would gleam as if brought back to life.

YOU MUST DO WHAT YOU THINK IS RIGHT

Aye, Clara, there's the rub.

He talked to her in his thoughts, and sometimes the thoughts erupted into voice, taking the form of real words, fragmentary sentences, even monologues, spoken with the speaker himself sometimes unaware he was doing so. Spoken words surfaced and submerged randomly, but to Kramer they were an unstoppable stream of fragments, a jumble of messages sent to Clara and received from her, a constant flow, an exchange back and forth. In this room, everything and anything was permissable. There was no need for silence, for pretence, for dissembling; no-one wore a mask here. There was no play-acting; they were frank with each other, as they had been when Clara was still alive. Nothing stayed hidden and nothing was too shameful. Today was special; it was the not just the day of Chelsea Mostert's murder but fittingly, the first anniversary of Clara's death.

He poured a generous dram of Jameson's into a teacup, enough for both of them, raised it and drank a toast as if she sat opposite him at the table.

'Tae you, Clara.'

He drank for himself, then for her.

'Here's tae us, old woman.

'Wha's like us – damn few and they're a' deid.'

Kramer left bottle and empty cup on the table and set to work, ripping down the mass of Chelsea Mostert's pictures from the cupboard and walls, then headed down the short flight of stairs to the bathroom and stripped the mirror. He gathered up an armful of images, made a pile on the table. He poured another dram. Later he would burn them. Nothing would be left, not a trace. They would not be missed.

*

He first encountered Clara in the summer of 2017 - no, that wasn't right, October '20, just after the sterling crash, and unemployment exceeding eight million, partly the delayed outcome of fleeing the European Union and Single Market in disarray.

Kramer had been promoted Detective Sergeant that week. He was crossing a small London square in Bloomsbury - barely a square - a concrete platform embedded with pebbles and with large concrete structures, reached by a couple of steps and rectangular in shape. He was so engrossed in his thoughts - he was leading his first big murder inquiry - that he failed to see them for what they were. Sculptures? Or air ventilation shafts to an underground parking lot, or both? It was a grey autumnal day, raining fitfully but not yet cold.

He heard voices, male and female, looked about him and there she was. She stood below him in the street, surrounded by three men. In whatever direction she moved, hesitantly, one or the other of the men would block her path. She was old, that was the first thing that struck him, her grey hair plastered to her face, a pathetic and troubling sight that provoked in Kramer pity, embarrassment, curiosity, irritation and a desire to do something, quite what he wasn't quite sure. So he waited and watched. The woman wept, tears mingling with rain on her cheeks, her mouth an ugly open wound of embarrassment, guilt, need. She uttered a high keening sound of despair.

She wore a summer dress, soaked, an open, lightweight coat which seemed totally inadequate and which she pulled around her as if it were a comfort blanket, but it offered little of that. Kramer's glance was drawn to something red she hugged to herself with both hands. It was a box, no, a rectangular tin, an improbable scarlet tartan tin of Mackenzie's shortbread biscuits and partly hidden by the coat.

The three men weren't aggressive so much as insistent. They repeated the same thing over and over. They were careful not to touch her. All three were black, all three were tall, and all wore white shirts, navy trousers, black shoes and there was the emblem of some or other private security firm on their shirt pockets.

Look, we're just doin' our job, see?

We don't wish you no harm, yeah, but you gotta come back to the shop, okay?

You 'ave to pay for them biscuits or we 'as to call the police.'

The woman turned this way and that, taking a few steps each time, but it was futile. They circled her constantly and it was obvious to Kramer there was no escape. The four moved up and down the street in a rotating formation, but made no actual headway in any direction. She couldn't escape. Until she spoke, Kramer had assumed she was an addict.

I'm hungry, don't you see?

That as maybe, madam, but you 'as to come back with us.

They were careful, scrupulously polite, even gentle. What was that old Anarchist trope? There's a worker at both ends of the bayonet. Something of the sort.

I just want something to eat.

Sorry, love, really, but we 'ave no choice, like.

Kramer took the two steps down to the street, held up his warrant card.

'How much are the biscuits?'

'She has to pay, sir, not you.'

Kramer turned his stare on the man. 'How much?'

'She owes the shop 9.99.'

'If I give her a tenner and she gives it to you, how would that be?'

The three security guards exchanged glances.

'Okay.' They and the woman watched him take out his wallet, fish a tenner from it.

So it was done. She handed it over. They had 1p change and gave it to her.

'Don't come back, love, will you? Not for a few months, anyhow.'

Kramer gestured with his head. 'You'd better come with me.'

'Am I under arrest?'

'No, you're not under arrest. I'm buying you lunch. You can't live on shortbread alone, no pun intended.'

Kramer was surprised at himself. The impulsive purchase was one thing, but this was surely going too far. Why did he do it?

She echoed his thoughts. 'What the hell are you? A policeman or a walking bloody food bank?'

Kramer took the shoplifter to a pizza place in High Holborn, a franchise he quite liked. She was reluctant to go anywhere at first, shy, unwilling to enter the place, to sit down, loath to pick anything from the menu, looking around her, embarrassed, trying to tidy her wet hair. It was as if she had the word 'shoplifter' or 'thief' written in capital letters on her forehead. She refused to remove her sopping coat.

Kramer waited, but when she still failed to select anything to eat, he ordered for her on the assumption she wasn't sure how much of his money she could spend: a side salad, a medium-sized pizza, garlic bread, a glass of red wine, a chocolate mousse.

She ate greedily everything placed in front her, and began to shed her sense of shame, eventually shrugging off her coat. Kramer watched her while pretending he wasn't. The expression on his face wasn't kindly, his tone wasn't especially sympathetic. Instead he was brisk, gruff to the point of rudeness. Kramer told himself he wasn't like this, he didn't do charity, he was nae do-gooder, and that anyway this strange old woman would feel patronised if he did display pity or sympathy. He told himself, not convincingly, that the sooner she finished and pushed off, the better.

'Don't eat so quickly or you'll be sick.'

'Don't tell me what to do. I'm old enough to be your mother.'

'How old are you?'

'Seventy-eight.' She looked at him squarely, eye to eye, frankly, for the first time, taking his measure.

'Grandma, more like. What's your name?'

'Cheeky bugger. Clara.'

'Kramer.'

They touched rather than shook hands across the table and her fingertips were icy. Clara smiled fleetingly. When she moved her lips, her cheeks revealed wrinkles deep as chasms in he skin.

'Nice to meet you, Kramer. Are you really a copper? You're far too scruffy - unless you're one of those sneaky undercover types.'

They both had coffee. With a full belly Clara seemed more relaxed, less guilt-ridden.

'Married, Kramer, are you? Kids?'

'No and no.'

'Wise man. I'd keep it that way if I were you. But there was someone, wasn't there?'

'What are you on about?'

'What happened? She's still on your mind, I can tell.'

'I don't do personal.'

'Fair enough. Grief never goes away. It just becomes more manageable, but the pain will always be there. You loved her and you miss her even now.'

Kramer grunted in response.

'You're what? Forty? Forty-three?'

Kramer didn't respond. He raised a hand, beckoned the waitress for the bill.

'What was she like?'

'Foreign.'

'Yes?'

'She was tiny.'

'Go on.'

Why was he telling her any of this?

'She had long black hair and a smile that lit up my days and my nights.'

'She spoke English?'

'Some.'

What did you have in common, d'you think?'

'Not much. A sense of humour.'

'What happened?'

Kramer took his time answering. It wasn't easy and he didn't like it and he

57

looked away when he spoke. 'Cancer.'

When he'd paid and left a tip they went out onto the pavement, Clara leading in her damp coat and still clutching the tin of shortbread biscuits. Kramer said he had to go to work. He took hold of her right hand, opened the cold fingers, pushed a banknote into her palm. 'Your bus fare.'

She made no effort to resist, to pull away. She looked up at him with pale blue eyes. 'It's not the first time I stole stuff, you know.'

'No?' He wasn't that interested in hearing her confession and his bored tone suggested as much, but Clara was not put off.

'I started when I was five or six. I didn't know my own name, or perhaps I did and had forgotten it. I didn't know my parents or where I lived. I stole then because I had no choice if I wanted to survive. It seems I've come full circle.'

'Where do you live now, Clara?'

'Brixton.'

'So do I.'

*

They were neighbours.

Whoever the architects were who'd designed the low-rise council estate, they had shown imagination. No one street looked like any other, and while the homes were very similar, given cost constraints, they'd managed to ensure that no resident overlooked another, that the homes, though formed in long, sinuous terraces, seemed individual, though in truth there was little variation. Some had their own garages. All had a patch of garden, back and front. The streets were quiet and shaded. When the estate had opened, sometime in the 1970s, all the tenants paid rent to the local Labour-run council. By now the vast majority were privately owned, and Clara was one of the last to rent her one-bedroom place and the council - no longer Labour except in name, certainly not in spirit - wanted her out so they could sell it on to a developer or investor and rake in a tidy sum.

Clara being Clara, she refused.

Kramer usually cycled or walked home. It was only a ten-minute stroll from Brixton Underground anyway, and whatever means of travel he chose, he passed Clara's door every time. It was a pretty grey-green compared to his council brown. The little garden was well tended, planted

58

with rose bushes and an improbable fig tree and unlike some, always clear of litter. All the front doors of the estate were protected by full length iron grills which spoiled the attempt to create a village atmosphere. So it was with the windows; even the garden plots had solid, four-foot grills around them.

Kramer usually left something. It was never very much; maybe a loaf of sliced wholewheat bread and a wee jar of marmalade. Half a dozen free range eggs, or the same number of pork sausages. A pre-washed salad. A few slices of smoked ham, a chunk of cheese, Tetley's Ceylon teabags. He rang her bell, usually, so no-one else would come along and steal his modest offerings.

She invited him to her place for coffee from time to time; it was her way of thanking him, of finding out more about him. He sat in her kitchen, looking out at the street, while she made it and they drank, sitting opposite one another, working their way through more shortbread biscuits.

'Steal these too, did you?'

'That's right.'

'Don't get caught unless I'm there to arrest you.'

'I know your secret, love.'

'You do? What's that?'

She'd found out practically everything else about him despite his efforts at keeping her at arm's length. She knew about his Cambodian wife, Pagna, her cancer, Kramer's efforts to get her decent treatment abroad with a particularly costly chemotherapy the NHS couldn't or wouldn't provide, thanks to the 'austerity' policies of the then Health Secretary, none other than Ryan Exeter, selling their home, the car, what little jewellery Pagna had, and how he'd stolen cannabis from the evidence room to cook up THC oil over a period of several months. None of it had worked. Pagna, his diminutive, brown-skinned, black haired wife with her stunning smile, her generosity of spirit, had died in agony, reduced to skin and bones, the morphine sulphate mainlined into her neck.

Clara leaned forward and whispered conspiratorially.

'You're a *Scot*. I know. You try to hide it - but I can still hear it in your voice. The Scots aren't terribly popular right now in England - but I can tell.'

'Are you going to inform on me, then? Denounce me to the

neighbourhood Party watch?'

'I'm seriously considering it, but I'd miss the prezzies.'

'They'll chuck me out of the Met and put me in one of their camps.'

'Don't you deserve it?'

For his part, Kramer discovered that Clara was not only the same age as his grandfather, that they were both born in 1938, but that Clara had been found wondering around the ruins of Dresden in 1945, aged six or seven, starving and incapable of speech. To survive, she had scavenged, stole and bartered whatever she could in the destroyed city. She put out fish hooks to catch, kill and eat any stray cats or rats. She did not know where she lived, or who her parents had been, or indeed, who she was. So too had Kramer's grandfather though in his case it wasn't post-war Germany, but post-war Ukraine. Perhaps it would be more appropriate to say temporary post-war Poland. The city of Lviv lay originally on the edge of the Austro-Hungarian empire and when it, along with three other empires, vanished in the aftermath of World War One, it became Lwow, in independent Poland. As Lvov, it became part of Soviet territory, and reverted to Lemberg under the occupation of the Nazis' so-called General Government and, in the summer of 1944, it became Lviv, in the Ukraine.

Grandfather Kramer had no name, no voice, no address, no family, and because the Central Tracing Bureau officer, an American named Ella, had the surname Kramer and had been unusually kind to the child, showing him the affection he'd either never had or couldn't recall, that was the name he chose for himself. He had given himself the first name Joseph.

'Being able to choose ones own name is rather special,' he told Clara.

'Yes, my son, it is.'

Eventually grandfather Kramer would discover that he had lost all 43 members of his family in the war, mostly just up the road - or rather the rail tracks - in the extermination camps of Sobibor, Belzec and Auschwitz.

None of it was especially abnormal, Clara and Kramer knew. According to one historian, in Czechoslovakia alone there were 50,000 orphans by 1947, in Yugoslavia, some 280,000. In Holland, no fewer than 30,000 children had needed help. In Germany there were 50,000 lost or unaccompanied children by the time the fighting stopped.

Many were never successfully traced, even as late as 1948.

While it was not an unusual matter, given the enormous suffering across the face of Europe, it did cement a bond between Clara and Kramer. He listened to her stories, and showed by his gifts that he cared, and that was all she ever really wanted.

*

As the months and years went by, Clara's situation worsened. With the Party in power, she lost much of her income. Her state pension was at first frozen, annual increments were cancelled, and finally her housing benefits were slashed. Once she'd paid her bills - her council rent and her utilities - she was left with ten pounds a week for food, for clothing, for transport. Prescription charges were introduced and for Clara it meant she could not afford medication for her arthritis. She gave up using public transport and walked instead when she was well enough, strong enough. She stopped going out almost entirely to try to save her strength and her pennies.

One day he noticed she wore a hospital wristband, but she would not be drawn, simply saying she'd forgotten to remove it.

'They've thrown us old folks on the scrapheap, my son. We're not wanted.' She had taken to calling him that because she said he was the son she'd never wanted. Her little joke. He said she was his mother from hell. Thus did they establish their affection for each other.

Kramer worried, though. He had little else to worry about, and he had a peculiar theory of his own that people have a capacity for worry and anxiety that requires an outlet to be found. Clara was his outlet. Once it had been Pagna. Now he had no wife, child or pet to worry about - they were an invention for his colleagues, to keep them at bay and out of his personal life. He tried all manner of ways to get Clara to accept money. She had half a dozen moth-eaten old rugs rolled up in the bottom of a wardrobe and he bought them from her. He didn't want them or need them - Clara certainly didn't - and that gave him an opportunity to pay her a generous one-off sum for the lot.

Clara's books provided another opportunity, only some really were worth something. Kramer tried to persuade her to sell them on the flourishing market for second-hand books, especially her first editions, convinced that a few at least were valuable; he promised to help by touting them around the specialist book stores in South Kensington and Mayfair. Clara wouldn't hear of it. She had no-one to leave them to, she said, and she wanted him to take all of them if only to deprive the council of her leavings once dead. He refused. He pretended to take an interest in one or two at a time, slipping her a fiver or a tenner. Of course Clara knew what he was up to, but she grudgingly accepted his ruse because at least it meant that while she had a little cash for her daily needs, including her meds, she could do so on her terms, and retain some measure of self-respect. He left the ones he thought were the most valuable, although in truth he knew very little about rare books and the market for them.

Clara loathed the Party and so did Kramer. At least he now had a fellow conspirator in whom he could confide his views.

They agreed on this much: there was the old way, the Britain of yesteryear, the way things used to be, the post war settlement, the welfare state, when people knew their worth, their possibilities, the changing order of things and how to adapt and improve them with hard work, climbing their flimsy ladders of hope for a better life for themselves, their children, trusting the rules they were born into and grew up with, believing in every man's home, and woman's, if not as his/her castle then her/his refuge if in a council flat, and trying to better himself or herself in a way most people understood by the term better; better in diet and in health, better in schooling, better in wages, in pensions, in paid annual holidays. A world of fridges and Morris Minors. That's what the war was about; that was the victory for the silent, broken spirits of those who stumbled back and couldn't speak of it and for those who never did come home. No way could they have known how everything would be taken from them, no way could they have even imagined such a thing.

Clara showed him a different world and she showed him how to see it differently. Both Kramer and Clara saw the little colour stickers on tree trunks, park benches, train carriages, bus shelters. Freedom! Equality! Democracy! Workers Unite! End austerity!

'Do you think they do any good?'

'No, my son. They make the people who make 'em and stick 'em up feel better about themselves, that's all. Self-therapy, I call it. Won't change a damn thing.'

'Futile, then.'

'Indeed.'

'But they could be shot for it.'

She was the first really old person Kramer had looked at closely with anything approaching attention. Age was repulsive if only because it was a foretaste of what was to come for him, indeed for everyone who lived long enough. In this case, however, he saw without disgust how her skin had thickened and pitted with age, darkening like rust, how the eyes were all but worn out with living, loving, fearing, wanting, the eyelids reddened, the mouth and nose wrinkled in a pattern that would tell, if Kramer could only read it, how she had lived, where she had been, how she had laughed and suffered.

'If someone is going to resist and risk life and liberty doing so, then it had better be worthwhile, don't you think?'

'Such as, Clara?'

'A bombing campaign, targeting security forces and law enforcement. You know, like the IRA.'

'On behalf of the Metropolitan Police Service, I thank you for your suggestion, though I do have great respect for the Republicans.'

'It's not personal, son.'

'What else?'

'I'm technically illiterate. I wouldn't make much of a terrorist. I don't know about you, Kramer, but I couldn't make a bomb if I wanted to. I'd be sure to blow myself up. I can shoot, though.'

'Assassination?'

'Yes, easier certainly, but harder to escape and remember they can replace one victim quite easily and the replacement might even be worse, hard though it is to imagine anything worse than this lot. There are plenty of ambitious sociopaths waiting for the opportunity to slip into any job you help someone vacate with a bullet.'

'It sends a message, though.'

'Better still, kill two. Or three. Make real inroads on the leadership. Scare the blighters, make them overreact, tighten security, take hostages, order reprisals. What a terrorist assassin must do is prompt a reaction that only increases popular opposition to the regime. Even if it means reprisals. I have thought about this...'

'Easier said...'

'Look, my son, only an idiot believes that as a result of his or her action alone the world can be changed. Unfortunately, the world is full of idiots trying to change the world for themselves. Anyone who takes up this fight must do so on his or own account, not for some creed or half-baked theory. This must be for oneself, a gift, like buying yourself a decent pair of shoes just to feel better about yourself. History is nothing more than another deception, another fiction. Forget posterity.'

Kramer must have looked puzzled.

'History is dead because responsibility is dead. How can events move forward if there's no longer any responsibility for the actions that take place? You can thank Richard Nixon and his successors, including our own glorious Party. Your pal Exeter will talk of deniability (that's not a real word, by the way). He will say mistakes were made - but what he won't do is accept the blame for the killings, the drones, the wars, the camps, the deportations, the failed states, the secret courts and executions or his precious guillotines. Srebrenica. Mosul. Aleppo, Tripoli. The list is long.'

'So I should kill for the personal gratification it brings?'

'Something like that, yes.'

Kramer went over the conversation many times in the year that followed.

She said on another occasion: 'Are you one of those cringing Christians or Jews who believes the mere *thought* of murder is a crime? Christ was a thought policeman, you know, he wanted to get into our heads so we would carry a little morality policeman around with us to control our behaviour and to stop us spitting or wanking. Or maybe it wasn't him. Maybe it was St. Paul of Tarsus, or the bishops of Niceae. Today it would be called an electronic chip implanted by the Party. If you're like that, Kramer, and I don't think you are but I am often wrong about people, if you've had the thought of killing - and I think you have, many times - then you will be punished for it anyway according to your Christian guilt. You might as well get on with the act itself.' She laughed an old woman's laugh, a wicked, throaty bubbling. 'In for a lamb...'

It was hard to know when she was being humorous and when she was being serious and sometimes it seemed she was both, simultaneously.

Then the eviction notice arrived, and the second. Finally a third warning, setting date and time in five weeks for the bailiffs to break down Clara's door and force her out along with her few belongings onto the street.

Clara told Kramer she'd had enough. At 82, it was time to go.

'The problem isn't death, Kramer. It never is. The problem is getting there.'

She was wasting away. Living no longer had a purpose. It was uncomfortable, often extremely painful, and there was no joy in it; it had become a burden and the great unknowing of annihilation would be a blessing. The last great adventure, she called it. Kramer argued with her, tried to intervene on her behalf, called the council a dozen times, wrote to the housing officer and to the local MP - all to no avail. A solicitor told Kramer - his advice was free - that there was nothing he or any other lawyer could do; the law was heavily weighted on the side of the council, on the side of all property owners, especially now the Party held the reins. The councillors had their small, grubby minds on the 300k Clara's little council flat would fetch, adding to a healthy bottom line. Who cared about an old woman of foreign origin without influence or the fortune to buy it? She wasn't even English!

For the very last time they had coffee at one of the chains on Brixton High Street. Clara even agreed without quibble to accept an apple slice with her overpriced cappuccino. She appeared to enjoy both. The sky was clear and eggshell blue, the sun warm. She seemed unusually cheerful and had visited a hairdresser's that morning, and kept touching her hair as if to reassure herself that she hadn't made it all up or dreamt it. She wore a pink dress and a silvery necklace around her withered neck. It seemed to Kramer that a transformation had taken place, some kind of physical and mental breakthrough, but it turned out it wasn't that at all. Clara had merely come to a decision that had relieved her of the burden of choice.

'I've come out to meet you, my son, because it's time and I do owe you an explanation. I've been diagnosed with stage 4 cancer. It's already spread everywhere. Just like your woman, only I deserve it. She was too young to die, but I've already lived too long. No - don't say anything, not now. *Listen.* It's in my rectum, uterus, colon, liver, lungs and lymph glands. My own body is in revolt and I can't even take a dump without pain. The prognosis is six months, but they don't know, the bastards are guessing. I've refused treatment except for palliative care because it's pointless doing otherwise, and they'll give me plenty of painkillers. At least dying is cheap. They promised me. I won't suffer my son, I promise.'

How could anyone promise not to suffer? It was ridiculous. Kramer was angry, with Clara, with the medical profession, with himself, with the world at large. He was on the verge of panic. For the first time in many years he felt helpless. It was Pagna all over again. A police officer was immensely powerful; he could take away anyone's liberty at a stroke, but this was no use to him now. He could not restore life to his late wife, let alone Clara. She gripped his hand on the table, her fingers misshapen and covered in liver spots, yet still strong enough to hold him still as if she understood how he felt as the world and things that mattered to him spun away, slipped out of his control. He looked at her hand, pinning his to the table top among the plates, cups and forks. He noticed for no logical reason that her rings seemed far too big and likely to fall off. 'It's what I want, son. Truly.' Her faded eyes held him fast more so than the wrinkled hand. 'Didn't Freud himself say the aim of life is death? He did. He really did. Please don't try to stop me. *Please*. It's the last thing I will ever ask of you.'

Kramer walked her home - it was only four doors down from his own place - aware this could be the last time they would see each other, each step a toll of the bell. Above them tiny scimitars flashed and scythed the blue sky, the Swifts' curved wings twisting and turning in pursuit of prey. Neither spoke. At her door, she turned to him and he felt her cool, powdery cheek brush his stubble. 'My son,' was all she said.

Clara accepted no more gifts and would not answer her door. He left food, but had to throw it away himself eventually when it went off or the neighbourhood cats tore at it, scattering it all over the pavement.

During the course of the month following the coffees and apple slice, Clara Weil starved herself to death and left him her scrap of a note just in time for the bailiffs.

Day Two: Tuesday, April 19.

'Who is set up for tragedy and the incomprehensibility of suffering? Nobody. The tragedy of the man not set up for tragedy - that is every man's tragedy.'

Philip Roth, *American Pastoral.*

6

'Boss.' Arden turned to face him, gave Kramer a puzzled look and tapped with two fingers of her right hand at her own chest, high up at a point where he thought her collar bone would be.

Kramer frowned. Had he spilled something on his jacket? He looked down, saw nothing and felt profoundly irritated. It was far too early for stupid games. It was too early to be awake, period, and he had been deep in thought.

He'd been thinking that considering how common death was, how universal, how inescapable, it amazed him that it was still a mystery at all, this final adventure of humanity, of every individual in a world of ten billion individuals - if it was final, that is, for there were those of a spiritual disposition who saw it as merely one of several such adventures, namely the cycle of rebirth - which was how Clara seemed to regard it, without fear, almost eagerly, as just another stage in the ordeal called life, a throwing off of ego, a dropping of the multi-coloured coat of personality until the next coming into being. What was personality but a bundle of habits - habits of want, need, dislike? Kramer had so many questions, though he of all people was familiar with the messy detritus of death: the bodies, the wounds, the fluids, the weapons, projectiles, bladed or otherwise, the stages in the process of decomposition, the stench, the inevitable pain and suffering of those acquainted with the newly deceased and left behind to grieve. He'd watched Pagna die, seen her in terrible pain, seen her hope, her courage, seen how death ignored her spirited resistance, ripping the life out of her with such violence, such indifference. It was the indifference that terrified him. He'd seen her body slowly shrink and shrivel and die even as he held her. But what happened to the rest of it, the parts that couldn't be seen, touched, smelled, heard? How could oblivion be oblivion if it was not experienced, and if it was, how could something that was experienced be properly called oblivion? Did the darkness and silence, the Emptiness, come quickly or slowly? What was the light people spoke of - was it simply the final chaotic salvoes of synapses, the last cerebral spasms before the dying of the light? Or was there something more, did something survive and emerge from the chrysalis of the fading body - call it consciousness, mind, soul? Whatever. Did Pagna still exist in some alternative universe? Did she still have that wonderful smile he'd fallen in love with? Of course not. Impossible. Was it better to depart quickly, in an instant, blinded and bowled over by axe, bullet or stroke, or slowly, withering away but fully aware, perfectly sentient, as the body burned up in agony with poison or consumed itself with cancer? Was it better to have time to prepare? But prepare for what? Sooner or later all his questions would be answered when it was his turn, whenever that would be, and he was confident for no particular reason that it was not far off and he was sure that in his case it would come for him when he wasn't ready, when he was sipping coffee or buying a newspaper, picking his nose or thinking what he would have for his supper. By then, of course, caught up in the trivia of his working day and confronted by its imminence, it was unlikely that he would be in a state of detached equilibrium in which he could frame such questions even if he wanted to.

Arden was speaking, her voice edged with annoyance. 'Did you forget again? The rose?'

She made him feel like a naughty child who'd forgotten his homework or socks.

Shit, she was right; he had forgotten. He pushed his fingers into his breast pocket and felt the cold metal of his spare, trying to hide a rising panic behind a wan and quite uncharacteristic smile. Thank god. He hauled it out and pushed it into his buttonhole, holding the little clip in his lips. Then he fastened it with fingers that felt too fat and clumsy.

Everyone over the age of sixteen had to wear the tiny white and red rose, indicating their birth in England and hence their English nationality, even schoolchildren had to display the flowers on their uniforms or they'd be sent home. Failure to do so would attract the interest of police and Party enforcers, and that would mean being publicly frisked and questioned and perhaps taken to the local station for a lecture from a desk sergeant who had better things to do. Party members were entitled to wear gold ones, signifying their superior and trusted social status. They were the Untouchables. It was one of the first regulations the Westminster regime had pushed through under the terms of the new national security act, along with nationwide issue of identification cards with biometric details. The 'smart' ID cards were colour coded for easy recognition: red and white for English of course, pale red for Welsh, green for Irish and blue for Scots, purple for everyone else, though there weren't many purple folk left alive or at large. The police were not exempt from these strictures, though Kramer had never known of a police officer being stopped by another for failing to wear a rose. Mind, it would be tough on those who were colour blind.

*

Exeter was on his way. The immense black saloon with Party pendants aflutter, slowed, slid alongside the kerb like some galley delivering royalty ashore without wetting the royal trotters. First two hard men with shaved skulls, white shirts and identical black suits sprang from the vehicle fore and aft, turning a balletic full circle, right hands crabbed and elbows cocked, ready to draw their sidearms, giving the empty embankment hard looks both ways with hard eyes. It was a wonder to Kramer that the very paving stones and lamp posts did not recoil in terror. The Chairman emerged from the rear. He took his time. An arm, then head, torso, legs, a graceful performance to be sure. Upright, he did not look anywhere but straight ahead, up the steps, his fingers touching first his tie knot, then the centre button of his three-button, two-piece suit with a sheen of midnight blue. He was slender, almost feline in movement, his steps oddly mincing, pleased with himself, a man used to being looked at, used to the deference that he thought was his due.

Kramer's view from above was steeply angled, looking down on the three figures so their heads seemed grotesquely large, bodies short and their limbs pitifully small. Two seemed to shrink, turning into dwarfs as they approached and the angle sharpened. Beyond them curved the river, at flood tide its brown waters rippling powerfully up from Westminster half a mile distant. The driver stayed where he was and prepared to light a cigarette; the second hard man followed with his passenger 's attache case and folded umbrella. These two dwarfs, Chairman and bodyguard, mounted the steps and were soon out of Kramer's field of vision. He turned from the window, caught Arden's eye and gave her the slightest of nods.

Exeter would have seen nothing amiss, he would suspect nothing. Arden had prepared for his arrival; the nearest military post was out of sight, opposite the Tate Britain, and no police were visible - the Party security personnel sat as usual behind the front reception desk, staring fixedly at computer screens, but the Chairman could not know the screens were blank, that the telephones in front of the security people were dead, the landlines disabled, the cellphones confiscated, the Party thugs disarmed. He would have left his bagman and brolly in reception, taking his briefcase from his minder and entered the lift. He didn't have far to travel; the Party offices were in the rectangular base of the 187-metre tall Millbank Tower, a Grade 11 listed column of steel and glass.

Kramer watched the security screens as Exeter rode the lift up two floors. The Chairman put down brolly and case, stood straight, apparently unaware he was on camera, and with the palms of both hands smoothed the hair on the sides of his sleek head, a narcissistic preening, a smoothing back from his forehead, something a male model might do before strutting his stuff on the catwalk.

He emerged from the lift, paused, glanced left and right, looking for his personal assistant, but her office space was empty. 'Angela?' Exeter shrugged, opened his office door and marched in.

Someone unfamiliar took the case and closed the door behind him. Exeter was about to protest, but his attention was diverted by Arden; she was wearing pink latex gloves and sauntered about in her black trouser suit, casually picking items up and putting them down again like someone housebreaking and inspecting the family silver and just occasionally, when something was of particular interest or value, did she drop it into a clear plastic bag.

'Who the hell are you?' The tone was authoritative, annoyed, and suggested that its owner could become extremely unpleasant if crossed. Obedience was assumed. It was directed not at Arden or the two other plainclothes officers present, but at the tatterdemalion slumped in Exeter's executive swivel chair, seemingly half-asleep, his legs crossed and his shabby boots - they hadn't tasted polish since they were bought five years previously - resting on Exeter's beautifully burnished desk.

Exeter's question went unanswered, the words left suspended.

Nobody said anything for a full half minute. Exeter looked at everyone in turn and they stared back at him with equal curiosity; he glared at the somnolent Kramer, whose eyes were shut, or seemed to be, giving the tramp - for that's what he appeared to be to anyone who didn't know who he was - the full treatment of disapproval, contempt, threat. 'I know you, don't I? Haven't we met…'

Silence.

Harkness and Seamarsh moved in, two detective constables built like grizzlies, sandwiching Exeter between them, pressing against him, frisking him, relieving him of two cellphones, a wristwatch, an old-style beeper, an expensive fountain pen, his keys, a leather wallet, even his precious gold rose. Mugged by the law would be one of putting it; the items were placed in a tray on Exeter's desk.

'What do you think you're doing?'

'This way, sir.' Harkness took a kindly tone, as if speaking to a mental defective.

'Where's your search warrant?'

Seamarsh smiled, his big hands pressing on Exeter's narrow shoulders. 'Won't take a minute or two, sir.'

'You'll regret this.'

'Yes, sir.' Seamarsh's gap-toothed smile widened. 'I'm sure you're right, sir.'

The Chairman was marched out, the officers on either side holding him up by the elbows sop that his feet paddled away, barely touching the floor, carrying him to the technicians who would take his prints, a blood sample, a DNA swab. He looked small, surprisingly ordinary, confused, angry; he tried to turn, twisting his head to look back, but he was pulled roughly on, hustled into the corridor. Kramer had shut his eyes again. He appeared to have gone back to sleep.

*

'I imagine you know this route pretty well by now.'

'I do, sir, yes.'

They seemed so extraordinarily high off the road and Kramer had to admit to himself; it was comfortable. What a change the Range Rover made from Arden's hatchback; this was luxury indeed; the huge vehicle hissed along on its fat tyres with barely any engine noise and it seemed to float over the potholes.

'And you always used to come this way in the mornings - when she lived here?'

'Mostly. It does depend on the traffic.'

'Yesterday?'

'Yes.'

'It was dark?'

'Pretty much. It was cloudy, so what little light there was…

'The street lights in Fentiman Road were working?'

'They were on, yes.'

The interior was immaculate; no empty crisp packets, no stink of tobacco, no empties rolling around by his feet, no clothing, hats, no toys - and the leather, real leather, smelled new.

'What time was it when you arrived?'

'A few minutes before seven.'

Patterson shifted in his seat, straightened his back. He was a big, red-haired man; it was the kind of bigness people found reassuring, both tall and broad, and there was a steadiness about him. Kramer was sure he was a good driver, no doubt about that, trained to an advanced level in evasive techniques, the kind of stolid Englishman who would make a very good shot if only because he would be calm personified, his nerves - if he had any - would never be permitted to get the better of him, unruffled to the point of dullness; perfect for the role of close protection officer, in short.

'Your shift began at seven?'

'You could say that.'

'What does that mean?'

'That's when she wanted me to start.'

Rain speckled the windscreen.

'And the others - your colleagues?'

'There were no others.'

'No others? Explain.'

Patterson sat well back, very upright, both hands on the wheel, arms fully extended, a position every driving instructor would applaud. Kramer felt Patterson's personal life might be like that; correct, ordered, formal, textbook and no deviations, no flair, one in which no doubt was ever allowed to intrude. There was Right and there was Wrong and nothing grey in between. Fortunate in a way, yes, but how bloody dull. Kramer hoped Patterson had not made the mistake of having fathered children.

'She didn't want the usual team of five officers, two off at any one time, three working eight hour shifts each. At a big event, we'd normally work as a team - two, three and sometimes all five. But she didn't want any of that and apparently she took it up with the Home Secretary to put a stop to it.'

Patterson kept his eyes on the road and his mirrors. He didn't look at Kramer at all, not so much as a glance sideways as if he didn't care how he reacted. Kramer was a supernumerary, an unnecessary and probably irritating distraction.

'She being your client, the deceased Chelsea Mostert?'

'Correct.'

'So you worked from seven - what, eight hours?'

'It was up to her. Usually it was seven or eight hours, yes.'

'And the rest of the time she was without any cover - from us, anyway?'

'Correct.'

'Why?'

'She said she wanted it that way. She said she wanted her privacy.'

'Bit rich coming from a very public politician, wouldn't you say?'

'Not for me to say, sir. I just do the job I'm paid to do.'

Kramer was impressed. Patterson showed none of the mannerisms of a man bothered by his interrogation; on the contrary, he seemed perfectly relaxed. His refusal to make quick judgements about other people or throw blame their way was also to his credit.

'Okay. So she called you on Sunday night - presumably you had the weekend off - and asked you to be outside her house at 7 a.m.'

'That's it. And yeah, I did have the weekend off. She was good about that.'

Patterson had turned the Range Rover into Fentiman Road. It was like riding in a big armchair, except for the hum of its enormous V-8 motor.

'Park where you did on Monday.'

'No problem.'

They glided past the house on the right.

'Here?'

'Yes.'

'You're sure. This very spot?'

'Yup. Right here. I'm sure.'

'But it's not outside her house, and we're on the wrong side of the road, facing the wrong way.'

'It's how she wanted it.'

'Are you serious? Do you have any of this in writing?'

'I do. I asked for a note from her, seeing as it broke all the rules, just to protect myself - you understand, I'm sure. I'm glad I did, seeing what's happened to her. You'd do the same.' Without taking his eyes off the road, Patterson drew an envelope from an inside pocket and handed it over. 'I can see her house using my mirrors, but I can't see the front door, not directly.'

Kramer scanned the note: 'Close protection officers are not to park or be physically present within 35 metres of my front door. They are to face away from my home when parked outside. Only in an emergency may they approach my home or seek entry. Only one officer is to be on duty at any time, and his or her presence will be limited to business hours.' She had signed it.

Kramer waved the note. 'Why do you think she did this?'

'She had a private life and she wanted to keep it that way, as she said.'

'Meaning what, Patterson?'

'Is this on the record?'

'All right. Off the record.'

'She had lots of friends, visitors, men friends. I mean, she's perfectly entitled like anyone else, and I think they might have been put off by a police presence right outside. Some of them, anyway. She had her reasons, but quite frankly if we'd been able to do our job properly and without interference, she'd still be alive. It's not as if she didn't have enemies.'

If Patterson had been loyal - and he seemed the type - the reference to 'men friends' was something of a revelation, albeit 'off the record'. Was he aware of what he was saying? Did he resent the fact that Chelsea Mostert took lovers? Was he envious? Or was this moral disapproval? Why mention it at all?

Kramer smiled internally, deep down. Yes, Patterson had a point about the lack of protection, certainly, but then again the killer would have made different plans if the Met's protection officers had been in close attendance, but Patterson was not the kind to allow himself to imagine such possibilities.

'How long were you here yesterday?'

'Twenty minutes, give or take.'

'What happened after twenty minutes?'

'There was a commotion outside the house, so I went to investigate. The neighbour had already called 911. Or so she said.'

'I noticed there are no CCTV cameras at this end of Fentiman Road.'

'There were, there used to be, but they were broken by vandals and had been taken away to be fixed or replaced by Lambeth Council. That was six or seven months ago.'

Patterson had a very slight northern accent, and like Kramer's Scottish burr, it had been almost rubbed away by years spent in the south, and it was impossible to locate precisely. If he had to, Kramer would have said West Yorkshire, Leeds maybe.

'Do you know the identity of these men friends who used to visit?'

'No.'

'Would you recognise any of them if you saw them again?'

'I very much doubt it.'

'Tell me about yesterday morning. My understanding is that she wasn't living in the house but wanted to sell it. Why did she ask you to come here of all places?'

'She'd had the cleaners in, so she told me on Sunday, and was making final checks before handing her keys over to the estate agent. They'd agreed a sale, apparently. I was going to pick her up and take her someplace else.'

'Where?'

'She didn't say.'

'Pretty early for a Westminster politician, wouldn't you say?'

'The Commons isn't sitting, and she didn't spend much time in the House anyway. She worked very long hours in the ministry, though, all night on occasion. I can vouch for that.'

'Did you see her arrive here yesterday morning?'

'No.'

'You missed her - or she was already inside the house?'

'I believe she was already inside.'

'Why do you think so?'

'There was a hall light on, and also in one of the upstairs rooms.'

'Maybe she had lights on in the house all night as a security measure.'

Patterson shrugged, said nothing.

'You didn't call to see if she'd arrived or to tell her you were waiting?'

'No. I would've given her another half hour or so. If I had called right away, she would have bitten my head off.'

'You were afraid of her?'

'Not exactly, but she had a terrible temper and was perfectly capable of making my life hell.'

'Did you see anyone else approach the house or leave?'

'No.'

'Did you hear a gunshot, or a detonation that might have been a gunshot?'

'No.'

'It was raining at the time?'

'Yes.'

'You had your windows open or shut?'

'Shut.'

'Did you have the radio on?'

'I did.'

'Catch a bit of shut-eye, did you?' Kramer added: 'I can't blame you if you did.'

'I did not.' Patterson gave Kramer a glance now. Kramer saw just a hint of defiance, perhaps anger.

'Did you see her ex-boyfriend, Ryan Exeter, at the house or in the neighbourhood yesterday?'

'I didn't, no.'

'You know who he is?'

'Everyone does.'

'Thank you, you've been most helpful. That's all, but we will need a short statement from you in due course.' A statement that would include, inter alia, Chelsea Mostert's instructions to her protection officers, Patterson's reference to the many 'men friends'. Off record remarks would go on the record - too bad if Patterson didn't like it. From Kramer's point of view, real progress was being made. The evidence - circumstantial as much of it undoubtedly was - was building up very nicely.

Patterson still didn't seem bothered, or if he was, he was good at concealing it. He took back Chelsea Mostert's note and placed it safely inside his jacket.

'Can I give you a lift back, Detective-Inspector?'

'You can, thank you.'

Patterson turned the key, paused, then as the engine warmed up he turned around in his seat and looked directly at Kramer, his brow furrowed. For the first time in their conversation, Patterson showed anxiety.

'I'm not in any kind of trouble over this, am I sir?'

*

The atmosphere in the incident room was edgy, expectant. Old hands only made it worse by putting on a display of being insensible, barely awake, or if awake then indifferent, supercilious, lounging on their chairs, tipping them back dangerously, throwing their arms wide or leaning back and cupping their heads in their hands as if sunning themselves on the Riviera - it wasn't sunlight, of course, but ranks of harsh strip lighting - exchanging the odd remark with the intention of giving offence, laughing needlessly and loudly, usually at the expense of a passing woman police constable or a particularly green police college graduate. Others played with their phones, smoked furiously, brazenly in defiance of the rules, made a point of ignoring the white boards and displays of maps, sketches and photographs; their manner declared that all such police apparatus, all the hard work, was beneath them. They knew better; they seemed to broadcast by their presence that they resented having been hauled out of their favourite watering hole, that they knew how the world worked, and there was nothing new under the sun; that, at least, was how these veterans wished to be seen and understood. Worldly wise. Cynical. Tough. To Kramer they offered up a different image entirely; they were time-servers, slack, ignorant, six pint, three-hour lunch habitués of the King's Arms awaiting their pensions, officers who'd pretty much given up on life. In a word, lazy. Kramer knew it. Arden knew it. Even they knew it and tried to hide it; somehow the more they tried to display a tough-guy indifference, the more surplus to requirement they appeared to be.

No less a figure than Detective Superintendent Malaparte had taken the trouble to quit his executive office, waddle down the corridor and enter quietly, preceded by his enormous battering ram of a belly, but both man and belly elected to remain at the back, leaning his back against the wall, hands behind his back - a glowering presence; most people avoided looking at him, but even so those at the back knew he was there and word rippled out to those at the front. The chief rat-catcher, no less; whatever this meeting was about, everyone knew, it had to be important; even the layabouts sat up, sheepishly dropped their fags and extinguished them underfoot on the brown tiles.

Arden strode to the centre, turned and faced the mostly male and almost entirely white gathering. She looked at the faces, remembering some, such as Harkness and Seamarsh, seeing others for the first time. Of the 26 plainclothes and uniformed officers present, only 17 had actually contributed anything to the inquiry, some being sight-seers and wannabe homicide detectives who'd sneaked in from other departments, from traffic to domestic violence.

'Our chief suspect in the Mostert murder.' She turned around whatever it was she was carrying and held it up - a large mugshot of Ryan Exeter, staring haughtily at the camera.

The impact on the room was almost tangible, rippling out from the epicentre in the slight form of Arden; a shocked silence, a sudden rigidity of the audience.

'You recognise him. You might even have met him. You can't fail to know who he is.' Arden turned her back, pinned the rectangle up on the board above the other photographs. She could hear the whispers now, the murmurs, the shuffling of feet. She turned around, smiled broadly - it was not a friendly smile, more one of ironic recognition. Yes, it said, you know full well what this means.

'Right now Mr Exeter is *kindly* helping us with out inquiries.' She paused, looked around at the faces, but avoided catching Malaparte's eye. 'In addition, he has, for now, waived his rights to legal representation because he insists he doesn't need it. He may change his mind of course when charged, which he almost certainly will be.

'Something you might not have known: the print found at the murder scene is a match. So is the blood type. AB negative. And,' Arden paused again for effect, 'we've just had word from our wonderful technicians who've been working around the clock on this case: Ryan Exeter's DNA was found in the blood discovered at the crime scene.' She nodded at Morrison. 'I'd like to take this opportunity to thank our scientific colleagues.'

An arm shot up, that of a detective constable named Giddis. 'Excuse me, but I understand Exeter lived with the victim in the same house. His prints would have been there, right? Same goes for the rest of it, wouldn't you say? I mean - ' He didn't finish. People shifted in their seats, shuffled their feet. There was an easing of tension, a settling in for the entertainment to come.

'That's correct. However, thy were no longer living under the same roof. A well known firm of south London cleaners dusted, wiped and scrubbed the place down just days before the murder. They did a thorough job.'

Another hand was flapped above its owner's shiny pate. 'Excuse me, DS Arden, but any prosecutor would have a hard task proving to the court beyond reasonable doubt that the evidence was not present prior to the clean-up. Cleaners are not infallible, after all.'

An anonymous voice: 'Maybe they were Polaks or Pakis, and we know how clean *they* are.'

General laughter. Arden looked over at Kramer. He had his arms crossed, his chin was on his chest and his eyes seemed to be closed. She could see little more than his silhouette against the blinds and grey daylight oozing through a dirty window. If he heard the remark, he gave no sign.

Another voice piped up despite the raucous merriment, this time a female police officer. 'Didn't the deceased have police protection?'

'She did indeed, but she had reduced the full team of five to one officer, and he had been given written instructions to work business hours only, not to approach the house except in emergency and to park on the opposite side of the road, no closer than 35 metres distant, facing away. He was there at the time but saw and heard nothing. We have his statement and the written instructions.'

'What can you tell us about the relationship between the victim and suspect?'

'We have a statement from the victim's brother, along with copies of emails from the murder victim to him indicating that Exeter assaulted Chelsea Mostert on a number of occasions, that he forced painful and degrading sexual practices on the victim - practices she she found repugnant, eventually withdrawing all sexual favours. We found certain transgressive objects and clothing belonging to Exeter in one of the cupboards.'

More shuffling, murmuring.

'Maybe the bitch deserved it.' It was the same anonymous voice. It prompted an immediate argument among the seated officers, with two women police constables jumping up and shouting at a uniformed sergeant who sat between them. He raised his arms to protect himself as one started punching him with her fists. Three more joined in, either to stop the attack on the sergeant or to add their blows. It wasn't entirely clear to Arden because she couldn't make out anything beyond the backs of those involved.

Malaparte propelled himself off the wall and walked to the front of the gathering. The mêlée quickly subsided and the group broke up. The sergeant wiped blood off his face with a handkerchief. One cheek displayed a long and deep scratch.

'DS Arden - is there more?' The little gold rose in Malaparte's buttonhole glinted as if winking knowingly at the assembled police officers. I'm *powerful*, it seemed to say.

'Not really, sir, other than to say the investigation has questioned more than 600 people, and taken prints, blood and DNA samples from 237. I should add that this inquiry seems to bear out the theory that 95 percent of murders are committed by people not only known to the victim, but in a close relationship. But we're not done yet - we still have more people on our list to get through and we will continue.'

'That's it then. Thank you. You have your orders.'

Malaparte waited until the room emptied, the departing officers picking up lists with the names of those they were charged with questioning. He pointed an index finger first at Kramer, then turned and jabbed the same finger at Arden. 'You. And you. My office. Now.'

What happened next was entirely unexpected.

7

The change in Malaparte was startling; Arden wasn't so much delighted by the deterioration in the detective superintendent's appearance as taken aback (although there was, admittedly, a measure of excitement), for her shock at the change was complemented by apprehension: what did it mean, not so much for Malaparte himself, the unadulterated shit that he was, but for Arden and for Kramer? Malaparte entered his office first, then trundled around his desk, wheezing audibly, one hand trailing along the surface like the float on an outrigger, stabilising himself lest he tip right over, and when he sat - collapsed was the word that occurred to Arden - in his executive chair, she saw that he was ashen. He leaned forward, forearms in front of him on the desk. He looked as if he might have a heart attack at any moment.

'Sit.' The order was hoarse.

Neither Kramer not Arden did so. Kramer had already taken up his usual defensive position to one side, with his buttocks against the window sill, his back to the window and the grey daylight, his arms crossed, and so too his ankles - a curious combination of the defiant and the determinedly casual. From that position he was able to watch both Malaparte and simultaneously the door to Malaparte's eighth floor office. He had only to raise his eyes to do so, but Kramer's head was down, his chin lowered, his eyes, if not closed (Arden couldn't really tell) then downcast as if he found his feet or the floor of immense interest. If he had also noticed anything out of the ordinary in Malaparte's appearance, Kramer gave no sign of it.

Arden expected a bollocking, a shit storm, a rant, a raised voice, threats, insults, a stream of obscene abuse, even suspension and demotion, anything was indeed possible and the cause would be Exeter's detention in the police cells; Malaparte was famous for throwing his teddy in the corner, and for ensuring that everyone else on the floor could hear it, too. It was part of his performance in belittling people, in taking them down a notch or two as he would have put it, in causing general embarrassment and public humiliation in what he regarded as a necessary discipling of his troops too wayward or too stupid to understand the political realties of contemporary England, for Malaparte habitually took it upon himself to rectify their incorrect views. It was more than expectation; it seemed a certainty - but it didn't happen. Why? While Kramer slumped like a boxer against the ropes, Arden had her weight on the balls of her ballerina's little feet; she adopted a position the military calls 'at ease'; relaxed up to a point, alert, with the license to move her head and her eyes, her hands loosely clasped behind her back, her shoulders straight and thus ready for anything, braced for the worst and determined to take nothing personally, to shield herself from the nastiness about to be unleashed.

It still didn't happen.

At last Malaparte spoke, but his words emerged as a croak. 'Do you have any notion, any notion at all, what you've done, the two of you? Have you?' It seemed to Arden less a rebuke than an appeal for sympathy, for reason, for a change of mind on their part, as if they'd done whatever it was specifically to spite him; that of course would have been perfectly possible, even highly desirable, had either Kramer or Arden been able to anticipate the effect.

Arden also expected that at some point in the inevitable harangue to come that they - Kramer and herself - would be given a direct order to release Ryan Exeter from custody.

But something else was of more immediate interest; Malaparte hadn't shaved that morning, and probably not the previous evening. His face was covered in stubble, an ugly mix of white and black, a messy salt-and-pepper beard in the making that contrasted with his bald pate. Under his dark and rumpled suit jacket, Malaparte's shirt looked as if it had not been ironed; on the contrary, it seemed stained, discoloured, by what she wasn't sure, perhaps sweat, or something spilled. Had he slept in his clothes? Was he ill?

He looked even worse than Kramer if such a thing were possible.

There was a long silence; no-one spoke. Arden stared straight ahead over Malaparte's dome like the good soldier she was; Kramer stared at his feet or the floor like a guilty schoolboy. All Arden could hear was the endless low grumble of London's impossible traffic beyond the filthy windowpanes and the laboured breathing of Detective-Superintendent Daniel Malaparte.

'It's out of our hands now.'

Our? What did he mean '*our*'? Arden bridled at the word, for it suggested collusion, teamwork, that they shared something, that were partners - in what, crime? What was Malaparte trying to slither out of, or perhaps he was trying to ingratiate himself, or implicate them in some horror - why, she couldn't imagine, but whatever it was, she felt the usual bilious and acidic dislike of the man rise in her throat so she had to swallow it down, stop herself from throwing it up on his desk - a desk unusually untidy.

Malaparte looked at neither of them when he spoke, but kept his eyes on the mess of papers in front of him. Whatever it was, he found it difficult to say. 'This is what you will do, you hear? You will formally interrogate the suspect, and you will do so now immediately on leaving my office, then you will charge him, read him his rights and place him under arrest. It will be recorded on video. You will make type up the interrogation and make two copies. You will deliver the original recording and report to me. Then you will absent yourselves from the premises until or unless you are summoned, by me or anyone else. Got it?'

Malaparte raised a hand and flapped it at them, a gesture of dismissal as if he were shooing away a couple of pesky servants. Get out.

Kramer pushed himself upright with both hands and away from the window sill; Arden brought her heels together, turned around, her back to Malaparte, and glanced at Kramer. Their eyes met, signalling that she should go first. Kramer followed. Arden realised in that moment - it was a strong feeling, no more than that - that there had been some sort of fundamental shift in power, quite what or how she had no precise notion. After all, Kramer was still a free man and still a serving police officer.

'You have absolutely no idea what you've done.' Malaparte was speaking to their retreating backs, but they didn't stop or slow down. 'No idea at all.' They did not look back even when they stood in the corridor waiting for the lift; it was almost as if they were afraid to do so for what they might see.

*

'What the hell happened in there?'

Arden's question went unanswered; they were alone and stood side-by-side in the metal box of a lift, staring up at the illuminated lights displaying the floor numbers and Kramer turned his head and looked at her with his flat, unblinking owl's eyes as the lift fell away, dropping giddily beneath their feet. He put a finger to his lips, dropped his hand and resumed his upward inspection. He was right, of course, the lift's interior was monitored by video and any chatter would be recorded. Arden didn't say another word.

What she would have said was that the most extraordinary thing about Malaparte was that for the very first time *he wasn't smiling.*

They hurried along the corridor, institutional drab green up to five feet, gloss white above that, with a cluster of pipes and tubes above their heads carrying god-knows-what wherever. His shoes squeaking, her boots clacking, and their breathing were the only sounds other than a background hum of machinery of some kind, probably emanating from an air conditioning and heating control room. Arden tried to break down the sour stench that grew steadily stronger as they moved deeper into the bowels of the place; for all the reconstruction and refurbishment costing the taxpayer some 58 million sterling, the stink's constituent parts seemed to include wet rags or wet dog - take your pick - urine, a million cigarettes, an over-abundance of shit in the sewers below, carbolic fluid cleaner, and rising above all of it, something deeply distasteful she couldn't identify - some kind of decomposition. Dead rodents, maybe. No-one in London lived or worked further than seven feet from the nearest rats, after all, and there were reckoned to be nine of them for every human Londoner.

A large, uniformed sergeant with a double-chin was waiting, cell door keys swinging from one hand. 'Exeter?'

'That's right.'

With a great clatter of metal - probably more than was absolutely necessary, the sergeant unlocked the cell door, pushed it open. Kramer paused, turned to Arden. 'You start with the usual-warm up.' Arden marched in. She waited for the sergeant to shut the cell door behind her. She knew Kramer would be watching through the one-way mirror.

She spoke for the benefit of the recording devices. 'Time: 14.38. April 23. Subject: Ryan Exeter. Investigating officer, Detective Sergeant Nicole Arden.' She sat down and looked at the prisoner.

His clothes had been taken away and replaced by striped overalls; they could have been hospital gown or pyjamas, for they were at least two sizes too large and there were matching grey slippers on his feet; Exeter sat on an upright chair screwed or somehow fastened to the concrete floor. They had taken his glasses. One arm, his left, lay on the simple metal table that was also screwed down, and he was turned slightly to his right, towards the door. He was shackled, both wrists and ankles, and a steel chain linked his fetters to a ring in the floor. To use the 'facilities' - a bucket with a lid in one corner, a narrow ledge or bunk at the rear of the cell, someone would have to unlock the padlock that secured his chains to the floor. It was in fact a double cell reserved for 'interviews' with its secret inspection section and window. Arden took this in with a single glance; it was not the first time she had visited police cells by any means, but it was unusual to find a someone detained on the grounds of 'helping police with their inquiries' chained up like a dangerous lunatic. On the other hand, wasn't that just what Exeter was, stripped of his Brioni mohair and silk suits, his Lobb hand-made brogues? A psychopath? No, Arden drew back from the thought - that was the kind of dangerous speculation Kramer liked to entertain. Imagination was a dangerous thing. It wasn't for her.

Arden went for the metaphorical jugular. 'Mr Exeter, did you kill Chelsea Mostert?'

The prisoner did not react. He didn't move. There was no sound at all in the cell - only vague voices from the corridor, echoes of shouts from a long way off. They hadn't shaved his head - not yet, for that would come later after he was charged and formally detained and taken away, ingested by the prison system - now his hair flopped messily down into his eyes. He needed a shave, a wash too, no doubt. She thought that despite all the other smells, she could detect his sour, masculine reek.

'All right, Mr Exeter. Let's go through this, shall we?'

For the first time since Arden had entered the cell, he looked at her directly; a cool appraisal, a measuring, a calculating, his eyes half-closed, glittering under their lashes, head pulled back a little as if sizing her up and Arden decided there was no fear in his face, no sign of nervousness, above all, no awareness of what might, what could, what would happen to him, for he still wore the mantle of his power as Party chief, a power that apparently seemed to him even now capable of reaching through steel cell doors, cutting through chains, and changing this state of affairs and subordinating them to his will - and certainly there was no sign he was at all willing to help the police with their enquiries. And Arden? In his eyes - those eyes now assessing her - she was a very minor servant of the state, an implementer of Exeter's will and desires, for his will and desires were synonymous with the will and desires of the Party, and the Party imposed its will and desires upon government. And it was true. That's exactly what she was; a black woman who followed the orders of mostly white males and she was following orders now and Arden was relieved that, unlike the man in chains before her, she had no responsibility for such decisions. All she had to do was carry out the instructions that emanated from above, a relatively simple matter for a relatively simple person like herself - and comforting, too, somehow. Something else occurred to Arden: or was it perhaps play-acting - mere bravado on his part? Did he conceal a quaking terror of this place, and what it implied? No - Arden did see contempt in that look of his, she was now certain of it, and she was interested to see for herself, in just a few minutes, whether that contempt for lesser mortals, that sense of superiority, that power derived from the Party, would still be in place once their one-sided 'conversation' was over and Kramer took her place.

Arden set out her stall, so to speak. She spoke from memory and did not consult her notes because she had no need. Briefly, coolly, factually, in a calm and dispassionate tone, sounding much more confident than she felt, she described the previous day's events: the discovery of the body, the manner in which Chelsea Mostert had been murdered, the nature of the weapon, its recovery, the forensic evidence linking Exeter to the murder in the form of a fingerprint and blood, the DNA match, the fact that Mostert and Exeter had lived together in the Fentiman Road property until they broke up, the fact that at the time of her death Mostert was paying a final visit to the house before handing over her keys to the estate agent, a buyer for the house having been found, and the fact that a man seen leaving the crime scene moments after the gunshot bore a striking resemblance to Exeter.

Arden took three minutes. Throughout this, Exeter barely moved. He said nothing. Curiously, he showed no nervousness; he did not tap his slippered toes, play with his fingers or clothing, bite his lip or cuticles, fidget on the hard chair, shake his steel cuffs or chain, laugh, cry or display any other emotion. He did not attempt to break Arden's flow by demanding a toilet break; he threw no tantrum, muttered no insults to undermine her, to cast slurs on her ethnicity, her sexuality, her profession, her looks. He did not look at Arden at all while she spoke - it was if they were passengers on a train and he just happened to be sitting nearby, within earshot, gazing out at the passing countryside or reading a paper, while she talked to someone else entirely; he was detached, unaffected, uninterested. Arden had to admit that she admired his composure; Exeter had given her a superb performance in playing the role of a man entirely innocent and quite indifferent to the 'facts' of the case against him. Someone guilty would surely have been intimidated, shaken, ready to make excuses, to argue.

'You done?'

88

Exeter still did not look at her when he asked the question, but instead had turned away, sideways to the table and Arden, and gazed upon the cell door as if he thought that if he could understand its construction he could use his immense power and charisma alone to blow it off its massive hinges. Mr Laser Eyes. She almost laughed out loud in mockery; Arden watched, waited for more - and there was more.

'It's all circumstantial, but you know that. Won't stand up in court, any of it - not that it will ever come to court, you can be sure of that.' He smiled, nodded, to himself it seemed, certainly not Arden, for she was beneath him and counted for nothing in his world. His confidence seemed entirely unaffected by his surroundings.

'We talked to your brother-in-law, Mr Exeter. Or should I say ex-brother-in-law? He consented to providing a statement as well as copies of communications between himself and his sister in the weeks and months prior to her murder. I think you will find we have ample evidence of your motive.'

Exeter appeared to laugh; his shoulders shook, he threw back his head, opened his mouth, though no sound emerged. He still kept his eyes on the cell door. Arden looked hard at the one way glass window and gave a quick, decisive nod. Then she stood up.

With a metallic clanging like a ship's anchor being hauled in, Exeter abruptly swung around to face Arden, planted both forearms on the table and beamed up at her, a wide humourless rictus.

'You've made a bad mistake, Detective Sergeant Nicole Arden. The worst mistake of your entire life. You no longer have a career as a police officer. In fact, you no longer have a life at all. Unless, of course, you release me. Now.' He rapped his knuckles on the metal table top and his wrist chain rattled merrily, reminding Arden of the Christmas nursery rhyme, *Jingle Bells*. 'It's your last chance. Take a moment to consider. There won't be another opportunity, I promise you.'

Arden looked at Exeter, her head slightly tilted in assessing the prisoner and his threat.

Yes, the contempt was still there, and so was a nervous twitch in his cheek.

Pompous ass.

But she did feel fear; she couldn't help herself.

They passed each other in the corridor, Kramer clutching two cups of institutional coffee, one of which he gingerly passed over to Arden. 'You did well.' He didn't look at her.

She was pleased, though she frowned; she didn't know why she was pleased and she told herself she didn't need praise, didn't seek it or want it, but for some reason when Kramer did praise her on the odd occasion, it was pleasing and this in itself irritated her, so much so it was sufficient to plunge her into a bad mood. Today was different, perhaps because she felt she hadn't made much of a dent in Exeter's armour, his self-assurance; a facial twitch was hardly enough, so the encouragement was welcome despite her feelings on the matter. Kramer seemed to sense this. 'You've shaken him more than you know; he's lost his cool'. Then he squeezed past without waiting for a response; he made his way into the cell, the sergeant ready to swing the door shut behind him, Kramer still carefully holding his cup.

*

For twenty years Kramer had been pursuing criminals of one species or another, and for the previous decade he had concentrated solely on killers, identifying them, locking them up, old and young, female and male and in-between, working class and posh, rich and penniless, the respectable and the disreputable, educated and clueless, giving evidence against them, watched them in the dock as they were convicted and imprisoned, and from their cells some had sworn to get even with him, to take their revenge, to stab, shoot, poison, bludgeon, strangle or run him down in their motors; doubtless they had plenty of time to fantasise about taking on the copper who'd felt their collars and causing him excruciating pain. Most passed on their threats verbally via the screws, visiting lawyers or relatives; with a minority it was an obsession and a few had even written him threatening notes, setting out in bloodthirsty detail what they or their muckers would do to him if they ever got the chance, including gang rape and being relieved forcibly of his epidermis with a hunting knife. One inventive little man, a bespectacled and middle-aged bank clerk, promised to burn him to death. Well, he would, wouldn't he, being an arsonist and repeat offender. Others were released depressingly early, and more than once Kramer had come across such characters, or they had come across him. Once, after a rare and agreeable pub lunch in Lambs Conduit Street, Kramer had decanted himself onto the pavement, a little unsteadily after a carafe of the house red, and had been confronted by a huge brown-faced man with a broad smile who filled the pavement, leaving no room for Kramer unless he was willing to step down into the gutter to get by. It happened too quickly to be frightened. 'Ello, guv'nor. Good to see ya - how's life, eh? How's the missus and the kids?' Kramer did not recognise his interlocutor, who then introduced himself. 'Yous sent me down for eight years, yeah, GBH, right? Remember?' Kramer did remember at last, yes, he most certainly did, and the giant before him smiled again, gratified. 'I'm ok, I was out in three, yeah, learned my lesson. Put it behind me as God is my witness. Good to see you, detective.' He offered his hand to the tipsy police officer, who took the huge paw; after all, why not? Kramer hadn't the heart to tell the giant whose name was Simpson that he, Kramer, had neither wife nor kids but despite appearances, he had indeed done surprisingly well out of serious crime, including Simpson's grievous bodily harm with a table leg, probably a lot better than the professional practitioners, that he was a detective-inspector on the strength of it and that nowadays he dealt solely with murders and murderers, thanks to scores of people he'd banged up like the friendly, forgiving and disconcerting Mr Simpson.

But here, in this cell, this was his moment, the culmination of all his work, his planning, his efforts, his putting into action those elaborate plans worked out in the solitary, silent gloom of his book-lined room in Brixton. This was what it had all been for. If Arden had played picador, pricking the prey, making Exeter bleed, forcing his head down, tiring him, setting him up for the coup de grace, here was Kramer himself, walking stiff-legged in his Suit of Lights towards the beast, his blade concealed beneath the heavy cape. A few beautiful, effortless passes, and the powerful creature should be ready to receive the final blow, the sword driven smoothly, quickly, deeply, fatally the full length of its fine, tempered and razored steel into the neck, between the shoulder blades and down into the heart muscle; his front legs would give way first, he would sink down, roll over onto his side, legs sticking out stiffly, the huge tongue protruding from a frothy mouth, the blood pulsing into the sand. Finis. Such a childish fantasy of cruelty would have made Clara laugh at him; perhaps, wherever she was now, if anywhere at all, that was what she was doing: laughing out loud from somewhere in the cosmos beyond space and time at Kramer's sadistic silliness.

But it wasn't yet finished: Kramer reminded himself that his prey was still dangerous while alive. Beware those horns! 'Would you care to change your mind, Mr Exeter, and have a lawyer present, as is your right?'

The only fly in this ointment was the unfortunate fact that while Exeter might deserve to die a thousand deaths for his innumerable sins, he was innocent of the charge of murdering his late girlfriend, Chelsea Mostert.

'I know you.' Exeter pointed an accusatory index finger at him with a shake and tinkle of chains, the prisoner's involuntary accessory. 'You were in my office chair, sleeping, or pretending to do so. And I've seen you somewhere before that, too, yeah.'

'Is that so? Do you want a lawyer now, Mr Exeter?'

Kramer did not sit down opposite Exeter; instead, he walked past the table over to the narrow wooden bunk and sat down. He put his coffee down next to him. He searched his pockets and at last produced a battered packet of Lucky Strike. He checked the contents; there were only four. He shook one out, tossed it to his mouth - the common party trick of a man who smokes far too much - and lit up, squinting against flame and smoke. He took his time; he didn't look at Exeter at all; he lifted his chin, gazed at nothing in mid-space, blew acrid circles with a pout of the lips. He spun the match in an arc to the floor. Then he absently picked up the cup with the hand that held the cigarette and sipped, once, twice, then put it down again. He leaned forward on his knees, eyes straight ahead, deep in meditative thought, or apparently so, drawing on the cigarette.

'Give me one of those, and while you're about it, get that fat sergeant to fetch me a coffee.'

Kramer gave no sign that he had heard Exeter. He continued to draw on the cigarette, occasionally taking it from his mouth and holding it out in front of him and inspecting it, tapping the ash off the end, resuming his blank stare as if he'd entirely forgotten where he was or what he was supposed to be doing. Took another sip, spat a grain of tobacco from his bottom lip; he seemed to be enjoying himself as if he were lounging on a public bench in Green Park, an idler watching squirrels and tourists.

'Please. Can I have one of your cigarettes?'

Silence.

'Does your boss know I'm here? I'm talking about Malaparte, Detective-Superintendent Malaparte, your superior officer.'

Kramer dropped what was left of the cigarette to the floor and put his foot on it, turning the toe of his shoe this way and that as if smashing a cockroach, then he raised the coffee cup to his mouth, head back, until he had swallowed the last drop; he crushed the cup in his hand and dropped it on the floor, too, then put his hands on his knees and pushed himself upright. His movements were slow, casual, performed with total indifference to the presence of another. He seemed to be headed to the door, but changed his mind, turning and placing both hands on the back of the empty chair opposite Exeter; he looked across the metal table at the prisoner for the first time, catching his eye and holding the look.

'I'm one of your admirers, Mr Exeter. Really. Are you surprised? You were always ambitious, determined, focussed with a very clear notion of what you call patriotism. I respect that clarity of purpose, I really do, so I hope you won't mind now that we've an opportunity to chat, if I ask you a couple of questions that have been bugging me. Do you mind indulging my curiosity? Please, as a fan of yours and Chelsea's?'

Exeter shrugged and looked away as if he didn't care one way or the other, but he was both irritated and interested; perhaps, Kramer thought, he was trying to work out just where and when they'd first met. Or maybe he was thinking about Kramer's remaining smokes and how to get hold of one of them.

'There's a lot about politics I don't begin to understand, you see, so maybe you can enlighten me on a couple of points. Of the dozen top Party policies supported by you and your then girlfriend, what would you say was the most important, the one that was most popular among voters, the one that really got you guys into power with such a large majority?' It wasn't large and it wasn't a majority, but never mind that - a mere detail. Kramer then did something that, for him, startled Arden on the other side of the one-way mirror because it seemed so unnatural and certainly out of the ordinary. Kramer actually smiled, showing his discoloured teeth.

'Was it by any chance bringing back the death penalty, do you think?'

'It might have been. I don't see what this has - '

Kramer finished his sentence for him. '...anything to do with you and I here in this cell, you being a suspect in the murder of Chelsea Mostert? You don't see it? Really?'

'No, I - '

Kramer interrupted again, raised a hand. 'Maybe it wasn't that. Maybe it was immigration. You a student of history at all, Mr Exeter? No? Well, perhaps that's why you don't see it. But you should know the general population of London was terrified by the Tyburn Tree from the 16th century when it was set up - close to what we today know as Marble Arch. They surely had good reason to be afraid. People, singly and in large numbers, were often strung up, and do you know why? There was a good reason for it, and it had nothing to do with what my trade calls common crime. It wasn't just theft and suchlike. Shall I answer the question? Okay, then, Tyburn's real purpose was to intimidate the poor into accepting the criminalisation of their rights and theft of their property without protest, without resistance. Tyburn was indeed a deterrent devised by the ruling classes. And do you know, like your precious American guillotines, Mr Exeter, the Tyburn Tree was an unusual apparatus because it comprised a horizontal wooden triangle supported by three legs, thus allowing the authorities to hang several people simultaneously, no doubt dragged out of Newgate Prison for the purpose. Useful, right? Do you now see any parallels with your restoration of mandatory capital punishment for murder? No?'

Kramer did an elegant little turn, swivelling on one foot like Fred Astaire, walking away to the far wall - which wasn't far - and then returned. He fished in his pocket for his smokes, then wriggled a finger into the packet and produced a rather crumpled cigarette. Once more he flipped it into his mouth, but he did not light it immediately.

'Two left.' Kramer's self-deprecating smile returned. Exeter's eyes were fixed on the cigarette.

Kramer flapped one hand in front of him, a gesture that seemed to say that he was happy to explain what he meant. 'Well, it's interesting because you're going on trial for your life, and by the very measures that you and the late Ms. Mostert worked so hard to pass into law, you will, if found guilty, find yourself on a latter-day Tyburn Tree. It won't be at Marble Arch, of course, but one of HM prisons where your guillotines have been set up and are awaiting their first clients. Or so I'm given to understand. Doesn't the irony strike you? No? Well, I can see you'd be upset, of course. I would be, naturally.'

'I didn't kill her.'

'No? Ah, well, thank you for that. I'm much obliged. I will record your statement. You'll be able to tell the court and clear everything up then.'

'I'll be out of here today. Then we'll see who's going on trial.'

'I'm sorry to tell you that habeas corpus, thanks to your government's emergency laws, has been suspended - what do they say, the lawyers, *sine die*? I'm merely a poorly educated layman, but I rather think that means indefinitely, so I wouldn't put much store by it if I were you. I very much doubt you'll be home for tea - at least not today.'

'Fuck you. You've no idea the trouble you're in.'

'Where were you at 7 a.m. yesterday?'

'Asleep. In my flat.'

'Can anyone vouch for that?'

'I'm not going to answer your questions.'

'I suggest that at that time you were very much awake and in the Fentiman Road property you used to share with Chelsea Mostert, and that you killed her with a single shot to the head on the doorstep.'

'Give me a cigarette. Please.'

'So sorry. I've only two left. Please answer the question.'

'You cunt.'

'Where do you get the replica pistol, Mr Exeter?'

'I don't know what the fuck you're talking about.'

'Why did you break up with Chelsea?'

'She broke it off.'

'Was it because you used to attack her physically? Was it because of your sexual demands, Mr Exeter, which she found physically painful and humiliating?'

With a jangling of his chains, Exeter turned away as far as he could, keeping his face averted, his back to the cell door and facing the slop bucket.

'Were you jealous of her success?'

There was no response.

'Or was it because of the several lovers she took to satisfy her needs?' Kramer leaned across the table and blew smoke into Exeter's face. Exeter shot up out of his chair, or tried to, but he only rose a few inches, dragging his chains as far as he could. He lunged at Kramer, throwing his body over the table and then fell back as the chains resisted. He tried again.

'Bastard!'

Kramer didn't move as Exeter flailed around, trying to regain his balance. 'In that case, I am going to repeat a question I asked you earlier, and if you have any sense at all, you'll answer. Would you like legal representation now, Mr Exeter? If you do not have someone in mind, we can appoint someone for you. You won't qualify for legal aid, of course, because you and your colleagues decided to terminate the funding.'

'Go to hell.'

'I'm sure that can be arranged if it hasn't been already. I must point out that I am

here on the express orders of Detective Superintendent Malaparte, and if it makes you feel any better, Mr Exeter, I can tell you I saw him less than an hour ago so he is certainly apprised of your situation. I can vouch for it.'

Kramer saw the blood drain from Exeter's face then the quick recovery and recourse to anger and defiance.

'You're lying.'

Kramer shook his head as if saddened and bewildered by such a refusal on Exeter's part to accept reality, to face up to his predicament. Kramer's smile evaporated and his tone changed from the conversational and self-mocking to the formal.

'Mr Ryan Exeter, I am arresting you for the murder of your former partner, Chelsea Mostert. You do not have to say anything. But it may harm your defence if you do not mention when questioned something which you later rely on in court. Anything you *do* say may be given in evidence.'

Finally, it was done; Kramer looked at the one-way mirror and Arden switched off the recording apparatus and opened her door to the corridor. Exeter struggled to rise again from the metal chair, dragging on his chains, but he remained hemmed in; he reminded Kramer of some ill-treated and vicious dog tied up in someone's yard and permanently at war with society, tugging and pulling this way and that in vain. Kramer ignored his struggle and walked out, not bothering to shut the cell door. Whatever it was Exeter was screaming at their backs, no-one could make it out and no-one would ever know. That he was innocent of Chelsea Mostert's murder was never in question, but only Exeter and Kramer knew that for certain.

8

In late afternoon sunshine, with the shadows of the plane trees lengthening on the grass, Kramer sat on one of the public benches donated by the virtuous and well-heeled 'Friends of Vauxhall' to improve the amenities and tone of Vauxhall Park and the neighbourhood generally. They'd even come up with the funds to employ a full time gardener, a young man in overalls with a ginger beard and beanie over his dreadlocks now smoking and leaning against a beech tree, unaware of being watched. Kramer stuck his legs out straight, kept both hands in his pockets, glanced over to the railings some forty yards away to his left but could barely see the house where the murder had taken place for the foliage. He couldn't make out the front door and step where Mostert had died at all. His bike was propped up next to him. Behind, four young people were playing doubles on one of the two community tennis courts and he could hear the regular impacts of rackets and ball, a popping sound like distant gunfire, interspersed with laughter. Something had occurred to Kramer while he was in the interview room with Exeter and he felt the need to figure it out right here, though it wasn't entirely clear to him why. It went something like this: if Mostert had presented herself to the world as an ever-changing series of carefully contrived and desirable masks of exquisite beauty and youthful sophistication; the same was true of Exeter. He wasn't beautiful or youthful, and certainly not exquisite in any department that Kramer knew of, and he didn't wear a mask, not quite, but nonetheless he was a man concealed, even from himself. Concealment was his thing, and it wasn't just the fancy cars and suits. He had designed his marketable public image - right in the glare of the spotlight of unceasing publicity, it seemed - as one of concealment, not just from others, but from himself, whatever that self was when it was at home. It was deliberate, calculated and it was entirely possible it had always been that way since childhood. Even in the cell, chained to the floor like a mangy circus bear, begging for a smoke, Exeter had remained concealed, despite the indignity of drab prison overalls, absurd prison slippers, the stink of his own body odour. It was hard - no, impossible - for Kramer to tell where the concealment ended and the man began. Only at the end, when his temper had got the better of him, had Exeter shown something of his real nature and then only for a few moments. Perhaps even Exeter no longer knew the difference or could tell them apart. The real question, Kramer decided, was this: if Mostert and Exeter had been drawn together by the attraction each power-hungry faker felt for the other's hidden and concocted identity, at what point had the mirror of illusion cracked? When did they cease to be dazzled by the other's fakery? At what stage was the make-believe of theatre tarnished? If attraction, even affection - conceivably, though improbably, the delusion of *love* two people might entertain in their feelings for each other - was based on a farce of misperception as was the case with Mostert and Exeter, what happened when the first fissures occurred, when her mask slipped a fraction, when his concealment started to flake, and their human flaws and weaknesses showed through the warpaint, when 'love' turned out to be nothing but insane narcissism? Did it happen when he first backhanded her, or when she failed to at least pretend to appreciate his predilection for anal intercourse, for strap-ons, whips, cuffs and black rubber, for threesomes with strangers randomly picked up in bars? How long had it taken for the beast to emerge in both of them? When did fear enter the room and join them in bed? It was no small matter, Kramer decided; the issue of sexual transgression and humiliation and pain, the steady or irregular process of intensifying alienation, would be vital for the prosecution's case.

He felt his cell hum and vibrate like a small animal trying to escape his jacket. He took out the device, flipped it open. It was Arden. Should he answer? Not to answer would prompt questions about where he had been and why he didn't respond. And if he did take her call, her first question would be where he was. Should he lie about his current whereabouts? If it came down to it, the call, and his location, could be traced without difficulty. It did not require a Home Office warrant to do so. It would almost certainly be safer to tell the truth. He grunted into the phone.

'Where are you, chief?'

'Vauxhall Park.'

'Jesus, why?'

'I wanted to think about the case, and it occurred to me that another look at the crime scene might help.'

'Help what?'

98

'Never mind.'

There was a pause. She knew his peculiar methods and work habits. He didn't have to explain. Kramer could hear her breathing and could almost hear her thinking.

'What's up, DS Arden?'

'Malaparte.'

'What about him?'

'He's disappeared. He's not taking calls. No-one seems to know where he is.'

That was *her* excuse for calling. She suspected him, that much was clear. The issue was what she would do with it.

'Alright. Does it matter to you - do you really need him? I'm sure there's a perfectly reasonable explanation. He's bound to turn up - unfortunately.' Kramer admonished himself; don't be childish, don't be an idiot, it will only get you into trouble.

Another lengthy pause.

'I guess you're right.'

'Okay then.'

'So, we just - '

'Do as we're told. Take some time. You heard the man. Stay out of the way until ordered otherwise. I'd catch up on some rest if I were you. You deserve it.'

'Are you really in Vauxhall?'

'That's what I said.'

'What's that sound?'

'They're playing tennis here, in the park.'

She was so suspicious - when had that started?

'You want company?'

'Thanks for asking, but thinking is something I don't do very often and when I do get around to it, it's something I do best alone. Nothing personal.'

'Almost forgot the reason why I called. Morrison phoned and asked me to pass on his apologies. He said he tried calling you. Anyway, something interesting has come up and he's sorry it took so long. You remember that Mostert was wearing some kind of two-piece suit - a top and matching skirt - when she was killed, yeah? The techies found something in the weave of the skirt. Turns out it was two hairs, two pubic hairs to be precise, and they came with their roots. So they've got the DNA, and we've a match. Someone living in Fentiman Road, would you believe it - the Fennels, husband and wife, two kids. Robert Adrian Fennel, architect. No form, no political history. They live seven doors down in the direction of Oval. If you remember we took prints, blood, a DNA swab and, in the case of males, we tested for powder residue.'

'Go on.'

'So that puts Mr Fennel right in the frame, wouldn't you say?'

'Seems so, yes.' Why wasn't he surprised?

'I thought we might talk to him tomorrow.'

'Why not tonight?'

'I don't know about you, boss, but I don't want to wreck a family - not because of a couple of pubic hairs. There might be a perfectly ordinary explanation.'

'Such as? We don't wreck families. Criminals do that themselves. There's nothing ordinary about leaving ones pubic hairs in a neighbour's skirt, especially a neighbour murdered on her doorstep. But okay, fine, let's be considerate about this for the sake of the kids and intercept Fennel on his way to work. Above all, let's be *nice*.'

Arden didn't react. 'He works at home, has his own company. An architect specialising in restoration and in great demand, so it seems. I checked. His wife is some sort of high end art dealer in the West End. According to the neighbours, she takes the kids to school around 7.30, so we could knock on his door around eight-thirty or nine. If you agree.'

'Sounds like a plan.'

'Okay, good. Don't forget the other thingy tomorrow.'

'Say again?'

She shouted as if he'd been struck deaf. 'Tomorrow! Don't forget!'

Bloody hell, yes, what was the matter with her? Of course he knew. The body was going to be released now the autopsy report was being written up and Chelsea Mostert' s remains were going to be cremated in Battersea, just down the road, at 1100 hours. They were lucky; there was usually a long waiting list. Her brother, David, would represent the family, and he wanted it done quickly - had insisted on it being done quickly - because he was leaving for Australia tomorrow night, his business in Germany having been completed. He would take the ashes back with him. Kramer had to be there, and Arden would be, too.

'I meant the King.'

'The king?' Kramer was becoming increasingly irritated by his partner's obtuseness, along with her mothering instincts, if that's what they were.

'It's the King's birthday, boss. His Majesty? Remember him? Yeah? Bloke with a crown? It's his official birthday. Trooping the Colour, fly-past, Buckingham Palace balcony, cheering tourists, adoring media, hours of it on the box, the new national flag and all that. Can't wait. Wear something blue. A blue shirt, a blue jacket, a blue tie. Anything blue, even blue socks will do. And black of course - for the funeral.'

He had forgotten, and that only irritated him more. Arden was right, as always, but he could do without the feckin' sarcasm. If you didn't wear something blue, royal blue, you were likely to get thrown off the pavement and given a thorough kicking in the gutter by posses of Party thugs - self-styled English patriots - roaming the streets while passersby looked the other way. The thugs seemed to be proliferating. They liked to congregate in the West End, showing off in their Party boots and combat pants, picking on shoppers who looked to them to be disconcertingly foreign and well-off. Party ideology was simple enough: rich meant foreign, foreign meant rich.

A white-haired woman, middle aged, passed Kramer's bench, almost at a trot, a small dog with fluffy white hair matching that of its mistress, pulling its owner along on its leash with a happy, malicious determination. No, Kramer didn't want to think. That was a lie. What he had to try to do was remember everything he could about the late Chelsea Mostert.

*

Kramer had pushed his recycled police card into Chelsea Mostert's hand on that wintry evening on January 14 without the slightest expectation that she would ever use the telephone numbers or email address printed on the thin, cheap cardboard with its 'making London safer' motto; why on earth should she? More to the point, why had Kramer bothered? He didn't know the answer then and he wasn't much the wiser now, other than the fact of his shortlisting the woman as a possible target. But she had. She called him on his mobile the next morning - January 15 - while he was on his bike and he didn't answer, being someone who didn't want to die messily under the wheels of a London double-decker or the 'bendy buses' that had cut short so many cyclists' lives - to say nothing of the heavy goods vehicles whose drivers seemed perfectly content to turn directly in front of cyclists without indicating, regardless of whether the latter were in an official cycle lane or not. It always surprised Kramer that so few cyclists did actually die on London streets - it averaged out at something like 30 to 35 a year - but he was determined not to add himself to the numbers of fatalities and injured. Kramer would choose another way to die if he could. So he ignored all calls and texts and concentrated on the street, on 'defensive' cycling, taking his territory mid-lane and not giving way, not allowing himself to be pushed or intimidated into the kerb, signalling assertively and making eye contact with drivers whenever possible. He didn't know it was her because he didn't answer when she called and later, over his first coffee of the day, he didn't recognise the number anyhow; it was only in the afternoon when Mostert called again that he realised who she was, and when he did he trembled at the sound of her voice and her name, a physical shock that seemed composed in equal measure of apprehension and a silly, adolescent sexual titillation.

Kramer was careful, though. He was careful getting there; he went over Battersea Bridge, through the park, then cut away from the South Lambeth Road through the Mawbey Estate and health centre, using the pedestrian walkways beloved by muggers and housebreakers because no police vehicle was sufficiently narrow to give chase, and in any case police officers with few exceptions hate leaving the comfort of their cars to pursue anyone on foot. Kramer should know, after all. He was careful, too, when he arrived, using the door knocker, not the bell (which would be audible to neighbours on both sides) and stood on the step, back to the door, partly hidden in the alcove, watching the road and the park opposite while holding onto his bike and waiting for someone to respond. Within a minute or so he saw through the glass panels a figure approach along the corridor; as soon as the door opened and then closed again so she could get it off the chain he asked if he might bring his machine into the hallway. He knew it was her by the sound of her voice, the slim shadow behind the glass.

- Do you mind? I don't want to lose it. Cost me four hundred quid.

- Of course, no problem.

She opened the door wide.

- Stealing bikes is big business in London and very well organised but it's by far the quickest way to get around.

- Really? Isn't it dangerous? It must be freezing at this time of year.'

At this point he was busy manhandling his bike in through the door, mindful not to gouge the expensive-looking wallpaper or muddy the expensive-looking blue carpet and relieved to have something to do to cover his shyness. He didn't really get a good look at her at all, and by the time he'd steadied the bike up against the radiator without damaging anything, removing his gloves, wiping his hands on his trousers, bending down to take off his clips, she had turned away, ending the pretence at mild curiosity, and as he took off his cycling helmet he followed her back down the corridor, through the kitchen and into the conservatory. She wore a simple white teeshirt and blue jeans.

'Thanks so much for coming - please, do sit down. I was about to make myself a coffee.' She was doing something next to the sink, and looked over her shoulder. 'Would you like some?'

'That would be great, thanks.' Kramer proceeded to sit down on a folding pine chair.

'How do you like yours? Black? White? Sugar?'

Mostert had her back to him and Kramer turned away rather than stare and looked out at the patio and decking, a couple of olive trees and a fig tree and a huge creeper on the rear wall prematurely covered with tiny white flowers, the name of which he'd forgotten. Jasmine, that was it. On the deck were pots, possibly for geraniums. Someone had wanted this expensive patch of south London to look, and smell, like the Mediterranean. He didn't think it a complete success, but he had to concede it would be a good place to sit out in summer.

Thus they renewed the silly, soothing smalltalk, creating the fake air of domesticity, massaging the strangeness of Kramer's being here, of her eccentricity in having invited him, blending it into a socially acceptable enterprise, and it wasn't until she brought the two blue-and-white mugs to the table and sat down herself opposite him, the pine table and coffees between them, that he really saw her, close to and close up. What he saw shook him; it was like jamming a fork in a wall socket. His first thought: is this Chelsea Mostert? Have I made a stupid mistake? Is this the wrong house? It rocked him, he felt the blood thunder in his ears and the sweat break out on his scalp.

'It's Colombian. Fair Trade. Hope that's okay.' Did Far Right politicians really prefer Fair Trade Colombian, no doubt bought from Waitrose?

The woman lifted her mug with both hands and sipped; she held it there as if hiding the lower part of her face and she studied him while doing so, the large blue eyes, their expression one of great seriousness, reaching out to his face; it was like being touched, he could almost feel her attention like a breeze, wafting all over his not-handsome features as if a fingertip examination was in progress and at last he felt like asking her - irritated, put out by this intrusive gaze - if he'd passed or failed this visual, almost tactile examination and what the hell did she mean by it anyway.

When she put the mug down he saw the bruising on her neck and jaw.

Kramer couldn't help blurt out, 'Who did that to you?' He pointed - rather obviously - at the big patch of discoloured flesh.

Perhaps what he really meant to ask was what she had done to herself. Gone was the makeup, the mask, the golden girl, the catwalk wonder, the photoshopped beauty queen of Instagram who needed no pageant to win prizes, the zestful, youthful, sun-and-sand, freckled, two-legged object of media panegyrics to female splendour, the wealthy Ayn Rand can-do-it and can-have-it-all heroine of the Far Right, the sensational goddess from the Commons front bench, slaying all dissenting dragons, Trots and Reds and wishy washy pinko liberals of all kinds, with her looks and her Valkyrie mission in life, sorting the living and the soon-to-be dead.

'Who do you think?'

Momentarily, Kramer was beyond thought and incapable of a coherent response.

What he saw - aside from the bruising - was a plain, pale, slightly built, undistinguished woman in her mid to late 40s, someone he would pass by on the street without a second glance, a woman without any makeup, not even a touch, the skin coarse, the colourless cheeks drawn, the eyes exhausted and puffy, the hair lank and lifeless, the shoulders drooping, the lips dry and cracked. The metamorphosis astounded him. To Kramer she appeared exhausted, harassed, and it wasn't the exhaustion of a couple of late nights, of a few too many drinks, of too much partying or work, of burning the proverbial candle at both ends. She looked deflated and battered by life itself, worn down - and, most recently, or so it seemed, by the boyfriend. What had happened to the confidence, the rude health, the sumptuous Caribbean tan? She didn't look like Chelsea Mostert; she didn't seem even remotely related to the pictures on Kramer's wardrobe and mirror. This was someone else, a lost and forgotten third cousin, perhaps, someone ordinary, someone unexceptional, someone in pain. Someone all too human from a Lewisham council flat.

'You met Ryan last night.'

'No, I saw him but I didn't meet him.'

'Don't think I didn't see you watching us. I'm sorry I was so rude, but you see I really had no choice.' She looked as if she might break down in tears at any moment.

'No choice - why?'

Kramer took a tentative sip of his coffee. It was very hot, very strong.

'He saw you, though, even if you didn't actually meet. He accused me of fucking you, you know. He accuses me of fucking every swinging dick that crosses my path.'

Kramer doubted that he qualified in any department of manhood as a swinging dick.

'Is that why he - ' She put her fingers gingerly to her jaw.

'No, that was earlier - three days ago. That was something else.'

Kramer had many questions, far too many, and it was hard to work out which to ask first. He decided it was best just to bait the hook, cast his line and sit back, wait. She would tell him what he wanted to know, eventually.

'How's the coffee?'

'Great.' Kramer lifted the mug again as if to prove he wasn't lying.

'Are you hungry? I could make some toast…'

'I'm fine.'

'It's no trouble. I think I've got some digestive biscuits somewhere, I - '

Kramer shook his head, smiled. 'No, thanks.' Did he look undernourished, as if he required mothering? Did 'swinging dicks' get fed toast or biscuits in the kitchens of strange, married women politicians at three in the afternoon?

'I know what you want to ask. You want to know why I called you, why I picked you and not anyone else. Don't you?'

'Yes.' Kramer saw that Mostert was nervous, almost frantic. She was holding onto her mug so he wouldn't notice her hands shaking.

'I know your boss, Malaparte.'

Kramer nodded, a nod that said, go on, do tell me.

'He's a senior Party member, very influential, but you know all that. I don't trust him, I *can't* trust him. He and Ryan are friends, you see, well, perhaps not exactly *friends* so much as partners in crime, as comrades united by the Cause.' She gazed down at the table as if she'd lost her train of thought, or she'd thought of something else she didn't care to talk about.

'You were saying? Something about the cause? It is your cause too, isn't it?'

'You're not a Party member, are you?'

'No, I'm not.'

'I thought so. I hardly know anyone who isn't any more.'

This was said sadly, as if she was hinting at how tough and lonely it was at the top, how she missed being an ordinary member of the human race - though Kramer thought it unlikely she knew, or remembered, anything about what it was to be ordinary and human; ordinary as in receiving unemployment and housing benefit, in being 'sanctioned' and refused those benefits, as in relying on the health service to treat a life-threatening condition, as in being mired in debt, in not having enough to feed her family for the rest of the week when it's only Tuesday, ordinary in having to work for nothing, or on zero-hours contracts - all of that and more besides. Kramer said nothing; he waited, for this was leading somewhere, but where he had no idea.

'Do you have a first name?'

'I do, but I don't use it. Nobody else does, either. I'm just Kramer.'

'I see. I checked up on you, detective inspector. I hope you don't mind. I know you have no family although you've told people you're married with a daughter, but that isn't true. I suppose you invented that story to protect you from gossip. I know you're a widower, that you live alone in one room in a Brixton housing estate. I know you're kinda anti-social, you don't have friends, or not many, that you don't have much money, that you live for your work, that you have an exceptional reputation as a detective, that you're of foreign origin though born in England, that you're single without siblings and without dependents. Am I right?' She seemed proud of her findings.

'You did all this since we met last night?'

'Oh, no. It took a couple of weeks. I had a look at your personal file. Surprised?'

Kramer pretended to drink more coffee. Pulling his file demonstrated her connections and power over him and that was why she had told him. She wanted him to know she had that kind of leverage. She couldn't help herself; a bad habit of her vocation.

'Do you hate me, Mr Kramer?'

'Why would I hate you?'

Mostert shrugged. 'I don't know. Maybe you hate the Party. Maybe you hate national socialists. Hitler gave us a bad name, sure, but really, we're not that bad and you shouldn't judge us by the mistakes of the past, but on the basis of what we've already achieved.'

So the genocide, the extermination and labour camps were just a blip in the national socialist popularity polls - an error, an unfortunate lapse in judgement, nothing more?

'We've got almost 100 percent full employment. Wages are up twenty percent and that's after inflation. We've built 120,000 affordable new homes for our own people. We've built new schools, too, we've invested in infrastructure, we've raised taxes on the rich, we've curbed the power of the banks, we've increased English pensions and, most important of all, we've stopped immigration. Totally.'

Kramer tried not to react, so he looked away, out of the conservatory and frowned at the empty flower pots.

'I'm sorry. I shouldn't preach.'

No, you shouldn't, you really shouldn't. No mention of the internment camps, the deportations, detention without trial, secret courts, mass roundups at night, systematic expulsion of all foreigners, mass surveillance, censorship, the collapse in sterling, with the pound now worth just under 50 U.S. cents and inflation hitting 29 percent and - or so he'd read in the papers - Scotland was about to break away, finally, from a discredited Union.

Kramer got to his feet, walked over to the kitchen and carefully, thoroughly washed out his mug, using detergent and warm water.

'You didn't have to.'

But he did; Kramer did not want to leave DNA or prints anywhere in this house. He told himself that when he left he must let Mostert open the front door; he'd avoid touching anything. Leaving traces of any kind would be unwise, unsafe. So she knew him by reputation, had done her research, had planned this. He didn't like it at all. He was in the home of someone who could end his career, take away his rights, his freedom to be himself, someone who could with just a word in someone's ear - Malaparte's, for example - have him placed in the limbo of what was now euphemistically described by this Westminster government as 'administrative detention' - that is, indefinite arrest without trial, without legal representation, without any court appearance and without any stated reason. He could quite simply be erased and no-one other than his jailers would be any the wiser.

'Can I trust you, Kramer?'

He resumed his place at the kitchen table.

'Trust me? Whatever for?'

Mostert's voice dropped to a quiet, confidential tone and she leaned forward on her elbows as if they were a pair of conspirators meeting in public, her bruised, wan face right in front of him, inches away, the famous, celebrated object of desire whose images decorated his bedsit. His obsession. They locked eyes.

'I need a favour from you.'

*

Kramer walked back under the street lights to Fentiman Road, keeping to the shadows of the side streets, pulling on his flat cap as he walked. Most office workers were home; television screens pulsed through panes of glass in tall sash windows and between hastily drawn curtains in front rooms, open plan kitchens, bedrooms. The streets were quiet, the clop and clack of hurrying pedestrians' feet had all but ceased, the irregular thumps of cars hitting the speed bumps were few. Central London still hummed, though, it would do so all night, punctuated by those wails of ambulances and police vehicles. The metropolis glowed, too, a yellow-orange blaze that blocked out most stars. Here, at least, on safe Party territory within the Division Bell, there were few troops.

He counted down the doors.

The Fennels lived in a tall, narrow mid-terrace Victorian redbrick. An elderly Volkswagen Golf and a Fiat 500 were parked outside, squeezed in side by side, on what would once have been a small patch of front garden and was now paved over like those of most properties in the street. Parking was so much more important than climate change, after all. The small size of the cars, their very modesty and their age, was for Kramer a statement of the Fennels' superiority, their awareness, their middle class willingness to sacrifice luxury for the sake of lower carbon emissions - without of course sacrificing personal mobility in any way. No doubt a fine antique barometer hung in the hallway, too, a contraption that was as useless as it was symbolic. The Fennels were sure to be people who knew which fork to use, and the fork would be nothing less than sterling silver. If the Venetian blinds drawn over the ground floor bay window were any indication, this was the area taken up by Fennel himself and his architectural business. Kramer could imagine why Robert Adrian Fennel's skills were in demand; restoration was safe because everyone, especially the English one percent, loved the immense and expanding nostalgia industry. The present was grim, harsh, terrible; the future was something to fear its sheer unpredictability, while the mummified past was all muted colours and easy sentimentality, a world of puppies, little girls with hoops and hats and horse-drawn carriages and Georgian homes, someplace where people never aged, never fell ill or died in agony; the people in this never-never land were beautifully compartmentalised by dress and accent and tethered by their respective classes, doffing their caps; good, church-going folk, patriotic to a fault, dying enthusiastically under the Butcher's Apron. Hey ho, upstairs and downstairs we go.

Kramer crossed the road quickly, looking down, taking a diagonal approach until he reached the far side where he could better make them out while taking advantage of the plane trees' shadow to hide himself from the street lights.

The family were seated in the bay window of the first floor. Two candles stood on the table. Robert and Clarissa Fennel sat opposite one another; the girl and the boy between them and on either side. Clarissa was serving something; her husband rose to his feet, leaning over and pouring what - wine? He wouldn't be a beer drinker. It had to be wine. They looked happy - smiles, laughing faces, a happy family, more than enough to make a loner, a solitary predator like Kramer, envious of the restrained human warmth on display, the sheer security of it all. If you don't like me watching, close your feckin' curtains! So, Robert, do tell; you're an adulterer, right, you popped out now and then, you did, walked over to Chelsea's house while the wife's at work and the kids are at school and you banged Chelsea -

what, out of boredom, curiosity, fascination? Was it just the sex? Were you infatuated? Was it love, Robert? Or are you a follower of the Far Right, too? Maybe you're a Party member. Did you whisper sweet racist epithets to each other between the sheets? Did you discuss autarky? The evils of immigration? Those wretched refugees? How many times, Robert? Did Clarissa never suspect? Have you put it all behind you? When Arden questioned you, you said nothing. In fact, you lied. You told her you didn't know Chelsea Mostert; you said you'd seen her a few times, but you didn't know her socially. You know who the boyfriend was, but you hadn't met him. You'd not spoken to them as far as you could recall. One lie piled on top of another, Robert. Once you start lying, you see, you can't stop. What would you say or do right now if you knew there was a Metropolitan Police detective-inspector watching you, a detective inspector who knew everything about your little off-the-books adventures? What would you do then, Robert Adrian Fennel? Choke on your arugula and parmesan?

*

'What is it?'

'Can't sleep.'

'What's bothering you?'

'Work.'

'Tell me.'

'I'm sorry. It's okay. I don't want to spoil your night. I know you're tired.'

'No, tell me.'

Beth turned over onto her side, facing Arden, who lay on her back, the duvet up to her chin, eyes wide, staring up into the dark

'Something's happening, Beth, and I don't know what.'

'Such as?'

'That pig Malaparte has vanished. He hasn't shown up all day, not since the morning briefing, and no-one knows where he is, or if they do, they're not saying, and in this business people only stay shtum when they're scared - very scared.'

'I would have thought that was a relief. Isn't it?'

'No, not really. When he called us into his office, Kramer and I, we expected him to give us a right bollocking. I thought he would suspend us, or at least Kramer, and that he would order us to release Exeter immediately. But he didn't. He looked shocked, beaten, like a whipped dog. He looked really sick. I was amazed by the change that had come over him, so much so I almost felt sorry for him - can you imagine? Sorry for Malaparte?'

'And?'

'He ordered us to question Exeter formally, then charge him with murder, turn over the recordings and then get out, make ourselves scarce, which we did. But that was only the start of it, you see. Malaparte must have received orders - and they weren't orders he expected or wanted. I only just realised on the way home. It struck me then in the car that it's obvious - it was staring me right in the face ever since yesterday morning, but I couldn't accept it, something in me refused to face up to it; a kind of wilful blindness, a refusal, you see, to embrace something so terrible so weird, so *perverse*. It made no sense - none - and it kind of went against the grain. It was disloyal to even think it. I suppose I'm a coward, really.'

Beth sat up, put on the bedside light, turned back to her. 'What *are* you talking about?'

'I'm scared, Beth.'

'Honey, I'm sure it's not that bad.'

'But it is. I feel the ground moving beneath my feet. It's horrible.'

Beth put her arm around Arden's shoulders, drew her closer, and Arden's words tumbled out.

'Kramer did it, Beth. He killed her, Chelsea Mostert. I needed to pee, and I went up to the first floor bathroom as I told you. Kramer said to go up. The techies were both downstairs in the kitchen area, and totally engaged in their work. The uniforms were outside. They weren't paying us any attention. I left Kramer downstairs - just where they later found the gun, the fingerprint and the blood. I was away maybe three or four minutes, but it was enough, more than enough. He'd put on his gloves for the purpose and tried to hide his hands when I came down. It was him. I'm sure of it.'

'I thought for a moment you meant Malaparte. You told me this already. Have you told anyone else?'

Arden shook her head. 'Only you. I'm so sorry. I didn't want to lay all this on you, not now, not so late at night. After a while you begin to think everyone's part of a conspiracy - except you - that everyone knows - except you. It's horrible, and I'm scared. Because they know. Malaparte knows. And if he knows, the fifth floor knows, but they've decided that Exeter will take the fall, not Kramer.' She rested her head on Beth's shoulder and her voice was muffled.

'Maybe you're just jumping to conclusions, though it's not at all like you. Maybe you're just tired, stressed out. You're normally so cool and collected, so reasonable - unlike Kramer and his bloody intuition. I think it's working long hours and the tensions of such a high profile murder. Anyway, what possible motive could he have?'

'No, Beth. No, I didn't see him *do* anything, it's true. But I know he did. I just *know*. What's even scarier is that it seems he's going to get away with it and I don't know why.'

Day Three: Wednesday, April 20.

'Dark nights of the soul are lit by inconceivable ideas.'
- Charles Baxter, 'The Art of Subtext'.

9

Fennel's reaction would be interesting; Kramer imagined how the man might feel at the sight of two detectives on his doorstep this morning, holding up their warrant cards, Arden using her left while her right rested on the butt of her sidearm, both looking at Fennel with that distinctive expression police adopt through the habit of long experience in dealing with suspects, a combination of stern, naked power and watchfulness, a wariness ready to detect any gesture, any hesitation, any threat, fake smile or facial twitch on the part of the interviewee that might give away a lie, a weakness, a failed effort to dissemble, a sense of his or her own guilt, an animal urge to make a run for it or draw a knife. Even in the best of times, in a democratic society, a police officer had immense power; nowadays that went a lot further; on the word of a sergeant, uniformed or otherwise, and any rank above sergeant - Arden, for example - anyone at all could be declared a terrorist suspect or a suspect extremist. No reason, no form of words were needed; the arresting officer required no narrative, no excuse, to exercise that authority. On the mere word of this same sergeant, or another, the 'suspect' could be held for 90 days without trial, and the process - again, on the word of a mere sergeant - endlessly repeated.

Fennel could not fail to have heard of Mostert's murder. In his first brush with Arden and her fellow officers in the immediate aftermath of Monday's incident, the record showed he had lied outright to officers canvassing Fentiman Road residents; yes, Fennel knew Chelsea Mostert by sight, he didn't know her socially, no, and he might have said 'good morning' or good afternoon' as one would to a neighbour, naturally, and of course he knew who she was from television and the press. But he didn't know her *personally*, no. They weren't friends. He was adamant on this point, and pretty sure Mrs Fennel (at this juncture she'd left with the children for school and then her own work) wasn't either, or the latter would surely have mentioned it to him, and she hadn't done so. He didn't know the boyfriend, Ryan Exeter, and had not seen them together in the neighbourhood, though of course he knew from the media who Exeter was. No, he hadn't spotted either of them at the local Sainsbury's supermarket at Nine Elms. These details were on the form filled in by a police officer on Fennel's doorstep within two hours of the killing. Fennel had initialled the form once all the boxes had been ticked and his comments written down in the large, child-like hand of the constable.

Fennel could not have known of the traces of his semen on the murder victim's clothing, but would have spent an anxious 48 hours worrying whether he had left at least some evidence behind of his sexual encounters with Mostert, evidence that would place him squarely in police sights as a potential murder suspect, and which would inevitably threaten his marriage and his family life. He could not know, of course, that Kramer already knew Fennel had not committed the murder, furthermore that Kramer knew in some detail of Fennel's encounters with Chelsea Mostert because she had confided in Kramer on the topic; how Fennel and she had coupled in her double bed on three occasions and once spent a few hours in a compact double room in 'boutique' hotel in Paddington which he, Fennel, had booked and paid cash for in advance. Nor could Fennel have any idea that Kramer was party to the very nature of the love-making, of the foreplay, positions, duration and quality of the coitus that had occurred, and the pleasure Mostert had derived from it, because Mostert had not spared Kramer any of the details; indeed, she seemed to have enjoyed telling him, revelling in the memory. And Fennel could not know that his emergence as a potential suspect was of considerable inconvenience to Kramer. For Kramer, nothing should be allowed to distract official attention from Exeter as the murderer and nothing, certainly not Fennel's adventures with Mostert, should be allowed to threaten Exeter's continued detention and his eventual fate. To that extent, then, Kramer had good reason to help Fennel get off the hook if he could possibly do so without drawing attention to himself and revealing himself to be uncharacteristically unprofessional - something he never was, or never seemed to be to others.

Arden posed a possible risk, though she didn't know it. Kramer had to be careful not to let the advantage of his inside knowledge of the Mostert-Fennel affair show; it must not be allowed to get the better of him when questioning Fennel in Arden's presence. He told himself he must not demonstrate any more knowledge than Arden had in her possession - namely, the forensic evidence of some physical contact of a sexual nature, but no more than this. She would lead the questioning, he decided. Yet what had Mostert told Fennel? How much did he know from their pillow talk? The uncertainty was troubling, but it occurred to Kramer that a statement from Fennel, properly assembled and carefully skirting some sensitive areas, could greatly increase the evidence against Exeter and make his release from detention more rather than less problematical for the authorities.

'Shall we?'

Arden stood back, slightly to one side, right hand hovering near her hip, her jacket pulled back so she could draw her weapon if needed. Kramer stepped up and forward and rang the bell, keeping his thumb there for three full seconds. Arden wore a black trouser suit and, in deference to His Majesty, a royal blue ribbon fixed to her lapel with a small black safety pin. Kramer wore his shiny suit, and had doffed his cap metaphorically speaking by wearing a washed out blue shirt - clean, but rumpled. Kramer didn't iron anything if he could possibly help it; the nearest he got to pressing his clothes was to place them under his mattress in the hope that they would emerge a little less creased than they had been when hung up over his single bar electric heater to dry.

Silence.

Kramer was about to ring again when the door opened. A very tall, pale and thin young man with long curly hair and wearing a white teeshirt, black jeans and a famous brand of trainers peered out and down at them.

'Yes?' Tone curt, expression hostile.

'Police. Is Mr Fennel in? We want a word with him.'

'One moment.' The stranger turned away and tried to close the door again, but Kramer was too quick for him and had inserted his foot and used one hand and his shoulder to keep it open. He pushed his way in and Arden followed. They followed the assistant or whatever he was into what would have been the living room but was now a white office space furnished with modern desks and chairs and some sort of expressionist abstract above the fireplace. Kramer recognised Fennel at once; he was sat at a large angled desk and a young woman was peering over his shoulder.

'They barged in, boss.'

'Robert Fennel?'

'You can't just walk in here…'

'We can and in case you didn't notice, we just did. We have some questions for you, Mr Fennel, in connection with Monday's murder of Chelsea Mostert. We can do this here, now, or you can accompany us to the

Yard. Your choice.'

Fennel shook his head irritably, rose to his feet, came around from behind the desk and examined their warrant cards. He took his time. He seemed perfectly in control, not in the least shaken, though visibly annoyed at the intrusion and, as Kramer saw it, channelling his fears into that sense of outrage to hide how he really felt. Close up, Kramer examined him. He was slightly above average height with a narrow face, a long, lantern jaw, and large, aquiline nose on which perched rimless spectacles. Doubtless intelligent, probably pernickety in matters of love and work.

'I'm Detective Inspector Kramer and this is Detective Sergeant Arden. This won't take long, but perhaps you'd prefer we do this somewhere private?'

Fennel turned, glanced at the architect's drawings on the desk as if reminding himself of the work he'd been doing when so rudely interrupted. 'Justin, Rose - carry on, will you please? You know what to do.' He turned back to Kramer and Arden with a scowl. 'You'd better come upstairs.'

*

They sat at the table in the first floor bay window where the Fennels had sat together *en famille* for supper the previous evening while spied upon by Kramer lurking under the plane trees on the opposite side of the street. Now it was just Robert Fennel on one side, faced by Kramer and Arden. He asked if his visitors would like tea or coffee, but they declined, Arden by raising her hand, palm outwards, fingers spread, Kramer by shaking his head.

Kramer: 'Your wife has left with the children?'

Fennel: 'You just missed them.'

Arden: 'She takes them to Hill House Preparatory School in SW3 and then goes on to her place of business in the West End - am I right?'

Fennel: 'Correct. Belgravia. She runs an art gallery there.'

Kramer: 'Nice. We saw them leave.' Arden couldn't tell if Kramer meant 'nice' in genuine admiration, or whether he was being sarcastic, though she suspected the latter.

Arden: 'We thought it best to wait and speak to you alone. For the sake of your family.'

Fennel: 'What's all this about?' Of course he must know perfectly well, Arden thought.

Arden: 'You told us on Monday you didn't know Chelsea Mostert. You lied to us.' This was stated flatly, without emotion. A fact.

Fennel, still frowning: 'I said to the officer I recognised her, had seen her in the neighbourhood from time to time and may have greeted her.'

Arden, undeterred: 'You specifically stated you didn't know her personally.'

Kramer: 'Do you still maintain you didn't know her, Mr Fennel?'

No reply.

Arden: 'When did you last sleep with her, Mr Fennel?'

Fennel flushed deeply, the blood enriched skin starting at his neck and spreading up all the way to the roots of his hair as if it had been rollered on like paint. He rocked back in his seat, as if he'd been slapped. That was all the answer the police officers needed; Arden's question had cut deeply - it was surely the one issue Fennel was so afraid would emerge from this interview and which he would have gone to extreme lengths to conceal. Clearly, he wasn't a good liar.

Arden: 'I'll ask you again. When did you last have sexual relations with Chelsea Mostert?'

A long pause.

Fennel: 'Am I under arrest?'

Kramer, with a bleak and humourless smile as if merely exercising his cheek muscles: 'Not yet, Mr Fennel. Right now you're helping us with our enquires.'

Fennel: 'I'm not going to say anything more. No comment.'

Arden: 'The right to silence is no longer on the statute book, Mr Fennel. It was denied to terror suspects at ports of entry for some years, but since then it has been withdrawn from the population at large. That means you.'

Fennel: 'In that case, I want a lawyer.'

Kramer pushed his chair back as if signalling an end to the discussion. 'That is your right, Mr Fennel. We'll come back tonight with our forensics people and we'll conduct a thorough search of your home and workplace. Your wife and children will be here, I imagine, but we can't help that. You'd better have your lawyer present from, say, 6 p.m.'

Fennel: 'Wait.'

Kramer and Arden waited, watching him.

Fennel: 'Am I under suspicion?'

Kramer: 'I would say so, yes. Definitely.'

Fennel: What can I do to persuade you that I didn't kill her?'

Arden: 'Answer our questions - truthfully this time, or you could very well face a charge of obstructing the police.'

Bullying was part of every police officer's arsenal. Fennel nodded, head down, eyes on the table where he had placed his hands, palms down like a card player hiding his trumps - if he had any.

Arden: 'When did you last have sexual relations with the deceased?'

Fennel, very quiet: 'Last Friday.'

Kramer: 'I didn't hear that. Say again?'

Fennel, looking up quickly at Kramer and then away: 'Last Friday.'

Arden: 'When last Friday?'

Fennel: 'It must have been early afternoon. Maybe two o'clock.'

Kramer: 'In Mostert's bed?'

Fennel nodded.

Kramer: 'Say it.'

Fennel: 'Yes, in her bed. It started in the living room and then - '

Arden: 'How many times in total, Mr Fennel?'

Fennel: 'I don't know.'

Kramer: 'Yes, you do.'

Fennel: 'Three or four times.'

Arden: 'That's all?'

Fennel: 'Yes.'

Kramer: 'Always in her bed?'

Fennel: 'No.'

Kramer: 'Where else?'

Fennel: 'In a hotel.'

Arden: 'Where?'

Fennel: 'Paddington.'

Arden: 'Name?:

Fennel: 'The Happy Unicorn.'

Kramer: 'When?'

Fennel: 'Three weeks ago, a Thursday.'

Arden: 'How did you first meet?'

Fennel: 'Borough Market. We chatted, then went for a drink, that's how it started.'

Kramer: 'You found her attractive?'

Fennel: 'Yes. Of course. Very.'

Arden: 'What did she see in you, do you think, Mr Fennel?'

Fennel: 'I don't know, do I? Someone sympathetic. Someone she could trust not to go to the media. Someone who would listen, who appreciated her the way she was.'

Kramer: 'Didn't her boyfriend appreciate her?'

For the first time Fennel looked directly at Kramer. 'No, he didn't. He beat her. He was some kind of sexual sadist. He liked to dress up, and he liked her to do weird stuff to her. She hated him and was afraid of him.' Kramer was struck by the similarity of Fennel's words with the terms of David Mostert's statement. He made a mental note to compare them later.

Arden: 'Did she know you were married and had children, Mr Fennel?'

Fennel: 'When I told her she decided to stop seeing me. She said my wife would find out eventually and it would destroy my family. She was right, but I still went to see her. I couldn't help it.' He looked away, out of the window at the trees, their new Spring leaves.

Arden: 'You had sex just four days before she was killed.'

Fennel: 'It was wrong, I knew that. We both did. It was that bastard she was with. He did it. He murdered her. When she broke up with him he threatened her. Told her he would kill her. That's what she said.'

Fennel was sweating.

Kramer: 'What was she wearing when you met on Friday?'

Fennel: 'Sorry - I really don't remember. Honestly.'

Kramer: 'Was it a pink suit - jacket and skirt?'

Fennel: 'I don't know. It might have been.'

Arden: 'We want you to make a statement now, Mr Fennel.'

Fennel: 'I can't. I really can't. I'm a Party member. It would ruin my business and end my marriage. I love my wife - and my kids.' He was badly shaken and looked as if he might cry. 'I'll lose everything if this gets out.'

Kramer: 'It's your choice, Mr Fennel. You make a statement now - keep it simple, factual, just as you told us - and sign it, or we come back tonight mob-handed, turn the place upside down and take you with us in cuffs, placing you under arrest right in front of the family on a charge of premeditated murder and obstruction of justice. It'll be in the morning papers, of course. It's up to you, Mr Fennel, but you must decide now.'

Fennel: 'You can't do that!' There was real horror in his eyes.

Kramer: 'Oh, we certainly can and we will.'

Fennel: 'How did you know Chelsea and I - '

Arden, giving Fennel her hardest and most puritanical look, and with more than a trace of disgust in her tone: 'You appear to have ejaculated on her Chanel skirt, Mr Fennel, the same skirt she was wearing when she was found murdered on her own doorstep two days ago.'

10

'This must be some kind of record, even for you.' They'd left the Fennels' house and were standing outside on the pavement, Arden about to go to her car, Kramer with key in hand, ready to unlock his bicycle. There was no wind and the sky was bleached white; it might only be April but it was going to be a very hot day - the forecast said the metropolis would experience yet another heat wave, the third so far this year. The London air was already foul. It wasn't so much the fact that each year was hotter than its predecessor as the sheer unpredictability of the weather that bothered Kramer; it was the uncertainty - it could snow in June and freeze in August. Kramer shrugged off his black jacket, revealing his rumpled blue shirt. He slung the jacket over his shoulder and started rolling up his shirtsleeves. He was aware that Arden was watching him, inspecting him with a curious intensity, from his scuffed police shoes all the way up - taking in the shiny, baggy trousers that sagged at the knees and bottom, the awful shirt, the open collar, his stubble. There was something mocking in her tone. Kramer didn't like it much; he ignored her remark.

Arden persisted. 'Are you pleased?'

'What do you mean?'

Kramer knew what she meant, but he wanted her to spell out her suspicion because he saw it for what it was and sought an admission from her, a declaration of where her loyalties lay and what she might do.

'I know you're some kind of intuitive genius when it comes to picking out murderers, boss - you always have been, I guess - but this, in less than three days, is truly unbelievable.' There it was, in the open, Arden's disbelief, spelled out with more than a hint of bitter sarcasm, but she retreated from it quickly, shifting gear as if afraid of being too forthright, afraid, too, possibly, of his response, though as far as Kramer knew, he'd never given her cause for trepidation. 'Why didn't you arrest Fennel? There's more than enough evidence.'

'He didn't do it.'

'You're so sure, aren't you?' Arden looked over his head up at the house they'd just left as if inspecting the gutters, avoiding his eyes now, her hands on her hips, and she was raising and lowering herself on the balls of her little feet as if exercising her calf muscles, the athlete and martial arts enthusiast always ready to spring into action. Her irritation seemed on the brink of boiling over into anger.

Kramer offered an explanation. 'Malaparte wanted an arrest by the end of the week. He's got one and it's only Wednesday. We don't need Fennel except as a witness. His statement is more than enough.'

Arden waved her hand dismissively. 'It's inadmissible. It's hearsay. No court is going to allow it.'

'Objection, your lordship. The witness's statement is testimony of the deceased's fear of the accused and of the latter's sexual cruelty.'

'Over-ruled, Detective-Inspector.'

'We'll see, won't we?'

'Same goes for the brother's emails.'

'I doubt that very much.'

Arden shrugged, turned away, and still avoiding him, she looked over the road at the park, but there was a fleeting expression Kramer caught that he couldn't decipher, something disapproving, something pained, disappointed, something that said Kramer no longer commanded her respect, her admiration. Why didn't she drive away? Why was she still waiting, and for what? Kramer wondered at it; to him it resembled the indefinable point a couple reach when they must accept the unpalatable fact that their relationship is broken, irretrievably so. Somehow, to Kramer at least, there was a finality to this moment, and it was not entirely unexpected. He bent down and put on his bicycle clips.

She knows.

*

The Battersea crematorium was busy, a conveyor belt of disposal, of waste management. People, mostly wearing black in some form or other, came and went, their expressions solemn, the close relatives in tears, clinging together and clutching tissues and handkerchiefs to their faces, holding the hands of bewildered children, crowding into the redbrick chapel, spilling out again minutes later and straggling away across the grass, heads down, drifting away as the next group hesitated, then headed for the door. Some groups numbered in the scores, others but a handful and they passed each other like blind armies, grappling with the mystery of death, each unaware of the other in their grief, confusion and, in some cases, embarrassment. Crematorium attendants like fallen angels, wingless, stony-faced and in black, shepherded them back and forth. Kramer and Arden stood silent, side-by-side, watching the proceedings over the low wall that separated the surrounding streets from the lawn, the shrubs and the building itself with its high, solid chimney that was supposed to take the smoke and stench of burnt coffins and corpses away on the breeze, only there was no breeze, just London's polluted air that was difficult to breathe at the best of times and made only more so today by the oppressive humidity. The bitter, charred stench was a bonus. Occasionally, snatches of music reached them as the doors opened and shut, sometimes jaunty guitars, once a tenor soprano, but more often fleeting cords both funereal and orchestral - Mahler and Bach seemed the favourites. Kramer thought he'd choose *The Doors* for his own bonfire, given a choice in the matter.

'Our turn,' said Arden. Startled, Kramer lurched into motion. His shirt stuck to his sweaty back. The heat slapped his face, sucked all the moisture from his pores. There were half moons of salt from dried sweat under his armpits earned from his two-mile ride over from Vauxhall. Should he have worn a tie? Should he roll his sleeves down, put on his jacket again? The public processing of death's messy detritus and all that involved made him unusually self-conscious. In the event, he did nothing - just ran his fingers through his unruly, damp hair.

The interior was plain; there was no religious iconography on display, presumably because the institution served all denominations, or none. It was a bring your own party, apparently. Put up your own crucifix, bring your own Zen Buddhist monk. Arden led, Kramer followed her, sidling into a pew right at the back. There were two other people present, and they weren't mourners. They sat near the front, on the left; they wore navy suits, were both in their late twenties or early thirties and looked coldly about them, the man on seeing Arden and Kramer nudging his female companion so that she too looked back over her shoulder to inspect them. They had hard, blank faces, the kind Kramer knew only too well, the faces of people whose humanity has been erased by their depersonalised servitude to the state. The Security Service, Kramer decided. That or Special Branch. Probably the former because MI5 staff were better paid and could afford to dress better than most police officers, even secret police.

Arden slid forward onto her knees, her hands together in front of her. She turned and frowned at him, and when Kramer took no notice, she poked him with her elbow, indicating he should get down on his knees and at least pretend to pray. Kramer had no intention of doing so; he moved further away, out of reach, and sat forward on the bench, ignoring her and looking around. 'Where's everyone?' His whisper carried to all corners of the hall or church or whatever it was. Even an attendant standing near the coffin turned his head to identify the whisperer.

Arden pretended she hadn't heard.

Well, it was a weekday. It was also a public holiday and the King's official birthday, but even so it seemed extraordinary to Kramer that the chapel or whatever people called it wasn't full to overflowing with Mostert's Cabinet colleagues, MPs, Party members and supporters, her friends and colleagues from the fashion world, her fellow models, the photographers and magazine editors, bawbags and bellends all, busily pressing the flesh, networking and playing with their bloody phones. Wasn't she a celebrity, after all? There were no media representatives, either, but perhaps that was because the police hadn't told them, and because it was all being done rather hurriedly. Their slot was only fifteen minutes. It was if Chelsea Mostert's murder had somehow signalled an abrupt end to her membership not just of life but of human history, the Party, the government, the national narrative - as if she'd never existed in the collective consciousness. Was it deliberate - had some powerful authority figure decreed that henceforth Chelsea Mostert was a non-person and had pulled down the blinds on her memory? And where, for that matter, was David Mostert? At this thought, as if on cue, the doors swung open and the burly figure of Mostert appeared, head down, not looking anywhere but straight head, hands clasped in front of him. He wore his black jeans and dark jacket over his customary black teeshirt. He moved quickly and settled in a pew near the front on the right, just across from the two secret policemen. They turned their heads as one and stared at him; he ignored them, unaware of the faux pas in failing to wear blue. Why should he? He was a foreigner, after all, and Australia no longer recognised the English monarch as head of state.

The attendant placed a wreath of flowers on the coffin, the only one; Kramer decided that David Mostert must have brought it with him.

The minutes ticked by in total silence. Finally, the attendant glanced at his watch and cleared his throat; oblivion must not be kept waiting, even for a corpse, so he approached David Mostert and bent to speak in his ear like some old and loyal family retainer, the very soul of discretion. Mostert shook his head and the attendant beat a dignified retreat, stepping backwards.

There was no music, none of Chelses Mostert's favourites, whatever they might be. The Carpenters? Massive Attack? The Clash? Land of Hope and Glory? The *Horst Wessel Lied*? Kramer told himself to stop this inappropriate line of thought.

The attendant, a pale man with a long neck and straggly grey hair, faced the five people present, his expression deadpan, and made a half-bow. He looked over at David Mostert and inclined his head again. Mostert nodded. Somewhere out of sight a button was pushed or a lever turned, for a low hum reached Kramer, and the doors of what he assumed was the furnace opened, revealing a white mass of flame; Chelsea Mostert's remains began to trundle forward in the varnished wooden coffin, bumping on rollers on their final journey to annihilation. It was a bit like riding a buggy to perdition. That should have been the end of it, but it wasn't; a regular tapping sound came from the back and those present turned, unable to help themselves. An old man tottered in, nether lip hanging loose like a camel's, eyes rheumy, back bent, one hand holding a black, silver-topped walking stick on which he leaned as he moved slowly down the aisle. A golden rose glittered in his buttonhole. He peered this way and that, his eye falling on Arden and Kramer as he passed, then he turned the other way to look at the secret police and finally, at David Mostert. Did he recognise anyone? Probably not. He stood immobile in the aisle, not bothering to take a seat, but quivering as he leaned on his stick with one hand, the other on the back of a pew. Instinctively, Kramer wanted to run forward and help hold him up before he crashed to the floor. The stranger watched the coffin and its wreath enter the boiling inferno, saw it disappear, the doors of the furnace close.

Kramer realised only then that this was the one person in England who could enjoy the privilege of not having to take orders, who had nothing to lose in turning a deaf ear to any calls to ignore the cremation; he was far too old and still far too powerful, a living legend; it was none other than the Party founder himself, Lord Henning of Dulwich, England's foremost fascist, the ultimate Untouchable, come to pay tribute to his protégée, his 'sweet girl', his acolyte and favourite ministerial nemesis of what was left of the welfare state, Chelsea Mostert. No-one could order him about; Henning could do as he pleased - he was above and beyond the law, a body celestial in the fascist universe.

The old gangster turned around, slowly, shakily, using his stick to steady himself with his left hand and in a surprisingly strong voice, addressed the multitude of six mourners as if they were six or sixty thousand, raising his free right hand, fingers together and palm flat, facing down, trembling yet thrust out straight from the shoulder as he called out: 'She died for England!'

*

Kramer hadn't noticed the flags, perhaps because he was preoccupied with cycling in such hot weather and regretting it. It only sank in as he peddled slowly along the Embankment, dodging pedestrians; the flags were everywhere, the huge ones hanging limply at regular intervals on both sides of the river, the small, triangular ones - strung closely together as bunting across side streets - giving neighbourhoods a festive air. Presumably that had been the intention. But the flags themselves were a shock, and although Kramer told himself he had expected it, just as everyone did (the design had been the product of a popularity poll among Party faithful), he wasn't really prepared for the impact. Nothing could have warned him just how radical the change would be, nor how violent. Of course the white Saltire on its pretty blue field had vanished from the Union flag - the Butcher's Apron, its critics had long called it - and that was only to be expected in the wake of the deal thrashed out in The Hague between representatives of Westminster and those from Holyrood. But the new design went a lot further; the once red St George's Cross of England was now pitch black, set on a narrow white background, and the four rectangular quarters were scarlet. Kramer stopped his bicycle and gazed along the Embankment, past the London Eye, the National Theatre draped with huge streamer-like versions, the restaurants and bookshops and gazed at the spectacle. Even in the heat, sweat rolling down his face, he had goosebumps. What had they done?

The Houses of Parliament on the far side were festooned with them, and so too the tourist boats plying the Thames flew them fore and aft. The new English national flag, incorporating what was in effect the Party's own pennant, might not carry a Teutonic eagle, but the similarity with Germany's imperial flag and subsequent Nazi symbol was nevertheless startling and not a little scary. As Kramer approached Westminster Bridge, where he had to dismount, the usual stall holder - a woman who customarily boasted a Union Jack bowler hat, selling Union Jacks and overpriced postcards - was holding out bunches of the red-and-black rectangles on short sticks to scores of Asian visitors. Apparently not everyone found them sinister; the tourists were buying them, chattering like sparrows and waving fivers in their enthusiasm - while the smallholder urged them on, 'C'mon love, only two for five quid' - the tourists unaware that they could have had them for free because the Party had paid for millions to be manufactured and distributed without charge to the populace up and down the country. As Kramer passed, the smallholder - a robust, red-faced woman - gave him a sly wink. She was making a killing, thanks to the King's birthday and the new flag; foreigners were fair game, weren't they? That hadn't changed.

*

Kramer was able to cycle in the midst of London traffic without any loss of awareness or attention and, with another part of his mind, he was capable of directed thought - in this instance, the Fennels' pleasant family home had prompted thoughts of the extreme contrast with his own Brixton mouse hole, his book-lined room, the dust and silence, the gloom, his narrow bed, the solitary nature of his existence. He reflected, not for the first time, that to be solitary, to be alone, was not in itself tantamount to loneliness. He was lonely at times, it was true, but it was an itch, a slight ache, but in Kramer's judgement, the odd pang of self-pity that had even brought him close to tears on occasion was a price far outweighed by the freedom it bought; the freedom to talk aloud to himself, to remain unwashed and unkempt if he so desired, to eat anything he liked when he wanted, not venture out at all when not on duty, to sit around naked or in his boxer shorts, to drink himself insensible, to sleep on a Caucasian rug on the floor wrapped in a blanket, to sing loudly in his flat voice, to play Shostakovich's 5th and 9th symphonies for hours, over and over, the volume up, and never be criticised or made fun of. Sometimes he needed to convince himself that this was his choice, and an hour spent sitting on his own in a busy pub or bar, listening to the conversations and accents around him and watching the other customers, their gestures, their expressions, the effect that drink had on them, the fighting and crying, the cursing, the pretentiousness, the insults, the groping and kissing and the gossip, did wonders, and was sufficient to cure him of the desire for human company for at least for a week or so - and as for sexual relief, well, Kramer found that now he was in his forties he could go for weeks without sexual contact with a foreign body of any kind, especially when working at full tilt on a new murder, and even in his down, 'black dog' periods between investigations, when the urge to find some relief became too insistent, and reached the point at which it dominated every waking moment as sometimes happened (it had been a constant of his adolescence), he had the mobile numbers of two sex workers he liked. Liked as in found sexually appealing, liked as in enjoying a pleasant and agreeable hour, liked as in being able to say goodbye without regret, without looking back, without recriminations, without anyone judging anyone else. If 'Tanya' and 'Julie' weren't free, then temporary relief in the form of Kramer's imagination and one hand in the shower was always available to him, though it left him a little ashamed of himself and out of sorts; he could never quite rid himself of the notion that masturbation was 'self-abuse' and somehow immoral and bad for him, although he knew perfectly well that this guilt was something he owed in part to his strict and puritanical father as well as the influence of Little and Large, the two anally retentive priests at his prep school who had always seemed to disapprove of all pleasure and not just the superficial joys of the flesh, but any kind of joy, even hot jam rolls (liberal quantities of the jam having impregnated the lapels of Kramer's school blazer). Enjoyment per se seemed to be a sin. Happiness was a sin, too.

These thoughts of pain and pleasure brought him around again to Chelsea Mostert and their second meeting, two weeks after the first, at the end of January.

*

By then she was in his sights, though Kramer hadn't yet made a final decision. Even so, he took every precaution, and planned the second encounter and all subsequent encounters as carefully as he could. He insisted towards the end of their first meeting that if they should call each other, and it would have to be in an emergency, only landlines would be used. No names would be mentioned. The person initiating contact would miss-call the other's cell, the party called would respond on the hour with a landline-to-landline call, both parties using London's dwindling number of public call boxes. Kramer recommended those at hotels and railway stations. When agreeing a time for a face-to-face meet, one hour and sixteen minutes would be added to the time agreed during the landline call. So a meeting set for, say, 2 p.m. would in fact takes place at 3.16 p.m. They would not arrive or leave together. Whoever remained behind would wait a full ten minutes before moving. Where possible, they would use separate exits and entrances. Ideally, meetings would be arranged face-to-face ahead of time, making calls superfluous. Chelsea was both amused and irritated by what she called his boy scout games. She accused him of being obsessive and tedious. That was certainly true. Kramer was obsessed by most things in life; he found himself reminding her in a tendentious tone -

Mostert of all people - that they lived in a surveillance state, that every electronic, digital communications device known to humankind was being watched. After all, she and her boyfriend Exeter had enthusiastically backed construction of the system with its close integration with its bigger American counterpart, all in the name of 'national security' and 'fighting terrorism', so she should know. The Internet was to be avoided at all costs. Kramer thought that if the relationship were to continue for any length of time, he would introduce her to the benefits of Wickr, though he even had his doubts about that, too, not least because he had reservations about the security of their smart phones' hardware . But he said nothing about this as yet. If they had to use names, either at the meeting itself, or on the phone, he told her he would be 'David' and she would be 'Angela'. When she giggled at his precautions and mocked him about the names, saying they were ridiculous, Kramer flatly stated it was that or nothing; take it or leave it and he didn't give a shit either way. She took it.

The location was always going to be tricky. It had to be within reach of Kramer's workplace - Scotland Yard, and it had to be a reasonable distance from Mostert's Vauxhall home. At the same time, he wanted to avoid places convenient in the lunch hour to the Security Service headquarters in the old ICI company building on the river in Westminster, as well as the Secret Intelligence Service south of the river at grandiose Vauxhall Cross, or indeed, other large police stations with Special Branch contingents. After scrutinising his London A-Z, he had settled for a pub in Pimlico. It had two doors from the street into the saloon and public bars, and a back door to an alley. Customers could see out into the street, but passers-by could not see into the interior, which was agreeably dark. For a clandestine chat, it seemed pretty good, and he doubted whether spies and secret policemen would venture this far away from their desks to meet undercover contacts.

Without further complications, they agreed both the time and place.

11

Chelsea arrived incognito. Trouble was, she looked like every celebrity trying hard not to look like a celebrity. With her silk headscarf, enormous designer sunglasses and collar turned up, hands thrust deep in the pockets of her pink cashmere car coat, she reminded Kramer of Jackie Kennedy trying to evade the paparazzi stalking her through the streets of New York. She *looked* hunted, and her expensive outfit seemed to shout out for all to see and hear: 'look at me! I'm trying to so hard to be conspicuously inconspicuous!'. As she slid into the seat opposite, Kramer asked himself the inevitable question, inevitable in the sense that he knew it had to come up and couldn't be ignored: how could he conceive of killing someone he pitied, and for whom he did feel compassion - not for her politics, of course not, but because of her status as victim trapped in a violent relationship? That was how she saw herself, and how she wished him to see her, and no doubt everyone else, too. How could he dream of doing such a terrible thing to anyone, let alone this slightly built, depressed and vulnerable woman? What kind of man kills a woman anyhow? He shrank from the notion. If he thought he could put her down like some sick or aged animal out of compassion for her suffering, a mercy killing, he was mistaken. You see, Clara, I do have a heart after all.

Chelsea lowered her shades and looked over the top of them at Kramer. 'I'll have a gin-and-tonic. Please.'

He got up without speaking, and as he went up to the bar and gave the order, he reflected on the fact that she had still not spelled out what she wanted from him, what the 'favour' was. Had she changed her mind? Had she forgotten? He turned and looked at her gazing out of the window. Had she asked someone else? He wouldn't ask or remind her of it - why should he, after all? Let her come on in her own time, walking unaided into his palisade, his killing ground, drawn within range of her own volition. Why make it easy for her? He ordered whisky for himself, a double, with one cube of ice. There were officers who wouldn't drink in order to avoid smelling of alcohol. Kramer wasn't one of them; he didn't care. He paid and carried the glasses to their table.

'Thank you.' She picked her gin up almost at once and sipped.

'Cheers.' Kramer smiled at her eagerness.

'Oh, I'm sorry.' She put the glass down.

'That's all right.'

'I was thirsty, I should have waited.'

Kramer responded with a non-committal grunt.

'Thank you for seeing me again. I wasn't sure you would.'

What did she want him to say? Don't be silly? It's nothing? Don't worry? Of course I wanted to see you? She wanted reassurance, that much was obvious, but reassurance without being frightened off or threatened in any way. What had someone called the complicated card game of Bridge? Socialising without intimacy? That was what she seemed to want, Kramer decided. They had that much in common. But he took it a little further this time; he reached across the table and took her pale, cold hand in his, squeezed it, letting it go at once. 'I'm pleased you came,' and almost smiled. He watched her to see if he'd gone too far this time, but she didn't react at all, at least not immediately. Kramer raised his glass, looked over the top of it at her, drank. The odd thing was he felt no sexual frisson whatsoever; he felt nothing at all - despite the fashionable outfit, the scent, the long boots, the sight of this posh woman slumming it in The Crown and Stag.

Slowly, deliberately, she took off her shades and looked at him.

The shiner was already a nasty purple and yellow, and the cheekbone below was badly bruised and swollen, the skin puffy and stretched tight like an apple.

'Nothing's changed, as you can see.' She put the sunglasses back on.

'When did that happen?'

'The black eye was last week, the cheekbone yesterday. He hit me with a vase. It fucking hurts, I can tell you.'

'What are you going to do?'

'What do you think I should do? You're a police officer. You tell me.'

'Leave him.'

Chelsea emptied her glass. 'Easier said then done.'

'You don't have much choice, do you?'

'He can make things very, very difficult. Leaving solves nothing.'

Kramer waited. She stared into her glass, turning it with her fingers.

'He controls me. He controls the entire fucking country. He knows everyone. He can do whatever he likes. To him, I'm just a toy, a plaything, a sexual object for his pleasure. God, I hate him.' She sat back, stared out of the window.

'Do you want another of those?'

'Yes. I'll get the next round. No, don't. I will. Please. Let me.'

When she came back, Kramer helped her put down the glasses and the bottle of tonic. 'What are your options? Let's make a list of them, starting with a divorce.'

'It would be very messy. It would get into the papers. You must understand something. I know you're a bachelor, so maybe I have to explain. The Party is very strong on family values. The family - and marriage - is central to our policy. It means that if I sue for divorce, I could lose my job in the Cabinet, even my seat in Parliament. They could take away my Party membership. Both he and I have plenty of enemies who wouldn't hesitate to use this to their advantage.' Kramer must have looked sceptical, or that was what she saw in his expression. 'Oh, believe me, they would. It would be awful. No-one's indispensable in this game.'

'Okay, so what else?'

'A court injunction - but that would be horrible, too. He'd persecute me. The beatings would only get worse.'

'You could move out, stay somewhere else. Put up with a friend for a while. Get all five members of your close protection team to be more pro-active. Even better, go abroad.'

'And you don't think he'd find out where I was - within hours? The Party has informers all over - every street, every block of flats, every exit and entry point. Heathrow, Gatwick, Southampton. You name it. He has eyes and ears everywhere. He'd know. He'd find me. You don't think my so-called bodyguards aren't on his payroll? These days, everyone gets a backhander.' She drained half her glass in one swallow, and the colour rose in her cheeks.

'Make a formal complaint of assault.'

'To whom? The police? You people? He controls the police, don't you see? Not directly, of course, not all by himself, but through the Party - people like Malaparte. Right up to the Home Secretary. All it takes is a phone call. Even if you wanted to help me as a police officer, Kramer, and do it all by the book, as you should of course, you'd be blocked. If you persisted, you'd be transferred or demoted, or both - just for trying to help. Or worse. Such things have happened. Trust me. It would go nowhere. We'd both be the losers.'

'So I can't help you - that's what you're saying.'

'Oh, but you can. You definitely can. You remember I asked you for a favour last time, but I didn't say what it was?'

Chelsea leaned forward to speak, but changed her mind and looked around to check if there was anyone within earshot. By now most of the lunchtime drinkers had gone. The bunch standing at the bar had thinned out. There was no one at the nearest table and no-one in the cubicle behind theirs.

Reassured, she leaned forward again, and Kramer followed suit so their heads were almost touching.

'You really want to help? Do you?'

'If I can, yes. Of course.' He put some enthusiasm and sincerity into it.

'Even if by doing so, you break the law?'

'Depends on the law, I suppose, and the chances of being found out.'

'I'll help you, Kramer. I will do everything I can to help you and protect you - and money would be no object. If you succeed, I will use all the influence at my disposal to get you right to the very top of your profession. You have my word.'

The word of a fascist. Terrific.

'And if I failed?'

'Then no-one could help you. It would finish me, too.'

That was frank, at least.

'So what have you in mind? What is this favour you want from me?'

'I won't blame you if you say no, if you walk out.'

'Tell me first you haven't asked this of anyone else.'

'Of course not.'

'Have you confided in a friend about how you feel?'

'No. I have no friends, not real ones.'

She pushed her glass aside, leaned forward as far as she could across the table and Kramer smelled the gin and felt the hot breath of her whisper; her fingernails touched, teased his wrist, stroking it. He felt as if he had been scalded.

'Kill him. Kill Ryan Exeter for me.'

*

Kramer sat back, withdrew his hand from the tabletop and looked at her. He rubbed his wrist where she'd touched it. He didn't say anything at first. He was surprised, but not as surprised or shocked as Chelsea probably thought he must be. He wasn't so taken aback that he failed to see the opportunity right in front of him. Her request was what decided him; it would have to be her, no doubt at all, for it opened the way, showed him how to reach his target, his goal. She had given him the means to achieve his ends, too; she had made up his mind for him without her suspecting it; she had showed her mettle, her true character. His pity was misplaced, always had been. This was no pathetic victim, an underdog cruelly whipped, a woman abused, no remorseful politician, far from it; she was one tough bitch and he was impressed - he admired the fact that at her weakest, at her most vulnerable, on the edge of tears and in pain, constantly shamed and humiliated and terrorised, she was ready to strike back against a far stronger foe, even if it meant using Kramer as a weapon, and he instantly understood her reasoning without her having to say a word, and her reasoning was inspired if not brilliant, or very nearly so. If she were indeed to hit back at her oppressor, and do so effectively, she knew she would have just one shot at it; it would have to be a lethal attack, it would have to be ruthless as it must be final. There would be no second chance. After all, he reasoned, if you want to commit the perfect murder - not there's ever such a thing because all murderers make mistakes - then you don't hire assassins or thugs, and you certainly don't do it yourself. She'd figured out that much. Instead, you persuade the country's top homicide detective to do it for you, someone nobody knows you know (except possibly the intended victim), someone you haven't slept with, don't socialise with, don't include in your network of comrades, friends, associates past or present, not an old school buddy, not a fellow Oxford alumnus, not even someone from your own class, pay grade or neighbourhood, no-one who drops round for coffee or supper, no-one on your cocktail circuit, no-one who turns up to your constituency meetings, no-one who sends you emails, or greets you outside a school attended by your children. It had to be an outsider, a misfit, a rogue copper, a freak, yes, he was all those things, a total stranger - well, almost, at least as far as everyone else was concerned. Finally, it had to be someone experienced, who knew what he was doing, who was such a success that he could do no wrong, whose judgement was never seriously questioned. Well, almost.

Oh, she was good was Chelsea Mostert. Soundlessly, mentally, he applauded her. Kramer had to stop himself smiling at her, partly out of amusement, partly admiration, partly because he realised the cold, calculating Secretary of State for Work and Pensions, in asking him to commit murder, hadn't an inkling of who or what she was dealing with, and what she was getting herself into. He even felt a tweak of desire for her. She had no notion, for example, that she'd just signed up to her own violent and sudden death, that she had offered herself up as a sacrifice on his altar, that at the very end of her own life the last thing she'd see of this world would be her executioner.

None other but yours truly.

For distraction he picked up his glass, tipped it up and swallowed the sliver of ice at the bottom. 'I think I'll have another. You'll join me?' He didn't really want another double, though he knew he would enjoy it, but he did want to play for time, to let her feel the tension of being forced to wait while he enjoyed himself even if it did make him a little tipsy. Chelsea shook her head. She watched him closely, screwing up her eyes; she wanted an answer, she was trying to work out from his expression which way he would go, but as usual his battered, enigmatic and blank, bird-like face gave nothing away. He slid along the bench, taking his empty glass with him. 'Won't be a moment.'

Did he have enough for another round? He counted his cash on the bar, taking his time, surreptitiously watching her out of the corner of his eye. He decided he did have enough, after all. She was sitting bolt upright, turned away, twirling her glass around and around with her long fingers, staring fixedly at nothing out of the window. She wanted his answer, he could tell. She'd been building up to this for what, weeks? Kramer changed his mind when the barman came over to him, ordered ginger ale instead, insisting on his customary single ice cube, paid and returned to the cubicle, put the glass down carefully, sat, offered up a twitch in the corner of his mouth that could have been an automatic smile, one without warmth.

'Cheers.'

Chelsea Mostert was in agonised suspense and not used to being kept waiting by anyone; she lunged forward. 'Well?'

He sipped his 'whisky', grunted with something approaching pleasure or approval, wiped his lips with the back of his right hand, a gesture he knew she would find uncouth which was why he did it. 'Well, what?'

'Will you, or won't you?'

Kramer put the tip of a forefinger with its bitten down nail into his drink, then sucked it. He was enjoying feeling her winding up tight like a watch-spring. Wait until I'm ready.

'I need to think about it. I need some time.'

'Oh, God. How much time?'

He scratched his forehead, the receding hairline, frowned. 'A couple of weeks? Can you survive that long?'

'Look, I'll help you, you know. I really will.'

'No. I want to make a couple of things clear to you right from the start. All right?' She nodded several times, quickly, anxiously. His voice was hard, commanding, the tone expressing Kramer's insistence that he was now in charge. He had control. This was his territory. 'Okay. Listen. No money is going to change hands. Not now, not ever.' She didn't react. 'Second, if I decide to go ahead, I tell you nothing. No details. And you won't ask. You won't try to find out. You won't even know me. I call the shots. All of them. I give you orders. And you stay the hell out of it. Got that?'

She nodded again, but it was a very slight nod, barely perceptible. It occurred to Kramer that it must sound to her like the 'yes' she wanted from him, but she wasn't sure and anyway, although he had already made up his mind he was going to play her on his hook as long as he needed to.

There was an edge to his voice now. 'If I do this, *you* are the last person on this earth who is going to help. Understood?'

'Yes.' Her response was testy, irritated.

'Right, then. Now we'd better talk about our next meeting and sort it. You want to make it a fortnight from now? Then I'll give you my answer.'

Keep her waiting, make her sweat, make her beg for it; yes, certainly - Kramer wanted her both compliant and a willing accessory in her own premeditated destruction.

*

The sky was dull steel, any colour sucked out of it by the heat, the river sluggish as mud. Kramer's shirt clung to him wetly. He reached the centre of the bridge, the highest point, moved to the kerb and stopped; dismounting, he looked forward and back, over his shoulder. He had been so deeply engaged in cycling on the one hand and remembering his initial meetings with Chelsea on the other that he'd failed to pay any attention to what was taking place. The first thing was the noise; the roar grew steadily louder until it was deafening and only when it seemed unbearable did Kramer understand what it was: a rehearsal of the royal fly-past. The first aircraft were the U.S.-built F35s, the most expensive combat aircraft ever built and almost totally useless. Three of them now tore overhead, followed by some obsolete fighters, F-4 Phantoms, at least forty years old, then, if that wasn't historical enough, the museum pieces lumbered by; a World War 2 Wellington bomber and a couple of Spitfires. They were all headed for Buckingham Palace where, at 11 a.m. sharp, His Majesty would appear en famille on the balcony, dressed not in military uniform this time, but Party regalia as honorary president.

Of greater interest to Kramer was what was happening at street level; groups of Party thugs were systematically clearing the bridge and embankment, several dozen of them working both sides, kicking and beating the homeless, demolishing their cardboard boxes, dismantling tents and seizing backpacks. Several of the last went into the river; the homeless themselves crawled, ran or hobbled away as best they could, trying to escape the truncheons, coshes and boots. Several had no chance; they were knocked down or tripped, curling up and protecting heir heads with their arms and receiving a thorough kicking as they lay prostrate by several young thugs simultaneously. Uniformed police - they were in shirtsleeves and caps - were present in considerable numbers but did nothing to intervene. All they did was watch. For their part, the thugs wore khaki shirts and navy combat pants, high, military-style boots, Sam Browne belts, and red-and-black brassards. Kramer knew His Majesty would wear something very similar, the only difference being the enormous number of awards and medals that would decorate the latter's shirt, most of which he'd awarded to himself.

Kramer remounted and freewheeled slowly down to the Westminster side. There was no civilian traffic, and he saw why. Cohorts of Party supporters, marshalled by their own kind in high visibility vests, were forming up, each group several hundred strong, and flanked by police officers. Each carried a banner announcing their origin: Wolverhampton, Middlesborough, Portsmouth, Cardiff, York, Liverpool. They marched six deep, and most carried ten foot poles bearing the new English flag. They too were headed for the Palace. Directly ahead of him, where the bridge decanted onto the Embankment, was a checkpoint built around the statue of Boudica and her chariot with its huge wheel blades, manned by both troops in camouflage combats and police. What would she have made of it? As he came within a few metres he noted two armoured personnel carriers, sandbags, razor wire and 44-gallon drums painted black and red.

He had his warrant card ready.

A burly police sergeant, peaked cap with its chequer board band on the back of his head, and a young soldier who could not have been more than 22 intercepted him, the soldier with his automatic weapon over his arm standing back and to one side, well-placed to shoot. The sergeant came right up, took the warrant card, gazed at it for a couple of moments, then saluted. He carried a pistol on his belt.

Instead of handing it back straight away, the sergeant looked back over his shoulder and raised the hand holding the card.

'Won't be a moment, sir.'

'What's the problem, sergeant?'

'No problem, sir.'

A plainclothes officer in teeshirt and jeans had come up and taken the card from the sergeant and held it up to his face and squinted at it as if short sighted. Kramer knew what he was by the shaved head, the tight mouth, careful eyes and the handgun in the back of his jeans.

'Headed for the Yard, are you, guv'nor?'

'That's right.'

'You won't get through, sir. Not on the bike. Not on foot, neither. We're expecting at least 60,000 more coming this way over the next hour and I wouldn't even try, if I were you. They don't take kindly to folk going the wrong way. Not safe.'

He turned - just as the sergeant had - and signalled to someone.

'No worries, Detective Inspector, we'll give you a lift and take your bike along, too.

'You don't have to. I can turn around and go home.'

'That's all right. Our pleasure.'

'It's not necessary. really.'

'You carrying, sir?'

He had to hand it to them; it was neatly and unobtrusively done with plenty of reassurance to keep him pacified; he couldn't have done it any better himself - in a second the sergeant had his arms pinioned behind him, and the plainclothes copper went through his pockets, leaving his cash alone but taking a pen and notebook. 'Clean,' he said. They had the van all ready; it had reversed up, the rear door was open and the young soldier helped his police colleagues by coming forward, picking up Kramer's bike and sliding it into the interior. The van was black, big, box-like, armoured, unmarked, with wire mesh over windscreen and lights.

'In you go, sir.'

Kramer was lifted up the step and pushed into the interior. 'What the hell are you doing?'

'I'm placing you in protective detention, Detective-Inspector. Don't fret yourself now. You're perfectly safe and I'm told it won't be for long and you'll back with us in no time.'

'Where are you taking me?'

But the door had shut before anyone had a chance to answer had they wanted to. Someone banged on the outside and the vehicle began to move, nosing its way through the crowds of Party faithful, many of them shirtless and clutching cans of beer. It was a public holiday, after all. Kramer was the only passenger.

12

After the visit to the Fennels' home, Arden drove back to Camden, leaving Kramer to his bicycle clips. She was very careful; she felt increasingly uneasy as she tried to evade the crowds of almost entirely white and male hooligans converging on the Mall and Buckingham Palace. She kept away from the main routes and stopped more than once to consult her London street map; it wasn't yet noon and many marchers were clearly drunk. God help any tourists foolish enough to turn up. There were scuffles with police on Vauxhall Bridge Road, and with one another - anyone, it seemed, who happened to be within range of their fists and boots and the two-by-fours they used for their English flags. All of Whitehall seemed to have been cordoned off, guarded by troops and their armoured vehicles. As a police officer, and a black one to boot, she did her best to stay well clear of both, reversing fast to get away from the marchers at one point, and she didn't hesitate to go down one-way streets the wrong way. Arden's palms were sweaty; the tension was getting to her. She felt vulnerable, and thought at first she might go home to her own tiny flat, but the sight of the mobs convinced her that Beth's was much closer and far nicer in every way; Beth herself might be there, or she might be out shrinking heads of whatever it was psychologists did to their clients (no, that was too unkind and not at all funny!), but she told herself she could nap, play music, read and wait for her - all the stuff she was always wanting to do and never getting around to. Now was her chance.

It was a relief to shut the front door and leave the world outside, but she hadn't been there twenty minutes before the silence of the flat got to her, so she hummed to herself, made coffee, drank it, put on an Aloe Blacc album to drown out the street sounds of cheers and chanting, and to the beat of *Wake Me Up* and *Ticking Bomb*, she swept, dusted, wiped, scrubbed and tidied, all the while humming along. She worked up a sweat, and under a cold shower wondered how Kramer had coped on his bike. She hadn't asked where he was headed; she assumed it was Brixton and felt better about it - he would miss the gathering masses.

Naked and still wet from the shower, she called him. No answer. She left a message. 'Let me know you're okay, boss, all right?' She knew he wouldn't, though. He never had, unless it was work.

No sooner had she finished and put her cell down, than it buzzed.

'Morrison here. Where's Kramer?' The senior technician had no time for pleasantries and from his blunt tone Arden could tell he was upset.

'No idea. Sorry.' A figure of speech, mind - Arden wasn't in the least sorry.

'Malaparte's vanished. I've got the completed reports on forensics and ballistics right here; you know we've sweated blood to get them out this fast, now both Kramer and Malaparte are out of pocket. I've also wasted a couple of hours looking for these gents. I've got work to do, for Chrissakes.'

'Can't help, I'm afraid.'

'Are you coming in?'

'No.'

'Nice for some.'

'I'm under orders from Malaparte to stay away until summoned. Kramer ditto.'

'Jesus H. Christ. So what do I do? Everyone's been press-ganged into crowd control. Or should I say riot control. It's crazy out there. This place is deserted.'

'Slide a copy under my door if it's locked. If it isn't, leave it on my desk. Keep one yourself under lock and key. If you have another, keep it for Kramer.'

'If you say so.'

'I do.'

'Look, Detective Sergeant, what the fuck's going on?'

'Meaning?' Arden didn't like talking to Morrison at the best off times, but certainly not while naked for some odd reason, and she was trying, unsuccessfully, to wrap a towel around herself while still holding onto her cell.

'Rumours. That Exeter has been charged with murder and detained.'

'Correct.'

'Bloody hell. There's talk Malaparte has been transferred or suspended and is under some kind of secret internal investigation.'

'I hadn't heard that one. It seems unlikely - he's Party.'

'And Kramer, snatched by Special Branch and taken off to Christ knows where.'

'I was with him less than two hours ago.'

'Okay.'

'Okay, then.' She cut the connection. It was never a pleasure dealing with Morrison, and it wasn't her job to reassure the man and, aside from that, she wanted to keep her line open in case Kramer called. Not that she really wanted to talk to him; her feelings about Kramer were particularly confused and contradictory, and she recognised that it was the strangeness of Beth's empty flat and the fact that she was alone with thousands of Neo-Nazis and diehard monarchists roaming the streets looking for trouble that made a conversation with him seem almost desirable. It wasn't, not really. She was upset, angry, disappointed, fearful, worried about him, too. Never before had her loyalty and her concern for him been tested to this extent. Not for a moment did she take Morrison's comment about him being picked up by Special Branch seriously. Anyway, what about her friends? Surely she could call someone. There was her mother in Croydon, but she hated talking to her if only because mum had the notion her only child was still only ten years old and needed a lot of fussing over, and the nagging was usually preceded by a lengthy interrogation of a personal nature. No, mum, not today, I haven't the strength or the patience. No, I don't have a nice, clever, rich boyfriend who wants to marry me. Sorry again, all right? Her mother simply refused to accept that her daughter's interests lay elsewhere. As for her father, she hadn't had any contact with him for more years than she cared to remember, and just thinking about him made her feel uneasy. He knew, he certainly did, and couldn't forgive her, as if her sexual inclinations were a matter for blame. Never mind all that shit now. As for friends, they were still in her contact book, but that was all. Names and numbers. She'd shed friends with an awful regularity once she had joined the Met. Police work and personal relationships did not sit well together. Some had openly and loudly disapproved of her chosen profession and they'd stopped speaking as soon as they found out. Girls' nights out were a thing of the far and distant past - she no longer recognised the outgoing, laid-back Nicole Arden of those days. She was tempted to phone Beth, just to hear her voice, but then she knew the kind of intensity Beth experienced at work. She hated being interrupted when she had a client. Best not.

Cheer up, she told herself. Don't be such a misery. Read. Sleep. Watch TV.

Outside on the street, glass broke, a popping followed by a tinkling, and again, each time to cheers and jeers. She peeked out, careful to disturb the curtains as little as possible. She saw they were using catapults to take out CCTV cameras, street lights, shop windows and car windscreens. Uniformed police did not intervene.

Arden turned from the third floor window, checked her pistol, taking it out of its holster, jacked one of twelve rounds into the chamber, put the Walther on safe and set it down next to her on the sofa, touching the cool metal with the fingers of her right hand; she felt somewhat reassured by its proximity. She lay back on the cushions, eyes on the front door, which she knew was double locked and on the chain. Finally, uneasily, she slept.

*

Something woke her; she lay perfectly still still, holding her breath, listening, but it seemed the crowds had long gone. Arden checked her watch; she'd slept for three hours. Kramer was on her mind - she told herself she must have been dreaming about him. Arden realised she was having doubts; yes, of course, he *could* have murdered Chelsea Mostert. He *could* have planted the evidence. He had opportunity, no doubt about it - but then so had she. So did several officers, come to that. But motive? *Why* would he? There was nothing to suggest Kramer and victim knew each other; quite aside from the odd and peculiar remark he'd made from time to time that suggested Kramer had a rather unconventional take on politics and the world in general, that peculiar episode on Monday outside the Commons, for instance, but there was nothing she knew that indicated he was linked to some extremist group or dissident organisation. He was too much of a loner for voluntary joint action; he didn't like people enough to work with them. He could have blurted out silly stuff from time to time because he was tired or stressed or drunk or all three - not that he'd ever really been properly drunk in her presence; tipsy, yes, loose-tongued, sure, but never - to use his weird phrase - blootered. She'd never seen him give money to the homeless, or express pity for the poor, and these days, you couldn't miss them in London; they were everywhere. There was nothing at all in his personal file to suggest radicalism. She knew - because three months ago she'd looked; she wasn't supposed to, but she knew someone who knew someone in human resources and she had been left alone with it for five minutes. There wasn't much there, in truth, and she didn't need five but around two minutes. There had been nothing to suggest that he was a closet Green or socialist. He wasn't Labour when Labour was still on life support and kicking feebly against the Party pricks. He wasn't CND, didn't join public protests over Palestinian ethnic cleansing, or cuts in the state pension and cancellation of benefits for the disabled. He was never one for trumpeting injustice. He was no Facebook activist. He kept to himself. All she'd found between the buff covers were several sheets setting out a long list of his successes as a criminal investigator, the official commendations and promotions, and despite the dull officialese and police jargon, it was still impressive - and she had expected nothing less.

Nothing about stealing drugs from the evidence room.

So what possible reason could he have? What had she missed?

There had been one odd, out-of-place entry in the form of a single, stained sheet of official paper featuring the words 'Harare Magistrate's Court' with the Zimbabwe national arms above the words. Apparently Joseph Kramer had been released with a caution for the manufacture and possession of five rounds of .45 ammunition. Only five rounds? And why . 45 - did he own a weapon of some kind? The manufacture of these bullets was the interesting bit; it meant Kramer had the tools and the expertise to mould the alloy, a press to stamp the cartridge cases, the chemistry know-how to mix the powder or cordite or whatever it was called (Arden knew next to nothing about firearms) - but if indeed he could do all that, why only five cartridges? Presumably such ammunition was unavailable in Zimbabwe. Where were the rest? And the real question was how someone had dug up this obscure official document and attached it to his confidential personal file? What had Kramer being doing there in the first place? She noted the date: September 9, 1999.

So, was there something right there, if not in his file then in Arden's scattered knowledge of the man, staring her in the face, hiding in plain sight? She found herself swinging wildly from this emotional conviction he had done it to a logical certainty that he couldn't have, not simply on the basis of a pair of disposable blue gloves. She recognised it said more about her current state of mind than it did about him.

Kramer was surely too intelligent to imagine that killing Chelsea Mostert would in some way damage the government, that it would make them rethink their attitude, revise their estimation of the effect of their policies on the working poor. Kramer couldn't be that naive. If the murder had any effect at all, it would most likely be the opposite of the desired effect; Arden reasoned that it would only encourage ministers to redouble their efforts in destroying what little left of the post-war settlement. Those people didn't care about half a million destitute, homeless kids. Did Kramer? Did he perhaps see himself as some kind of avenging angel, visiting retribution on the guilty, someone who dedicated himself to righting social wrongs, to seeking vengeance for those unable to stand up for themselves? Nothing he'd done or said in Arden's company supported this notion. He wasn't altruistic in that sense; he didn't submerge himself in causes, charities or humanity's failings as far as she could tell.

No, she had no solid grounds for suspicion, not really, though she *was* suspicious; unlike Kramer, Arden regarded herself as a rational and reasonable person. Intuition and instinct weren't enough. She left that stuff to Kramer. It might work for him, but not her. Suspicion alone wasn't enough, she decided, not when it came to someone she'd worked with for almost a year, someone she had - until now - respected, trusted. Face it, girl, you've benefitted from his success; his success has been yours, too. Getting up from the sofa, she decided she'd been unfair to him. Ungrateful. She went over to the kitchen sink, filled a tall glass to the brim with tap water and drank it down in one.

What she should do, she told herself, was write down everything that had happened since Monday, every detail, step-by-step, every single action that she could remember. She was missing something; it was the kind of minor thing in the corner of her eye, something innocuous, the kind of thingy that Kramer would have pounced upon immediately, but which she had to reach in her deliberate, slow, dogged and reasoned way. What he saw in an instant and could use to build an entire case would take her hours or days to find, and even then she'd be full of hesitation. Very well. Never mind all that; she would do it the hard way, and not for the first time. She would find a pen and paper and start. It would at least occupy her until Beth got back, whenever that was.

Her cell beeped and she put the empty glass down, turned back to the living room. That must be Beth now and she hurried to pick up.

'DS Arden.' She spoke in a deep, mock-serious voice.

'Porter. Dave Porter. Don't think we've met, Detective-Sergeant. I'm ADC (Crime).'

'Sir.' Oh, no. What the fuck. Arden resisted the urge to snap to attention.

'Can you come in?'

'Now?' Arden closed her eyes, took a deep breath.

'If it's not too inconvenient. If you have nothing more important to do. I know it's a public holiday.' Smooth, public school, authoritative, the sarcasm carefully controlled, hidden, a graduate no doubt in criminal psychology or sociology. What he was really saying (she reminded herself that members of the white English middle classes never ever say what they really mean, they'd rather die first) was that if she wanted to stay a copper and a detective in the Met, she'd bloody well better jump to it.

'I can, yes.'

'Would you like us to send over a couple of officers as an escort?'

'No, I'll be fine. Thanks.'

Arden was sure that the last thing she needed when it came to her own security was a police car and two uniformed officers. They'd attract the kind of attention it would be best to avoid.

She knew the name and the rank of the voice, but not the face. Assistant Deputy Commissioner, with special responsibility for violent crime, including homicide. Malaparte's boss, up there among the gods. Positively celestial.

'You know where to my find my office?'

'Yessir, I think so.' Of course she effing did.

'Excellent.' That cool exaggeration again. 'We'll be waiting. Walk right in.' His voice was like a cold, sharp blade pressed against the back of her neck and Arden shivered.

'Right.' *We?*

'To put your mind at ease, DS Arden, it's good news. So relax, all right?'

'Sir?' Who said she wasn't relaxed? She was perfectly goddam relaxed.

'You're being promoted, DS Arden, and with immediate effect. Let's talk, shall we? I'll expect you in what - thirty or forty minutes? Be careful out there, wont you?'

Patronising sod. She supposed she should have been excited. She wasn't, not one tiny bit.

Arden stood at the window, forehead against the pane; despite her long snooze she felt both light-headed and numb, unable to make sense of anything; the hottest day of the year was at last giving way to long purple shadows in the deserted streets and broken glass littered the pavements, winking up at her like rippling water in the softening light. The pollution, the heat, the dust - it splashed the western sky above London rooftops a gory red: a blood-sodden sunset.

13

Whoever they were, they weren't taking Kramer to the Yard - that much was evident in the first few minutes. He tried to make out where they were going, hurting his wrists and fingertips by throwing himself up at the side of the van and clinging to the tiny aperture, jumping up and hanging from it for a moment or two before he was shaken loose; it was little more than a ventilation duct - it was barred, and covered with heavy mesh not only to keep passengers in but projectiles out. He felt they were heading south, across the river, then they seemed to turn east. He tried three times; he had glimpses of shadow and sunlit pavement, that was all.

Kramer felt like a parcel, a sack tossed this way and that.

Some thirty minutes later the van halted, the rear door swung open.

'Out!'

He had only to look up to know immediately where he was as the uniformed screws emerged from the reception block to take possession of the latest arrival. Someone held a clipboard, someone else scrawled something, then two of them grabbed his arms, frog-marched him to the first of 13 gates and doors that barred the way between freedom on the outside and his cell deep within. He knew Belmarsh well; a Category A men's prison, built in the 1990s, and like the rest of them hopelessly overcrowded, a sprawling complex of red brick built on the site of what had once been the military's Woolwich Arsenal. It housed especially violent prisoners, child murderers and rapists in particular, as well as those deemed to pose a threat to 'national security': spies, saboteurs, war criminals, convicted terrorists, high-level dissidents and subversives, corrupt politicians and businessmen. Difficult journalists, also, such as Julian Assange.

One prison officer marched a little way out in front, unlocking, drawing bolts, then waiting for the escort and prisoner to move past while locking up again after them.

The escort: two on either side, in step, gripping his elbows, hurrying him along. They kept turning to look at him, zookeepers practised in anticipating how a predator is going to react from one second to the next. Are you going to give us any bother was what their eyes asked. Kramer wasn't; the odds were not in his favour.

A fourth came up behind, the one in charge, keeping a little space between them, truncheon drawn; a shaved head, pockmarked face, thin mouth, a stout HMP Service man with sergeant's stripes. There was some sort of reception area and Kramer was searched again, more thoroughly this time, and ordered to strip. His captors formed a circle around him; he noted they were equipped with Tasers as well as truncheons, but no firearms that he could see. His bits and pieces taken when he was detained - without the bicycle - were listed and placed in a brown envelope. A folded grey blanket, orange prison overalls, prison slippers - well, that's what they looked and felt like - were thrown at him so he had to bend down and pick them up off the tiles while they watched him. Nothing was said; Kramer matched their blank expressions with his own - there was no fear, no anxiety, no anger, no curiosity on his beaky face, and he made no effort to ingratiate himself. He said nothing, asked nothing. Nothing for them to use because he knew they were on he lookout for that. He didn't fiddle or fidget. They were reading him; they wanted a handle, a way in, a means of getting to him at the outset and he was not going to oblige. He had made up his mind; they'd have to work hard but still they'd get nothing out of him.

His cell offered no surprises; it was standard single-occupancy and he could count himself fortunate that he was indeed alone because most prisoners had to double up. It was painted white, and recently: narrow bunk, steel toilet, washbasin, tiny desk screwed into the wall opposite the bunk, also steel, stool ditto, two small shelves, on the bunk a thin foam mattress covered in plastic, a small barred window, high up on the back wall. A central electric light and one over the desk. There were no signs of previous occupants. When the screws had gone, and slammed the cell door behind them, he lay on his back on the mattress, hands behind his head, as countless prisoners had done before him in this very cell. Kramer told himself he should get some sleep because he was going to need it; they'd come for him, sooner rather than later, and he had no doubt it would be a very long night. There was no television - that was something that had to be earned with merit points, and they knew what they could do with them. He loathed television anyway. His gut rumbled - he'd had nothing to eat since he'd been detained save for an apple and a cardboard cup of cold, unsweetened coffee.

*

At first they were civil.

'Let's start with Monday morning. Okay?'

Kramer looked at him, said nothing. The interrogator was almost bald, and had sensibly cut whatever survived of his hair very short. What there was left was silver on the sides. He was clean-shaven, had brown eyes, thick brown eyebrows, and an uneven, nobbly sort of face, as if whoever had put it together hadn't organised it properly. Nothing seemed to fit, particularly the cheekbones and jaw. The nose was large, blunt, slightly upturned, like the prow of a trireme, made for ramming. He wore half-moon spectacles and his hands were big, like a farmer's or labourer's. Only they were very white. The hands and their fat fingers ceaselessly shuffled papers and waggled a felt-tip pen. There was a gold signet ring on his left pinkie. He was overweight, the flesh of his neck straining at his collar. To Kramer he looked very English. He gave the man a nickname: Yeoman. His companion was a woman, thin, straight-backed, middle aged, dark-haired, dressed in black with what looked like a blue silk scarve, in all, severe-looking. She looked back at him, said nothing. Kramer dubbed her the Spanish Widow.

The male interrogator, Yeoman, stopped his fiddling and looked up expectantly at Kramer over the top of his glasses.

Kramer met his look with his own expressionless, owlish stare.

'So who ordered you to take on the investigation?'

Kramer held his stare, said nothing.

'Was it Detective Superintendent Malaparte?'

Yeoman was turning his pen end over end.

Kramer kept very still, breathing lightly.

They had taken him from his cell close to midnight - by his estimate - and still groggy from sleep, cuffing him for the short walk down a corridor, then unlocking and removing the restraints and shoving him none too gently into what he was supposed was an interview room; bare save for a one-way mirror, table, three chairs, two of which were occupied by his questioners. The strip lights made him wince and squint at his questioners.

'We're waiting.'

151

'Who are *you*?'

'We ask the questions. You answer. I repeat: who was it who ordered you to take charge of the murder inquiry on Monday morning?'

Kramer was a police officer of some years' standing, and he knew better than most that when questioned by police officers the very best thing for a civilian to do is not answer, to say absolutely nothing, unless of course the individual being questioned has an inclination for self-destruction, because everything and anything said would be used against that individual. Each and every utterance would be snapped into bits, taken out of context, misinterpreted, edited and reworked to mean something else entirely. That was the way the system worked. Even if the right to silence had been scrapped - in itself a grave violation of civil rights and common law across the rest of Europe - it was still a first line of defence, and an important one. The only really justifiable information to give up was one's name and address, that, and certainly nothing else.

'The right to silence has been abrogated, Detective Inspector. You are obliged to answer.'

'And if I don't - what then?'

Kramer looked first at Yeoman, then switched his attention to Spanish Widow.

'What am I charged with?'

'We ask the questions.'

At this point Spanish Widow leaned forward, raised a bony hand. 'You have not been charged. You are not under arrest. You are helping us with our inquiries.' She seemed so firm, so reasonable. Matron handling small boys suffering from homesickness.

Yeoman pursed his lips, took a deep breath; he didn't approve of concessions, but the intervention suggested to Kramer that Spanish Widow was the senior of the pair.

'What inquiries?'

Spanish Widow spoke again. 'We can't share that information.'

Kramer addressed himself to her. 'If I am charged with no crime, and I am not under arrest, and you won't inform me what these inquiries are that I'm supposed to be assisting with, then I have every right to walk out of here and you have no legal right to prevent me.' In his own ears, Kramer sounded like one of those legalistic young students trying to argue his or her way out of indefinite internment in the wake of some public protest. He knew it was pointless. Under the Emergency, no-one had any rights.

Yeoman almost smiled. He threw down his pen, expanded his chest and leaned back. 'You really don't seem to understand your situation, Detective Inspector. Under the terms of the National Security Act of 2020 you have no such right. You are detained as long as we choose to hold you.'

'Who is 'we'? Who are you people?'

Silence.

Spanish Widow, softly, almost kindly, as if addressing a rather dim child, offering sweeties if said child would comply with the omnipotent adult's request: 'We simply want your help. Do you understand? That's all. If you answer our questions fully and honestly, Mr Kramer, I can promise you that you will be out of here and on your way home in a matter of hours and certainly in time for breakfast.'

What was such a 'promise' worth in this place, and from such a person? Nothing. Double nothing. Less than double nothing. Kramer did not respond. His strange, flat, unblinking eyes watched them.

*

Kramer had no inkling how long the questioning had lasted, or what time it was when he was taken back to his cell. If there was something that struck him as odd it was the silence. All the prisons he had visited during the course of his police work had been intolerably noisy, from Wandsworth and Wakefield to Wormwood Scrubs - the hard brick walls and cement floors, the metal bars, the big spaces were sounding chambers and every shout, scream, cry, fart, blow, profanity, racking cough and insane laugh seemed magnified, and when multiplied by the number of inmates, usually in the hundreds or even thousands, it was an inferno of human misery, with at least one death in custody every other day in English jails. But not here, not now.

There wasn't a sound.

He slept, despite the heat which made him thirsty, the rumbling of hunger, the glare of the central ceiling light that stayed on and over which he had no control, though he had looked for the switch. He slept, turned on his side and facing the wall, arms folded and feet to the door, a corner of the scratchy blanket over his eyes.

*

Kramer heard them enter, though they tried to take him by surprise; it was the metal door squeaking open that woke him, but by the time he had lifted his head, squinting at the bright overhead light, his left hand raised to shield his eyes, they were already standing over him and the first blows had started falling. His assailants battered him all over, using long rubber batons and - yes, he saw them rise and fall - a rolled up telephone directory that he knew would leave no marks. He couldn't make out his attackers' faces; the floor was not the best place to recognise anyone, and Kramer used his arms to shield his head - only later would he reflect on the fact that they seemed to deliberately avoid striking his face, which gave him some idea what this was all about. They wanted him presentable, apparently, at least superficially. For further questioning? For a court appearance, perhaps, as witness or the accused?

But while it was happening, all he could do was concentrate on self-preservation. That meant tumbling off the bunk immediately it started, falling to the floor and taking his blanket with him, scrabbling as far as he could under the bunk like a dog trying to evade his master's whip, rolling up like a centipede under attack, making his priority the protection of head and his balls. He was struck hundreds of times, at least, that's what it felt like, a blizzard aimed at legs, shoulders, back, arse, thighs, arms. He couldn't fight back, and didn't try. He made no protest and did not cry out.

All he could hear were the smack of the batons on his body, and his attackers' grunts as they flailed at him. They grabbed him and dragged him out from under the bunk, clawed the blanket away, though he clung on as best he could, then they switched targets and struck his hands to make him let go.

They were gone as quickly as they had arrived; it was impossible to tell how long the assault had lasted. Two minutes? Twenty? He thought there must have been four or five of them, taking turns to keep up the momentum of the beating because he reasoned that only three at most could actually crowd into the cell with enough room to use their batons effectively. Who were they?

He was conscious and wasn't bleeding at the end of it, but the pain was like fire in his muscles and bones; Kramer groaned from the pain, unaware of doing so, and tears sprang from his eyes.

Would they be back? Silly bloody question.

He wouldn't sleep. Mustn't. He pushed himself into the corner of the cell, at the end of his bunk farthest from the cell door, huddled there, his back wedged into the right angle of the two walls, knees pulled up, waiting for the next attack. He had nothing to defend himself with; he had an empty box of matches which he crushed in his right hand so that bits of it protruded from between his fingers. He would try to strike the first intruder in the face, hit him in the eyes and gouge as best he could. In his left he held a tin mug and with this he planned to ram the open end into an attacker. He would lash out with his feet. His blanket was folded and wrapped around his torso as protection. None of this would be effective, he knew, but he had to try.

Kramer waited.

*

Yeoman and Spanish Widow were in precisely the same place behind the table. It was as if they hadn't moved but had been there the whole time - through his sleep, the assault. They were dressed the same way. Nothing about them had altered in the slightest; there wasn't so much as a cigarette end or an empty coffee cup to indicate they'd taken even a breather - they did not look at him as he was half-carried in, pushed down into the vacant chair opposite his interrogators. They didn't bother with manacles this time. Yeoman's big fingers played with the cuffs of his shirt, Spanish Widow stared down at her bony white hands resting on the metal table.

Were they ashamed, embarrassed?

Kramer was in pain. Whatever way he held himself, he was racked with shooting pains, especially his ribs; if his attackers hadn't cracked any, they'd certainly succeeded in bruising several, and no matter how he sat or slumped, he had to grit his teeth not to cry out or moan. His back was burning, his arm muscles quivered involuntarily, even his legs twitched as if needles were being driven into them. Every part of him was alive and crying out in agony, and every breath - in or out - was a cruel flash exploding in his brain. Those rubber truncheons had certainly proved their worth.

'How many detectives did you have to help investigate the murder of Chelsea Mostert?'

Kramer did not seem to hear the question, and if he did, he paid it no attention whatsoever. He was swaying back and forth in his chair, his manacled hands pushed down between his thighs. At the end of every forward motion, he grunted. He wasn't sure if they could hear him and he didn't care; somehow this expulsion of breath at the back of his throat seemed to help. He ground his teeth together in his effort not to moan loudly. He put all his pain into his hate for the two interrogators. He focussed on them without having to look at them; they knew what he'd been through, they'd ordered the beating, the 'softening up' and now they were studiously avoiding looking at the results. Gutless they were. Fuck them and their questions. He fantasised about paying them back in kind, straddling them and beating the seven holy shits out of them until they are unrecognisable. This vengeful little fantasy made him feel a little better.

Did they know he was a murderer? Did they suspect? Had Arden talked? Even if she had, he reasoned, she didn't know his ultimate aim, his real target, and the way he planned it. How could she know?

'How many uniformed officers were you assigned that first day?'

Kramer continued to sway like a trawler's mast in a storm twelve gale, back and forth, back and forth, bows pointing into the enormous North Sea waves of pain. He squeezed his eyes tight shut, and his lips were pulled back, revealing his irregular, stained teeth, a rictus of pain coupled with the resolve to control it. His throat was dry and he was angrier than ever. These seemingly trivial, inoffensive questions, he knew, were designed to get him talking.

'Did Detective-Superintendent Malaparte play any active role in the murder inquiry?'

Kramer's response was to throw himself back against the chair and emit a loud grunt, though it had nothing to do with the question, only the pain. Then his rocking began again, backwards and forwards.

'In total, how many officers would you say were working on the case?'

'You received some help from local police stations, didn't you?'

'And Transport Police? How many officers did they provide?'

'What precisely were your orders as given to you by your superior officer?'

'Did Malaparte say he wanted an arrest within the week?'

The questions continued. This was not about him. They weren't interested in Kramer, and that was a huge relief. They didn't suspect after all. They were after bigger prey - Malaparte, for one. That was all to the good, but Kramer was too preoccupied with his shrieking flesh and bones to care very much one way or the other, though he knew it was going to happen again if he stayed silent and he dreaded another session of the same. These people wanted whatever he knew, and they were in a hurry; he reasoned that they must have a deadline.

'Why didn't you detain Fennel for questioning?'

'Who ordered you to question, charge and arrest Ryan Exeter? Was it Malaparte, or someone higher up the chain of command? Who was it, Kramer?'

He said not a word, not an intelligible word, that is. He moaned to himself, a deranged humming on a bass note, the volume low, throat singing the Sami called it.

When they took him away this time, dragging him by the arms because his legs failed to work properly, his slippers left behind and his bare feet scraping the floor, Kramer fully expected another thrashing. But it was not to be; it would be far worse.

*

At about the time of Kramer's introduction to the delights of His Majesty's Prison Belmarsh at Woolwich, Arden knocked and entered Porter's office to find three men and one woman sat at a conference table, in addition to the Assistant Deputy Commissioner himself, a tall, imposing figure in full uniform, who rose from his chair immediately, came over to welcome her, shook her hand in a friendly fashion, introduced her and led her to a chair. Having driven through almost deserted streets - deserted except for the occasional tank or armoured fighting vehicle crunching its way through fields of broken glass, tattered English flags and other detritus left by the hordes of drunken 'loyalists', Arden was in no state of mind to remember names or ranks. The other faces at the table were simply a blur.

'Tea or coffee?' Porter was already hovering over a tray on what looked like a sideboard, a cup and saucer at the ready.

'Coffee, thank you. Sir.'

'Sugar?'

'Nato standard, thank you.' Where, she wondered, did she get that phrase from?

The four other people stared at her curiously, but their expressions didn't seem unfriendly, merely inquisitive. A black detective, no less; whatever next?

Porter placed her coffee before her, along with a paper napkin and a chocolate biscuit wrapped in plastic edged into the saucer. She was grateful that he had not handed these to her or asked her to help herself; she feared she was shaking too much, and would have made a scene by dropping everything - as it was, she hid her hands below the table top, waiting until her heart settled to its usual, steady beat.

'We're so glad you could make it. How was your trip over here?'

'Nothing untoward.'

'Streets empty?'

'Pretty much, sir. A few military patrols and roadblocks.'

'Ah, yes. Our army friends.' It was said in such a way that it was clear to Arden that they were anything but friends.

Porter smiled, showing gleaming and regular white teeth, so regular and white that Arden had to wonder if they were his own - she couldn't tell. He was playing the gentleman, the kindly host, trying to put her at her ease, draw her out, give her a few moments to collect herself. Perhaps her nervousness was all too apparent, after all. Or maybe, Arden wondered to herself, this was how the fifth floor lived - tea parties every day with Earl Grey or Fair Trade freshly ground coffee and chocolate cookies, served by all the people with egg on their hats. Now jolly *nice*.

'Can I help anyone else with a refill? Feel free to help yourselves, won't you? Mabel...' the grey haired woman around 60 nodded and without a word got up at once and proceeded to do just that, pouring herself tea out of another jug. Mabel Fletcher, Arden realised, deputy director of Human Resources. Short, plump, able, aggressive, no fool, a long divorced mother of two grown-up children with a doctorate in sociology and from the East End, one of very few women of modest origins to have made it to the 5th floor.

Porter sat back down at the table.

'Perhaps I might recap very briefly for Nicole's benefit. I can call you Nicole? We're all friends here, and we needn't stand on ceremony.'

'Of course.'

Of course *not*. She hated the male assumption that females in subordinate roles could and would automatically acquiesce in being called - uninvited - by their first names, but what could she realistically do? Not much. Malaparte had done so, waving the carrot of promotion before her as a bribe to let him put his disgusting hands on her, and breathe all over her,

158

rubbing his belly up against her. A disgusting beast.

'First of all, Nicole, let me congratulate you on your promotion to detective-inspector, with immediate effect. Everyone here has helped put your name through the various hoops to get you the job, and you passed the *nihil obstat* process without a hitch. So well done.' Porter beamed.

'Well done,' said Mabel Fletcher.

'Well done, well done,' said the others. 'Bravo.'

'Sir - '

'Questions all in good time, Nicole. If I may set the scene for you, very quickly, that may answer some of your queries right away.' Porter steepled his fingers under his chin, the gesture of a high priest of law enforcement - these days, more enforcement than law. 'It could save us all some time. All right? Yes? Well, then. Here we go - and anyone please jump in if I go astray - the first thing you should know is that there's an internal inquiry underway into the murder investigation; the murder, I'm referring to is of course that of Chelsea Mostert, one in which you played your role very effectively, I'm told. Now, the inquiry is looking into the failure to provide sufficient resources, notwithstanding the extraordinarily rapid and conclusive result thanks in large measure to you and your senior partner, Joseph Kramer. Notwithstanding his undoubted abilities as a detective, he is detained while helping the authorities with their inquiries - '

'Detained? Where sir? What authorities?'

'Questions later, Nicole. Please. This won't take long.'

Her nerves now steadied in large measure by focusing on her concern for Kramer, Arden lifted the cup before her and sipped the coffee. Had these people come to the same conclusion as she? Did they too conclude that he was the murderer? Was that what this was about? She decided the coffee tasted a lot better than the usual brown dishwater to be had from the machine on her floor.

Porter turned in his chair and spoke directly to Arden. 'You'll also want to know about Detective-Superintendent Malaparte, who headed your department. He is suspended, subject to the results of the investigation, and when that happens - and I'm confident he'll be exonerated - he'll be no doubt be transferred. I don't think I'm violating any confidences when I say that he himself recently asked for a transfer, incidentally, prior to taking early retirement. That is his wish, not ours.' Porter looked around and no doubt to his satisfaction, other heads around the table nodded in agreement.

'You have replaced Kramer, Nicole. Your first task is neither easy nor particularly pleasant, I have to admit. You might say that your new status is dependent, though, on being able to carry it out. I wouldn't call it a condition, exactly, more an understanding among ourselves. Which brings me to the next point - this matter is known to only those present. It does not leave this room. Is that understood?' Porter glanced around the table.

'Yessir.'

'Good. Excellent.'

'Has Ryan Exeter been released?'

'Once again, you have anticipated my next point, detective-inspector. You must understand that although the Party in power has created a mass movement, a popular movement that transcends the usual bounds of politics in this country, rightly so, the leadership is still very much concerned with public opinion. It cannot be seen to grant special favours to senior Party members. An example has to be made, and seen to be made. Too often in the recent past there has been a perception that there's one law for the public, but that for certain influential figures, exceptions are made when it comes to justice. That cannot continue. Yes? Understood?'

'I think so.' Since when did truth and justice have anything in common?

'In the same way, the Met cannot afford another scandal. The Police Service in the capital is under tremendous pressure from all quarters. I don't have to spell that out, at least I hope not. For one thing, the military is on the streets. We cannot have one of our very best officers - our best detective, certainly - brought into disrepute and held up to ridicule. It would undermine the state's authority and our reputation as an effective crime-fighting force. Secrecy is paramount, therefore. Are you with me?'

'I must be a bit thick, sir, but I am groping my way towards the light.'

The other officers smiled at this, Mabel even allowing herself a chortle, quickly cut short by a look from Porter.

'Then these are your orders, Nicole. They fall into two parts, stage one and stage two. If you have a problem, if you need clarification with any or all of it, you must let us know now because there won't be a chance to do so once you leave this room.'

Two sheets of paper were pushed towards her across the table, each covered with typewritten instructions.

Arden tore open the plastic with her teeth and ate the biscuit. She'd been given the carrot; now she would be shown the stick and she told herself the infusion of sugar might help her cope with whatever was to come. She started reading.

*

'Where are you bastards taking me?'

'Who you calling bastards, eh?'

'Where are you taking me?'

'That's better. keep a civil tongue in your 'ead. Seems to me you're in enough trouble as it is.'

'So? Tell me. Where?'

'To the pens, mate.'

'Pens? What pens?'

'You'll find out soon enough.'

Kramer did find out and far too soon; two minders or warders or whatever they were dragged him down a flight of stairs, along a very narrow corridor, then he was stripped roughly and pushed, naked, by men wearing pink rubber gloves into what at first glance might have appeared to be a wire mesh pen made for a dog, something to be found in any common pet shop. But this was curiously shaped, and its dimensions were soon to make themselves felt; Kramer could not stand, nor could he sit or squat. He hung somewhere between the two positions as if crucified. Already in pain, his ribs felt as if they were on fire; wriggle, twist, turn - it made no difference. It was as if he'd been forced into a miniature coffin, only he'd been forced into it upside down, and when they switched off the lights, he suffered in pitch darkness.

Kramer knew post-imperial, post-industrial and post-Christian England was a world leader in torture of a special kind, often called sensory deprivation which in itself sounded rather pleasant, sleepy, mild, even comforting. In fact, it was a special technique, or several versions of the technique, to induce exquisite physical and mental anguish and exhaustion. The 'counter-insurgency' operations in Northern Ireland had provided ample opportunity for experimentations in torment without any effective legal constraints.

Kramer's body and mind - his whole being, in effect - reacted to the pen

161

in a curious fashion; curious to those who have never witnessed such an ordeal especially designed for its special effects upon the living organism. In a matter of minutes he started to sweat copiously, a little later he felt a terrible pain develop in his jaw and teeth; this soon spread to his head, especially down the centre of his forehead. He felt as if he'd been axed, and his head and brain had been split in two. Now he did scream out loud; he could not help himself and was beyond caring who heard or what impression he made on his captors by giving in in this way. He bared his teeth, his lips pulled back in a rictus of helpless agony. A little later and he couldn't help notice that his heart beat was rapidly increasing. He was unable to control it, though he tried by forcing himself to breathe deeply, slowly, regularly.

His heart raced, and it palpitated irregularly, now at at once he started to experience spasms, his head was twisted this way and that, as if by its own volition, the sinews of his neck stood out, and his arms became rigid. Starting with hands and arms, he started to shake violently. Though he wasn't aware of it, his eyes were wide open, the pupils massively dilated. He saw a train of still pictures, like a film slowed down - he would not remember what they were and he didn't recognise them as anything he could describe when this actually happened to him, except that they were dreadful; it was a visual nightmare. Kramer shouted 'no!' in terror several times. He did know they were simply terrifying, and he tried to turn from them, not to see them, but he had no control over his own body or consciousness any longer. Finally, his eyes rolled back into his head, his head flung itself back, mouth open, he lost all semblance of consciousness and his spittle burst from his mouth in the form off foam running out of the corners and down his chin, finally his lower jaw and mouth twisted to one side as if someone had been repeatedly been punching him in the face.

When a jailer bent down to look at him, Kramer stared back but did not see him. He saw something, but whatever it was he saw and stared at, it wasn't human.

A bucket of icy water was poured over him, and he came to, teeth chattering, body shaking. Almost immediately, he started to warm up as the water dribbled off him, and the same thing happened again, almost exactly as before, though Kramer sensed what was coming and was desperate not to let it happen. But it did. He couldn't stop it any more than he could have escaped his pen. The rapid increase in pulse, the headache to end all headaches, the rigid neck and twisting head, staring eyes, the shaking and rigid arms; the terror at his own internal movie and finally the blackout.

Kramer was dragged back to his cell, thrown on his bed, his blanket tossed over him. A young man in black framed spectacles, white coat and armed with a stethoscope listened to his heart, took his pulse, set up an intravenous saline drip, then made a note. Kramer breathed deeply, his mouth open, his breath rasping, then snoring. Now and again he seemed to shake himself into wakefulness, only to collapse back into sleep. From time to time his hands twitched, his lips moved, his teeth bared, his chin moved up and down, his eyes fluttered; Kramer shook - he seemed to be dreaming and whatever it wash was experiencing in his sub-conscious, it wasn't pleasant.

One phrase scribbled on the page of the notebook held by the man in the white coat: *'some impairment of short-term memory, probable hallucination, dislocation of facial features, especially eyes and mouth.'*

It was almost midnight.

He slept without meaning to; he woke in turmoil, thoughts raging through his mind. No such thing as a perfect murder; no such thing as a perfect murderer - he certainly wasn't. His victim, Chelsea Mostert, had known him, of course she had, and there had been no other option open to him but to make contact. It was an essential part of his plan, but a mistake all the same. He had also returned to the crime scene, had he not, sitting on a bench in Vauxhall Park that evening and admitting as much when Arden had called? You're a fool, Kramer. What did you have to go and do that for? And those silly things you said outside the Commons - bloody hell, man, that alone could have sunk you good and proper; a good thing it was only Arden who heard you blathering about politics. Three mistakes right there, but what else could he have done? There was more - he had solved the case far too quickly given even with his reputation, and come up with the culprit with extraordinary ease, as his tormentors were finding out, and he had done so with far too few resources; that in itself was ample grounds for suspicion. It hadn't taken Arden long to work it out. Idiot!

Was that why he was here, in Belmarsh?

Kramer knew he couldn't stay alert and so he rolled off the bunk and huddled under it instead in case they came for him again; hoping to sleep, he shivered and sweated by turns, throwing off the prison blanket damp with his fever, then rolling himself up in it as the shakes returned; he tossed on the hard floor this way and that, staying out of the light and sliding in and out of a shallow doze illuminated by nameless terrors. He heard part of a conversation right outside the cell door, or thought he did;

two male voices, probably those of the prison screws, passing by, not hurrying, perhaps pausing at his cell.

'Blood moon, they call it.'

'Why's that then?'

'It's big and it will look very red. They say it's gonna be the biggest moon we've seen in two 'undred years.'

'Yeah? How's that then? The moon don't change size.'

'Atmospherics, see, and the orbit changes, yeah? Like it's a lot closer to earth now. It's something to do with a lunar eclipse.'

'That right? How can you see it if it's an eclipse?'

'It's a shadow, like a copper disc, see.'

'Uh-huh. No, not really, to be honest. Blood moon, eh? When is it, did you say?'

'Tomorrow night. Keep an eye open for it.'

The voices faded, and somewhere, beyond the prison, a bell chimed midnight.

Day Four: Thursday, April 21, 2022

'Men are so necessarily mad that not to be mad would amount to another form of madness.'

Blaise Pascal, *Pensées*.

14

Arden didn't get much sleep; she told herself that was all right because it was worth it; in the end she'd come out of it looking pretty good and there'd be plenty of time to catch up. She had lots of accumulated leave and that might be a good time to take some of it once this was over - with Beth, of course, somewhere really nice. She would pay this time. Her treat. The Amalfi coast, perhaps. She'd seen the pictures and had always wanted to go; it seemed so romantic. They'd given her a challenge, a task of some considerable importance and she had to be prepared, and it would take her much of the night; she couldn't tell Beth, naturally, and although at one point she considered asking Beth if she could borrow her car, but she decided against it. The less Beth knew the better, and taking Beth's car for the long drive might only incriminate her. Arden's own police issue Skoda was too easily recognisable as hers, and the registration plate recorded on a dozen or more CCTV cameras would lead any interested parties straight to her. She would have to avoid using her mobile, too, and the usual social networks were off limits for obvious reasons. Nowadays no driver could escape those video cameras, to say nothing of police checks and army roadblocks. So she signed out a battered little Fiat from the car pool, the sergeant-mechanic who had a rather soft spot for her - well, he was Jamaican originally, and a grandfather - reassuring Arden it might not look much and was rather long in the tooth, yes, ma'am, there are some dents and scratches and the tyres are worn, for sure, but hey (running his big hands fondly over the paintwork), it was dependable - more than that, it had a surprising turn of speed. He also let her take it under the previous user's name, someone named Brown, keeping it off the books, and though the sergeant didn't know it, that modest act of kindness on his part could save her life and career.

It turned out that the Met's resources extended to all manner of weird and wonderful things, including a wardrobe stinking of mothballs that was apparently mined from time to time by undercover types and that would have done a film studio proud if sneaky, seedy and sordid was the cinematic theme. She had to wait two hours for someone ordered to come in and open up to actually bother doing so - and Arden wasn't popular. But in a 40-minute search, during which the sullen civilian, a Mrs Woodrose, who looked after the place, pointedly refused to help, Arden found a man's dark grey suit - actually, it wasn't a suit but a pair of woollen trousers and a woollen jacket that, put together, closely resembled one - that would fit someone of middling height, say five nine, with a 34 inch waist, a black leather belt in case the pants did turn out to be too large, a pair of black size 9.5 brogues, black socks (they didn't smell too clean to Arden), a brand new white shirt still in its plastic wrapper and with a size 16 collar and a plain black tie with what seemed to be a soup stain though barely visible to anyone but the wearer, along with a rather crooked wire hanger for it all and a brown paper bag for the shoes and socks. Arden had to try to picture the wearer she had in mind, and guess both size and weight. Undertaker or professional mourner was the image that came to mind. Finally, she had to list the items herself and sign for them, in triplicate, the stout curmudgeon in yoga pants with a stud in her lower lip looking on, arms crossed, and Arden lugged the gear out to the Fiat herself, making two trips of it, throwing the gear onto a back seat built for Lilliputians.

From a public call box - the first two she came across had been badly vandalised, but the third, aside from stinking of urine, was at least operational - she made two collect calls to Edinburgh. To anyone eavesdropping, the conversation appeared to be a boring affirmation of some dull plan to visit a favourite uncle in the Scottish capital, involving rail and coach services. Finally, the documentation, neatly gathered in a file and prepared by the helpful Mabel Fletcher, she placed under the driver's seat. Arden drove to an all-night garage, checked oil and water, filled the tank and drove on to Camden. It was 2 a.m. by the time she opened the front door with her key.

'Well, I didn't expect you this late.'

They brushed cheeks in the hall, then hugged a little awkwardly, Arden unsteady on her feet, Beth groggy with interrupted sleep.

'Sorry, Beth. I certainly didn't mean to be so late.'

'You might have called, honey.'

'Best not in the circumstances.'

'Like that, is it?'

'Afraid so, love. I was right all along. About Kramer. I wasn't imagining it.'

They looked at each other, holding each other's arms.

'Drink? There's some supper, too. We better call it breakfast.'

'You're a life saver. I haven't eaten a thing for twelve hours at least.'

'Help yourself to the wine. I'll get your food, such as it is.'

'I'd prefer a glass of milk or yoghurt.'

'You are in a bad way.'

Beth, in rumpled white and pink striped pyjamas, was drooping from interrupted sleep, Arden dizzy with a desire to sleep. Beth held her head up with both hands, elbows planted on the table, battling to keep her eyes open. Arden dipped her spoon tentatively into what seemed to be chicken and vegetable soup but gave up after a couple of polite mouthfuls.

'This is about your boss, isn't it.' It was stated as fact rather than as a question.

'Partly.'

'Tell me, love.'

Tired as she was, and dying to share everything with Beth, to unburden all of it to someone trustworthy and much loved, but Arden knew she couldn't. This was unchartered territory, and hazardous; she dare not risk the one thing - the one person - who mattered to her more than anyone and anything else. More than the Job, even. As for Kramer, he had no idea what was coming, no idea at all. He was going to get the biggest shock of his miserable life. Served him right, though, didn't it? Arden felt a savage surge of pleasure at the prospect. 'Come on Beth, let's go to bed. I've only got a couple of hours and then I've got to get going again.'

'You're not going to tell me, are you?'

'I can't Beth. It's for the best. Sorry.'

'You're a masochist, honey.'

'What does that make you for putting up with me?'

'A bloody fool, I suppose.'

She went to the window and looked down at the street and saw a large, familiar shape in the shadows. David Mostert. It looked like David Mostert, but that simply wasn't possible. He must be back in Australia by now. Cairns, wasn't it? Arden told herself she was seeing things. When she looked again, the man-shaped thing had moved away.

They came for him at 4.30 a.m., but there was a distinct change this time in his visitors' general demeanor. They weren't hostile, but Kramer was extremely cautious.

'Wake up, sir, you've got to get yourself ready.'

Kramer rolled up into a ball under the bed, braced for another attack.

'Sir, you've got to get up. We've got some breakfast for you.'

Impatience, insistence but no aggression in the voice, Kramer noted.

'What's the time?'

'Four-thirty.'

'What's going on?'

'You've got to get yourself tidied up, sir. You haven't much time.'

'For what?'

'You're an official witness, sir.'

Sir. Why the sir? Why the sudden deference, and what had happened to detective-inspector?

When they finally coaxed him out of his lair, they helped him to his knees and then to his feet and lifted him onto the steel stool and desk. Kramer felt twenty years older and his muscles seemed unable to obey his instructions. He could barely take a single step unaided. No, he wasn't hallucinating; they really did have hot, strong tea in a mug and a plate of scrambled eggs, grilled tomato and toast. The eggs were the real thing, not the usual institutional powdered stuff. Someone held up the mug for him until he could get a grip on it. The edge rattled against his teeth. Kramer couldn't help himself; he fell on the food and hungrily devoured everything, shovelling it between numb lips with a plastic fork, shaking so much he had to lift the plate to his mouth, though his face and teeth hurt. He looked quickly over his shoulder; there were two of them, uniformed, one by the door, the other in the corridor.

'Witness?'

'Yessir. That's what they said. You're a witness. Official witness. Barber's here, sir. He'll give you a quick cut and shave. Smarten you up.'

'I need a shit.'

'Can you manage by yourself?'

'I think so.'

'We'll be outside.'

They did wait outside the cell, too, though one kept looking around the edge of the door to make sure he hadn't fallen flat on his face or pissed himself.

'Time to clean up, sir. You've had the shit - now for the shave and the shirt.'

Kramer didn't object. He was sore all over and he had no fight left in him. He let the convict barber - he wore prison clothes - cut his hair and shave him with an electric razor; there was no other option but to put up with it. Kramer endured it in a stupefied, passive fog of bewilderment. There had been some kind of regime change as far as he could tell; these guards with their respectful, even helpful behaviour weren't the same people who'd welcomed him to Belmarsh the previous night with rubber truncheons, or were they?

'This way.'

He had to lean on the arm of one of the guards as he limped along. He wasn't cuffed, and he thought it was because they judged him rightly as harmless, as someone who couldn't have run anywhere even if there was somewhere to run to. With a great metallic whanging and banging, doors opened and closed as he went along.

A white, tiled room, cubicles.

Naked, he was blue and yellow, a damaged animal of the striped kind, a wounded ocelot or jaguar trembling all over.

Then he was in the shower, though he couldn't remember how he'd got there. Somehow he'd stripped, and stood, or rather staggered, under a blast of hot, steamy water that struck hard, stung his skin, his eyelids, his scalp, his bruised ribs; he gasped at the shock, at the pain, at the relief; it was hateful and wondrous, simultaneously - he tried his utmost but couldn't lift his arms above his shoulders but that was okay, really - he told himself he could manage, of course he could. The sound he heard was himself, groaning or singing or maybe both. He turned slowly, swivelling like a pig on a spit, holding onto the wall with one hand so as not to fall, letting the water strike him all over, washing away his stink. What was he doing, what was being done, and where would it all lead? Above all, why? He grappled with the fog in his brain, tried to make sense of everything, achieve a sense of timing, of cause and effect, how come he'd got to this point, and where would it take him. He was holding a large bar of soap, he discovered, and tried, not with much success, to rub it over his hurting body while he remembered the last meeting.

*

Where to hold a final clandestine meeting in London? It had to be somewhere Kramer and Chelsea Mostert were most unlikely to be seen by anyone they knew, or anyone who might recognise either of them. It had to be somewhere they would be alone, more or less, where they could talk, or at least whisper, where no-one would be likely to bother them, and while cameras might cover the approach and exits, they would not be observed together while in discussion, and finally, it had to be somewhere convenient to both. Kramer, after much reflection and study of his London A-Z, and a brief reconnaissance of two likely spots, had the answer: St John's Church in the Waterloo Road, SE1, in the Borough of Lambeth once again. On a weekday morning it would meet all Kramer's stringent requirements, or should do so.

St John's was handsome, at least Kramer imagined many would think so; it was built along classical lines; six immense columns supported the triangular Greco-Roman portico and it was one of the few Christian places of worship still in use and open to the public. Its Sunday services were popular and its bells famous; inside, instead of wooden pews there were individual chairs made of light wood with blue-grey upholstery, giving the place a cheery, contemporary feel. At the far end, on the wall behind the altar, was a colourful triptych of some kind. Kramer arrived by bicycle (there were plenty of bicycle lock-ups out front), Chelsea Mostert by taxi, but at least she stopped it well short and walked the last stretch, fifty metres or so, still looking like a starlet trying hard to be spotted as someone trying not to be, that please don't see me but please do see me false modesty; Liberty silk scarf, shades, pale green outfit, gold sandals, fancy purse that could have paid for a slap-up meal for London's immense army of homeless were all part of the performance. Never mind all that, Kramer had told himself, watching her enter, removing her sunglasses, looking around like a lost and carelessly elegant tourist, seeing him and clacking over in her sandals.

We're past all that now and at least she's on time.

She dropped down next to him, glanced around. She didn't bother to lean forward or kneel, put her hands together, pray. Party high-ups and government ministers were too important for that; maybe, Kramer thought, they saw themselves as being on equal terms with God. Poor God; the stuff he had to put up with.

'Well?' The word was a pant, a fish of expelled air.

'Well what?' Kramer knew perfectly well, but he wanted her to slow down, to calm herself. She was pent up, bursting with it.

'What's your answer?'

'You still want this, really?'

A nod.

'Are you absolutely sure? I can't afford the luxury of last minute doubts.'

'Never more so.' She used a trembling finger and its long pink nail to move a stray strand of blonde hair behind an ear.

'And you accept my conditions?'

'You mean - '

'Look at me. That's right. Now, you won't ask questions. You won't contact me. You'll do exactly as I say and we'll both be in the clear. Understood?'

'Yes.' She kept looking at him, and he could see the fear, feel it in her. She was quivering slightly, like someone who's cold and doesn't want to show it.

'Then I'll do it.'

'You want - '

'I want nothing from you. Nothing. I have some questions, though.'

She shuddered as if a gust of wind had swept in from the traffic-clogged street - a shudder of relief, or horror? No that it mattered to Kramer.

'Okay.'

'When are you next going to your house in Fentiman Road?'

'Oh. Monday week. The 22nd. It will be the last time.'

'Why then?'

'I'm having the cleaners in - Mops and Dusters. You might know them.'

Unlikely - Kramer wasn't on familiar terms with either. He couldn't remember when he'd tried to clean his own dingy flat. Dusting wasn't his thing, and neither was mopping if it could possibly be avoided. Then he realised she was talking about a professional cleaning company.

Not noticing his confusion, she rushed on. 'They're good, or so I'm told. I want to check their work. I will probably spend Sunday night there and be up at four or five to have a final look round, then just after seven I'm going to hand over the keys to the agent who'll pass it to the new owners - once all the moneys paid and contract signed. You know - the usual process. I've got to be at the ministry really early. There's still a couch in the house I can use. It's comfortable.'

They were interrupted by footsteps. A figure in black swept down the aisle, his shoes rapping on the floor. The footsteps paused, turned. 'Can I help you?' The voice was deep, masculine, confident and filled the church. It was a voice that was used to being heard, liked making itself felt, there was ownership it, a proprietary sense that this was its owner's undisputed bailiwick; here, it said, was Authority of a different kind. Kramer looked up and saw a bearded priest looking down at them, a broad, impressive figure well over six foot and in his late 30s. He looked like an All Black prop forward and he held prayer books or hymnals in his hands; his smile was curious yet sympathetic.

'No, thanks, father.'

'You're not seeking confession? Don't be shy now.'

Irish accent, softened by years spent away from home, Kramer guessed, gently mocking.

'No, not today. Later, perhaps.'

Later, Kramer thought, I will need it.

The beard split open as the smile widened. 'All right then. Looks like you want to be alone. If you do want anything now or later, just ask.'

The black shadow swept away; the sharp, marching footsteps faded. What did he imagine? That they were lovers, having extra-marital relations?

Kramer turned back to Chelsea Mostert, who was hunched up on her chair, all angular knees and elbows folded up like a beaten child trying to hide itself from the world, twisting her hair into rats' tails in her fingers. 'So you'll be there overnight, up at four or five and then you'll leave at what time?'

'No later than seven. A little before.'

173

'Good. Very good. Then this is what I want you to do.'

She was his, and so was Ryan Exeter.

15

Kramer struggled into the crisp new white shirt, helped by two guards. He found it difficult to lift his arms and thrust them into the sleeves, and when they tried to help by doing up the cuffs, he shook them off. The same went for the collar. For God's sake, he hissed under his breath. He let them loop the black tie around his neck, but he wasn't having them doing up the knot. Fuck that. They were trying to get him dressed, to be fair, to make sure he was on time - but on time for what? They wouldn't say. They led him to a mirror, a polished steel affair embedded in the wall of the washroom. He didn't recognise himself - just the bent and twisted nose, the unblinking stare. He wasn't impressed at all by the stranger's close-shaved face staring back at him. He had less of a prison pallor than a death pallor - he looked exhausted and to Kramer, ancient. Then they struggled to put on the jacket, Kramer cursing, groaning.

Fact, Kramer thought as he zipped up the black woollen pants all by himself this time, fact: the police had been the making of him. He'd amounted to nothing before that, not as a child, not as a man. He'd been useless at his studies, hopeless on the playing field; he'd always been a loner, a misfit. His headmaster had turned to his mother during a cricket match (Kramer loathed cricket along with most sports) and said of him that he had two speeds: slow and dead slow, and they'd both laughed, or so his mother told him later (Kramer had not found it in the least funny). He seldom passed any exams, and then inadvertently, only scraping through when offered the possibility of escape from institutional life. He was an atheist from very early on; he detested the Jesuit fathers and their teaching. He thought Christianity a fairy story for fools and weaklings. His father had him down for the Royal Marines and kept sending him glossy brochures about the 'sea soldiers', but the sea terrified Kramer, and always had, ever since as a child Kramer had sat on his father's knee and had been shown pictures of a man in an old fashioned dividing bell standing on the bottom of the sea surrounded by terrifying sea monsters of one kind or another. Of course he'd not confessed his weakness. He was a poor swimmer, too, and that hadn't helped. He wasn't good at anything, really. But the police had changed all that.

At first, he had been no more than mediocre as a uniformed officer pounding the pavements of Southwark and the Elephant & Castle in south London, true enough; he admitted that he was a bit slow to act on occasion, a little lacking in decisiveness. Always the observer, he had a habit of standing back, of being distant, uninvolved and taking in detail - such reflection and hesitation cut no ice with his sergeant. It was only his constant questioning, his ideas, his imagination, that started to make itself felt and won him a chance at crime detection. He had come into his own almost immediately. His colleagues thought him odd, always had, always would, and he didn't mind that a bit as long as he was good at what he did, and of course he was. Very good. The best. Homicide was the obvious place for him, the minutae of crime scenes fascinated him and he had the patience and careful attention to detail that put him head and shoulders above his inattentive and lazy competitors. People started asking him his views, for his opinions, and he was careful how he responded. Kramer was never flash, never showy; He kept it quiet, understated, brief. That too worked.

So why, after all these years, had he risked throwing away his career, to say nothing of his liberty? Why had he turned on his vocation in such a self-destructive way? He wasn't sure. As he put on the black shoes they gave him, grunting at the pain of his bruised ribs as he forced his feet into them, no socks, no thanks, he thought he had a rough idea, no more: it wasn't enough. That was it. It had never been enough; there had to be something more, a lot more, though he had no idea what. Yes, he had immense power as a cop, of course he had; he could deprive a citizen of his or her liberty on a whim, on instinct, and he could enter anyone's life and wreck it on impulse, force his way into someone's home (under the Emergency), and he could make himself a thorough terror to anyone he wished. He had that power, certainly, but it was a shoddy kind of bullying, uncouth and inelegant. It was nothing but brute force, and Kramer did not see himself as a thug. Kramer had always felt that abusing his position while hiding behind his badge was the courage of the coward. He wanted more, much more. He wanted to have an effect on the world. He had to admit that he had reached a point at which he actually envied the power of some of the people he'd put away; villains who regarded respectability with contempt, who simply didn't care for society's rules, who obeyed their own laws, such as they were.

He had never been political until Clara.

176

'This way.'

They were leading him outside into a chill, foggy morning, keeping an eye on him because he wasn't steady on his feet, lurching rather than walking, swearing to himself under his breath about the pain. The downlighting on the security fencing was reduced to a series of furry cones and the fog drifted through the patches of illumination like smoke; it was an escapee's perfect weather.

Fact. Kramer had never been political, not really. The politics came after the fact, they could be used to rationalise what he'd done. Had he killed for Clara? Perhaps he had, for he'd been outraged by her end and had genuinely mourned his friend. But wasn't that just self-justification after the act of murder?

They had the rear door open.

Fact. Yes, he had killed, but how many had Chelsea Mostert killed - how many disabled people had been driven to suicide? How many pensioners had frozen to death through lack of the wherewithal to pay for heating, for food? How many starved themselves so they could pay the rent or clothe their kids? How many lives had he, Kramer saved, by removing Chelsea Mostert and her erstwhile lover, the ghastly Ryan Exeter? Dozens? Hundreds?

'Where are we going?'

'About four hundred metres.'

'Where to?'

'You'll see, sir. Get in, please.'

He hurt too much to resist or object. He wasn't handcuffed and his escort was civil.

Was it vengeance on his part? Retribution? Big words, but what did they really mean? On the other hand, killing her had made little if any difference that he knew of.

A uniformed officer climbed in next to him. As the car rolled, he turned to Kramer, out of breath and wheezing, his gut straining against the black knife-proof jacket he was wearing.

'Your first?'

Kramer shifted in his seat, gave his burly companion a long, owlish once-over.

Nothing further was said for several seconds.

'First what?'

'Your first execution, pal. Is it your first?'

*

Kramer held on to the top of the car door with both hands. It was cold in the open; the metal and glass of the door were cold, too and he could feel the blurry sodium yellow mist on his face and neck. His legs quivered; he felt the chill through his borrowed pants even though they were wool. He knew he wasn't quite right - it wasn't so much the bruises he'd sustained but the dizziness, the sense of being out of it, not of this world. They didn't touch him, though. The driver watched, lit a cigarette in a gesture that seemed to signal that he couldn't care less what Kramer did or didn't do, and Kramer's backseat escort moved his weight from foot to foot, hesitating, unsure how to manage Kramer. In front of the car was a tall red box of a building with some kind of corrugated skin, and no windows. Just a door, also red, and it was closed.

Did the officer say 'execution', and if he did, and if Kramer wasn't imagining all this, the next question was obvious. *Whose?* Who was going to be executed? Kramer clung with his fingertips to the open rear door like a man hanging from a high window ledge, terrified of falling. Why am I terrified, he wondered? Then he reminded himself - something about an execution.

Was it his? Do they mean me? Really?

Had he been tried by one of the secret security courts that very morning - no accused, no witnesses present, just a pile of paper and a special judge - and found guilty on charges he would never be told about? Was this it? Was this what the beating and interrogation had been about? Dredging up stuff to use against him in a hearing while he slept uneasily under his bunk, waiting for the next assault?

'They'll be waiting for you. We'd better be going,' said the stout prison officer or whatever he was. 'There's a woman in there already, a witness. She's probably waiting for you.'

What woman?

None of it made any sense. It felt like a dream. The fog swirled through the high security fencing, the razor wire, past the very solid looking guard towers, so big they looked like those old water towers Kramer had seen in

178

Africa. The vapour left droplets on his face, his eyebrows. Had that stuff about being a witness been a lie to secure his cooperation?

'Come on, sir.' The guard or whatever consulted his watch for the millionth timed moved a little closer to Kramer. He seemed nervous and he had a look on his face that said he wanted to peel Kramer off the car door if he could, even if it meant doing him some violence. 'It's time.'

But Kramer did not want to let go of the car door, or move away from the warmth of the car's heated interior. In the four days since the Chelsea Mostert murder, they'd experienced exceptionally heavy and prolonged rain in London, local flooding, a brief heatwave and now a winter fog, one of those old 1950s pea-soupers, and it was late April and bloody cold again.

'Let's go.' The uniformed officer had had enough; he made a grab for Kramer's arm, but Kramer sidestepped, releasing the door, evading the man by stepping back and to his left. His hands were open, slightly raised, fingers extended, a fighting posture which the officer recognised as a willingness to brawl despite his diminished capacity.

'Easy does it,' said the uniform. 'They don't want me in there, sir. They're waiting for you. You're going in there, not me. You're a witness, remember? They're not going to cut your head off, now, are they?'

Kramer wasn't sure. He turned his back; he walked slowly, gingerly, towards the door, aware that the two officers were staying put, watching.

*

Arden wanted to be in bed, Beth behind her, feeling that long, lean and naked body against her own, legs entangled, those hands of Beth's around her and holding her breasts, Beth's light breath on the back of her neck. She loved that position, the warmth, the comfort, the desire, the silent communing, the possessing and being possessed, as if no other world existed and certainly not this one. Loving each other. That was the reality worth having; that was where she should be now, Arden told herself, not perched on a dark blue moulded plastic chair in this sinister place. Each row had four chairs fastened to a horizontal black bar, with legs at each end, and there were three rows like a well-drilled platoon stood at attention. Arden was quite alone in the front row, at the far end.

In her lap she held a buff file.

Arden was aware that there were two doors, one external, the other internal, and by each door stood an armed prison officer. She didn't look at them; she faced forward, eyes down at the tiled floor. She'd been waiting half an hour already, having handed over the clothing at the prison guardroom, watched by officers in black, bulky with body armour and helmets, clutching those obscene German machine pistols beloved of the security services - phallic things with nasty muzzles, and she wondered why they didn't stick them in their trousers for greater effect. *Pricks.*

They'd invited her to leave her car, to raise her arms and two female officers had searched her carefully, then they'd gone over the Fiat, four of them, inch by bloody inch, running metal detectors and mirrors under it. They'd even had a German Shepherd sniff the seats. They'd checked her sidearm, then returned it.

Now she used her cellphone.

'DC Harkness? Nicole Arden. Sorry to wake you.'

'You didn't. What can I do for you?'

'A favour. Check to see if David Mostert has left the country.'

'I'll call you back.'

Her palms were moist; she was anxious. She raised herself just enough to slide the file under her buttocks rather than smear it with sweaty hands. She had so much to do and with every minute that slipped by the prospects of success were reduced. Arden would do her utmost, of course she would - but some things were beyond her; she was being carried on a tide not of her making. If they were late, what could she do? Absolutely nothing; she told herself not to worry about things she could do nothing about. It didn't help, not really. She tried to force herself to relax by shutting her eyes, breathing slowly, steadily. She tried to occupy herself by thinking of Beth, of their life together, and she did not look at *IT*, though *IT* demanded her attention, insisted on her horrified fascination. I won't look. I won't.

Come on, Kramer.

*

Those few steps were difficult, and the door itself was a bit of a mystery; it had no knob or handle to twist or turn but an indentation for the fingers, a sliding door, he realised, his mind sluggish, unwilling to focus. It was so unlike the territory he had traversed by bicycle on Monday, so well known, so well planned and reconnoitred that he could have done it blind and backwards if he had to. But nae this, nae here. In the weeks and days preceding Monday, he had practised leaving the A3 a dozen times, coming north from Brixton, disappearing into streets to the right-hand side, crooked residential alleys and crescents that had no CCTV and mostly no traffic, certainly not at that hour. He could vanish off the police radar, so to speak, and reappear again at will in Fentiman Road and be away, back into the alleys where he felt safe, unseen, within a couple of minutes at the very most. He had timed it, too. Even now, standing before this strange door, he could picture the byways in his mind's eye. Carroun Road, Rita Road, Meadow Road and Meadow Muse, Palfrey Place, Claylands Road so close to Oval, and Richbourne Terrace. He had had access to video footage at the Yard without having to answer to anyone, or leave his signature, and he knew perfectly well what the cameras that did exist revealed, and what they did not show, and he had made full use of that.

Now Kramer pulled; the door slid half way; his view of the interior was almost completely blocked by the back of a black uniform, the cloth shiny from use. The form inside the uniform was so immense that Fraser wondered how on earth the man inside it could possibly get into it in the mornings. It fairly bulged in the arms, shoulders, back and thighs. The prison officer, if that's who he was, must have been an amateur weight lifter or something of the kind; he was the human version of a Charolais bull, all muscle and fat, and he shifted to his right, looked back to his left at Kramer, and the massive neck, when twisted, revealed a giant and inflamed boil. It must be painful, Kramer thought, especially when turned against the tight white shirt collar that seemed too small to contain such a vast human being. The officer was still moving; he took half a step backwards with his left foot, turning also to his left, but Kramer was so fascinated by the huge size of the stranger and his inflamed neck, that he was almost inside by the time he first caught sight of Arden, seated alone in the front row of seats. At once he forgot about the prison officer and made his way past him and towards her. With relief he bent down and hand over hand like a hospital patient too weak to stand up from a bed, leaning on his palms, letting his arms take much of his weight, he made his way towards her, walking his hands over to her, moaning gently to himself with the effort, finally settling himself next to her, leaving one vacant seat between them out of a sense of respect for her personal space. He didn't like being crowded and took for granted that other people felt the same way. Sitting on his buttocks - a simple act in itself, surely - turned out to be extremely painful, and Kramer held his breath again as he tried to find the position that caused his ribs, both the ones in front and in his back, the least agony.

Oh, Jesus.

Like his cell, the floor was tiled, but it sloped towards the centre and a groove - well, more than a groove, perhaps a narrow gutter would be a better way to think of it - ran down, yes, ran down the slightly sloping tiles to a large rectangular grate in the centre. There were four such gutters or groves, he saw, equidistant, starting at the centre point of each wall. Now the officer had resumed his position before the sliding door, there was nothing obstructing Kramer, and he saw the pièce de résistance for the first time.

The apparatus looked to him to be one of those very large, expensive and comprehensive fitness machines to be found at the best gymnasia and sports clubs in the West End; the compactness and strength of it allowing for every muscle known to humankind to be put through its paces, exercised and strengthened with loops, wires, seats, weights, pulleys and straps. It was painted a bright red and looked new. It didn't soar. It didn't tower. It crouched. It squatted like a malign, metallic insect on its numerous steel legs, braced and ready to spring. Clearly more than one person could use it at any one time, just like its twin on Westminster Green. But of course it wasn't an exercise machine at all. It took him several seconds until he found the modern equivalent of the charmingly named bascule and lunette, but sure enough, they were there. That much, at least, had changed little since Dr Joseph-Ignace Guillotin had introduced his Machine in 1789 - and it must be said in fairness to the inventor that he did so in the belief that his equipment would provide the condemned with a relatively merciful end. Relative, that is, to the sometimes blunt axes, bad eyesight, intoxication and the several blows sometimes required of an executioner to hack a head from its neck with sword or axe. This was to the original, Kramer thought, what the modern compact bow must be to the medieval longbow.

16

The internal door slid open, its sentry stepping to one side and looking back as his comrade had done on Kramer's earlier entry through the external door. Arden and Kramer turned their heads as one to the right; there was some kind of commotion in the corridor and at first it seemed to Kramer that several prison officers were attempting to enter simultaneously, or were squabbling for precedence. This made no sense, of course. After a moment or two it became apparent that the officers were trying to propel and pull a reluctant party with them, someone obscured by the dark uniforms and peaked caps. Said party, as yet unidentified (though Kramer fully expected to see Exeter), tried to cling to the doorjamb itself, but his hands were roughly torn away and he burst into the chamber, or more likely, he was pushed forward from behind with some violence, looking up at the double-height ceiling as he entered, the immense windowless walls and finally, directly before him in the centre, the scarlet Machine, squatting hungrily on the white tiles. Immediately he recognised the last for what it was, he tried again to hurl himself away from the officers, to break free, but he had no real chance at all. They had him an arm lock and quickly fastened his arms behind his back as he entered the execution chamber, and it was apparent to Kramer that he was not in full possession of himself. He'd been sedated. His reactions were slow, like a submerged man trying to swim fully-dressed against a powerful current. His slippered feet slapped the tiles like someone not sure of his own ability to judge precisely where the floor was. That burst of energy, of resistance seemed to have deflated him, left him exhausted. Muffled sounds came from him, a moaning and the muffled yelps of a puppy; he had been gagged, Kramer thought.

Ryan Exeter wore red overalls with a deep V-neck at the neck and no collar. His head had been shaved. Something resembling a horse's bit between his teeth, pulling his cheeks back and secured behind his head, prevented him from saying anything that could be understood, but it did not stop him trying. He ducked, shook himself, tried to turn, to call out.

His eyes started from his head - he looked towards Arden, then Kramer. Under the strip lighting his face was without colour. Did he recognise them? In any case, his efforts were to no avail. The officers on either side almost lifted him off the ground, taking at least some of his weight, but not quite all - and he seemed to paddle across the tiles as he was propelled forward.

When he reached the gutter, though, he held back for a fraction of a second, tottering and swaying and only prevented from losing his balance by his escort; and in the next instant he seemed to make up his mind - he stepped with some delicacy over it, first with his right foot, then his left, and the procession continued onward as if nothing had happened, but now there were only half a dozen yards still to go.

*

His final journey on foot complete, Exeter came to a standstill before the Machine and his legs were immediately buckled together tightly above the ankle with what appeared to be a wide leather strap - this was done very swiftly by an officer kneeling behind him - and Kramer saw that he was lifted bodily by the officers on either side and placed face down on the bascule, a move that was done with care (presumably to ensure he was centred on the board), and then the bascule or bridge was tipped forward and down and slid forward until it reached its end point and Exeter's pale hairless head emerged from the lunette, ensuring his neck was positioned under the blade, in effect, a giant razor blade still sheathed. It was a process that seemed so smooth and continuous - and indeed so quick - that Kramer thought it must be automated in some way.

Kramer was totally engrossed in the proceedings, yet he did cast one swift glance to his right, at Arden. She sat bent forward, her head resting on her knees, as if praying or feeling ill - or perhaps both. Her eyes were shut, or seemed to be. She was sitting on something that looked like a file. Kramer looked away, wanting no further distraction and concentrated on the activity before him. Yes, he thought it quite likely that the human brain would have sufficient reserves of blood to provide five to seven seconds of consciousness immediately following the fatal blow. It made sense. Five seconds was an eternity, wasn't it? He counted slowly, trying to imagine the passage of time. Kramer was determined to see everything for himself, to be the witness he was supposed to be and more, much more. After all, this was the culmination of his plans, his true triumph, and he had never really expected that he would actually be able to observe Exeter's end. It was quite an honour! He had months ago accepted that to experience the

184

satisfaction of Exeter's death on his own Machine, Kramer would have to rely simply on his imagination in the same way that sexual pleasure had all too often to be limited to images conjured up in his mind, aided and abetted by pressure exerted on the organ in question. A very different pressure was about to be applied to a different organ entirely, and like Arden, but for different reasons, Kramer leaned forward in his avid concentration. He was too wrapped up in the details, in the procedure, to wonder at his own sense of taste, his moral state of mind, his emotional reaction, whatever it might be - if indeed, there was any at all. He had invested immense amounts of time and effort to bringing all this about and he was damned if he would miss any of it through inattention. Kramer believed he deserved to be a witness, regardless of what might happen to him later. He quite appreciated that Arden would share none of his enthusiasm; of course he expected - knowing her as he did - that she was probably disgusted, appalled, dismayed. She was basically decent, as decent as was humanly possible. Kramer accepted that. He accepted that he wasn't. Indeed, he admired her good qualities. She had had no hand in any of it - she could not be expected to show anything like Kramer's enthusiasm and he thought no less of her for her likely disgust and moral outrage, if that's what it was that made her close her eyes and lean forward until her forehead rested on those pretty knees. If anything, she went up in his estimation. Did he imagine it, or did he just hear her groan? Ah, well, Nicole, never mind; it'll be over soon. So sorry, but you do see, don't you, that I've been waiting for this.

*

What could Exeter see?

It seemed to Kramer that the condemned was trying to turn, but he was severely restricted in his movement by the lunette and the straps that held him fast; he could not turn his head from side to side. He was trying to lift his head vertically, straining his utmost, the back of his head bumping against the metallic surface of the lunette, painted red like the rest of the Machine. What did he see? Kramer and Arden would be beyond his range of vision and so too were the prison officers. Exeter would be faced by the plain wall of tiles opposite. He certainly could not see the blade suspended above him. What would he see if he looked down? Was that why he was trying so hard to look up - was it to avoid seeing whatever it was that would receive his decapitated head, for whatever it was it would be directly below - a bucket, a basket, a receptacle of some kind. Kramer was anxious to see whatever there was; he almost stood up with the notion of coming

185

closer, of walking right up to the Machine and Exeter held so securely in the midst of its mechanical workings.

Kramer did not have a chance to indulge his curiosity. The four officers took up position - they resembled a well-drilled gun crew serving a historic 25-pounder gun for a salute on the ramparts of Edinburgh Castle. Each knew his place. One knelt. Three stood, two opposite one another on either side of the Machine. The fourth stood by himself and Kramer took him to be in charge, the chief operator of the device, perhaps.

They were motionless, as if at attention. Kramer leaned forward, apparently smiling to himself, wondering if Exeter had ever seen this done to another human being, and he was still smiling as something clicked, followed immediately by the swift rasp of metal on metal, something Kramer associated with a short sword or large knife drawn rapidly, forcefully, from its scabbard; the rictus - there was no humour in it - remained in place even at that scrape of steel on steel which lasted a fraction of a second and was immediately followed by a thud as the head was detached from the body, hanging for a moment, then gone, followed by a horizontal cascade of blood, a kind of projectile vomiting of life torn from its host, Kramer nearly falling forward, mesmerised, horrified, stunned yet exalted, jerking back in his chair as the grate in the floor gurgled greedily with Exeter's lifeblood..

Exeter's torso twitched and jumped.

Kramer counted up to seven, giving each digit a full second, his eyes on the fountain of blood gushing like a hydrant from the neck of the corpse, then slowly dropping until it became a trickle. The bound feet performed a very brief and staccato dance.

Tickety-tock, Kramer whispered until he estimated the seven seconds were up. Tickety-tock.

Arden lurched, threw up between her feet and splashed her shoes with the puke.

Day Five: Friday, April 22.

'We have to distrust each other. It is our only defence against betrayal.'
- Tennessee Williams, *Camino Real*

17

'Stick close.' An ashen-faced Arden hissed the words at Kramer and held the material of his jacket, the arm, just above the elbow, a strong pinch between thumb and forefinger. It was a command, not a request. Kramer did as he was told, adjusted his direction to the pressure she exerted on his upper right arm, propelling, pushing, pulling or turning him, keeping him at her side. No-one stopped them or showed the slightest interest in the two official 'witnesses'; they exited from the door through which they'd gained entry. He went first, Arden close behind, still holding him as if he were a toddler likely to run off at any moment. Was she holding him captive, or clinging to him in case she fell? They walked out into the night air at a natural pace and over to her car, only separating when they reached it - Arden to the driver's side, Kramer waiting at the front passenger's door. Whatever she felt inwardly, Arden seemed to be trying to maintain a calm, unhurried exterior, with her free left hand holding a tissue to her mouth. She unlocked the doors with her electronic key.

'Get in'. Her voice was muffled.

It was still dark outside and the prison yard glimmered with with pools of rainwater reflecting the perimeter lights; the fog had cleared and turned to a fine drizzle, but it was a relief to Kramer to be out of the execution chamber notwithstanding his personal interest in events, his bloody triumph. It felt good to be alive, to feel the icy droplets on his hot skin.

Arden threw the buff file on the back seat and the balled up tissue out of the window.

'Belt.'

She'd said the same thing, issued the same order, on Monday morning. Then, just after having killed Mostert and pedalled away on his bike down the ratlines behind Fentiman Road, and over Westminster Bridge, finally along the leafy Victoria Embankment to the Curtis Green Building (the rotating 'New Scotland' sign had been retrieved from 10 Broadway and placed outside the renamed and relocated Scotland Yard headquarters) Kramer had found her Skoda to be a refuge, a return somehow to good manners and decency and everything normal and companionable, the reassuring, trusting, never-never fantasy world of Dixon of Dock Green. He did of course feel a little apprehensive that some of Mostert's blood might have attached itself to his clothing, his shoes, his skin, and if it had, that Arden would have spotted it as she surely would spot anything out of the ordinary. She was like that; she was one of life's noticers. Then they'd driven to the crime scene he'd left thirty-five minutes earlier. The murderer became the investigator. The imperfect killer transformed himself into the infallible cop in pursuit of evil. Kramer loved the irony, then and now. He felt no little pride in his achievement.

No-one stopped them at the prison gates. The gunmen in black kevlar helmets and body armour showed little if any interest in the Fiat, Arden keeping strictly to the 12 miles per hour demanded on the notices and painted onto the tarmac as she approached the barrier. She kept her lights dipped. The boom went up, the nasty muzzles of those sub-machineguns or whatever they were and the guards who toted them turned away as if at a signal, and Kramer caught a glimpse of one surreptitiously lighting a cigarette in his cupped and gloved hands. They said not a word to driver or passenger. No-one waved. There were no salutes. The Fiat rolled sedately out of Belmarsh.

Arden gripped the wheel tightly, glanced in the rearview mirror, put her foot down hard, changed down and the little car leaped forward with a throaty growl. The acceleration was enough to press Kramer back into his seat.

'Happy now, Kramer?'

'Meaning?'

'Got what you wanted? You looked as if you did. You lapped it up, didn't you, every gory moment?'

Kramer didn't answer.

The Fiat was still gaining speed as Arden slammed the gears into fourth.

'I get it, Kramer, I really do. You wanted Exeter on one of his beloved guillotines, and you murdered Chelsea Mostert to put him there. Brilliant. Fucking masterful. If I wasn't driving, and if we weren't in such a rush, and if our progress wasn't being watched, I'd stop just to applaud. Really I would. Fiendishly clever if I may say so, with the emphasis on fiendish.

And I'm not going to apologise for spoiling your little party by throwing up.'

She didn't look at him. She concentrated on driving, on watching the deserted road ahead, her mirrors. He didn't turn his head to look at her, to check her expression.

The Mall, Constitution Hill, Knightsbridge.

'You'll be wanting an explanation but you're going to have to wait. In the meantime, you can keep yourself occupied by reading the contents of the file on the back seat. It'll help bring you up to speed. One thing I will tell you for starters: The Met has washed its hands of you. You're fair game.'

Kramer did not react. 'Mind if I smoke?'

'I certainly do.'

Her cell buzzed.

'Harkness here. No sign of David Mostert leaving the UK on any flight in the last 36 hours, and no booking in his name for any outward flights over the next week. Same for ferries to the Continent and Ireland. He's still here.'

'I was afraid you'd say that.'

Piccadilly, left into Park Lane, left into Cumberland Gate, then Lancaster Terrace and the A40.

Kramer reached back and grabbed the file.

Further to your request for early retirement, I can now confirm that this has been granted with effect from Friday, April 15, 2022. In line with the rules governing Metropolitan Police Service pensions as negotiated with the England Police Federation, your payments will commence immediately, paid in monthly and in arrears, based on a scale comprising your seniority and years of service as well as the additional voluntary contributions you contributed to your personal pension....

Kramer had made no such request, of course. He looked up, stared through the windscreen.

'Finish reading, then we'll talk.'

'Where are we going?'

Left into Gloucester terrace, signs for Oxford via the A40.

'Don't worry, Kramer. I'm not going to draw my sidearm and shoot you

190

while escaping - though you deserve it and much as I am tempted. And you're not heading for the police cells, either. You're too much of an embarrassment. You're a dirty cop and beyond the pale. '

He looked down at the file and read the second memo, shorter than the first, signed by a senior officer named Porter and dated Monday, April 18, the day of Mostert's killing.

On behalf of His Majesty's Metropolitan Police Service, I would like to thank you and congratulate you for your distinguished and meritorious service as a detective in the capital. You have achieved much in your many years with us. I wish you every success in your early retirement from active police work._Your *colleagues have asked me to pass on their best wishes.*

'Bloody hell. What is this?'

'A clean bill of health you don't deserve. All in good time. First I have a question.'

Kramer said nothing. He saw they were heading north for the M25 and Birmingham.

'What were you doing in Zimbabwe all those years ago?'

'Police exchange program. For junior officers.'

'I see.' Arden said it in such a way that she might believe it, but then again she might not. 'Why were you making .45 ammunition - illegally?'

'How do you know that?'

'It's on your personal file - or was. It was a copy of the magistrates' caution you received in Harare.'

'I made the cartridges for a farmer who was a friend of mine. He owned, perfectly legally, a Thompson submachine gun, obsolete and almost an antique. I did it as a favour and got caught. A copper's nark. I think they suspected I was single-handedly plotting a coup against Mugabe. No point in owning a wee weapon like that and not being able to fire it once in a while, wouldn't you say?'

'I wouldn't know, to be honest. The point is that someone disliked you enough to attach it to your file and it worked; I mean that's what persuaded me you shot Mostert with a modified replica. You had the skills to do it, you see.'

'Anything else you want to ask?'

'Not for the moment.'

Beaconsfield Services ahead at Junction 10 of the M40 and Arden turned off the motorway.

They stopped; Kramer had his first smoke in ages, relieved himself. He still ached all over, but coffee and the distant relative of a cheese and pickle sandwich helped. He watched Arden top up the Fiat's fuel tank.

'If you're using your card, they'll be able to track you.'

'Makes no difference. They're doing that anyway.'

It was almost dawn, a grey affair, and to use Kramer's word, Baltic. There were banks of fog rolling in, clearing, then rolling in again. Arden had to reduce speed each time it happened. A military checkpoint loomed abruptly out of the murk - a wall of sandbags, razor wire, 44-gallon drums painted white and red, but there was no sign of life, and no lights. The boom was up. It seemed deserted. They drove on past.

'Well, yes there is something else. Something I'd like to know. Personally.'

Kramer glanced at her.

'What went through your mind when you killed her? What did you feel, Kramer? Did you feel anything? No sorrow, regret, mercy, pity, compassion? None of that? Nothing? Jesus. How's it possible? Tell me. I'd like to know how it feels.'

Kramer didn't respond, not because he didn't like the question, but because he took it seriously. It required some thought. The fact was that he was too wrapped up in the timing, in the seconds and minutes he had to complete his task, the moments he stood there in the alcove. It was not a time for reflection. Anything could have happened. Some kid on a bicycle, the milkman making his delivery (they still did deliver pints in south London, despite everything). That's what preoccupied him: the unexpected, something not in his script. Technical issues of the mission were what mattered. He'd tapped on the glass pane of the front door as planned, and she'd come immediately and opened up. So far so good. Kramer took her arm, pulled her out so they stood so close together in the alcove they touched. He noticed she was shivering. His own heart was beating fast, so much so he thought she would sense it. He forced her down, then, using his thumb to dig into a nerve in her neck, painful but effective. 'What?' She had said just that one word - in surprise, in pain, in protest. He spoke to her in an urgent, commanding tone. 'Not a sound. Be still.' Or words of that sort - he couldn't remember exactly. And she had obeyed, looking about her as if expecting to be found out by Exeter and his cronies arriving on the scene. Kramer drew the pistol. The rest of it was over so very quickly, and Kramer didn't hesitate or pause to examine his handiwork; he walked away, his stride brisk, heading for his bike, jumping on it, pedalling away, telling himself to keep it steady, not to rush it, to seem normal, just another commuting cyclist trying to get to work on time.

Arden shook her head. Kramer could tell she was furious. 'You don't want to say. That's okay. If you were ashamed I'd say there might be some hope for you as a human being. But I do want to say something now. I want to tell you that I always thought that you, more than anyone else I'd ever known, lived up to your character, to your sense of who you were. But what I didn't realise in the year I've known you - until this week - was what a vicious, sadistic bastard you really are, Kramer. How could you kill a defenceless woman like that? How? How does one human do that to another? Especially someone like Chelsea Mostert - a victim twice over.'

They passed Beaconsfield Services at junction 10 of the M40.

Kramer laughed, though it came out like a pent-up explosion of air deep inside him; there was no humour in it at all. It sounded like a bark. 'Defenceless? Chelsea Mostert?'

Arden spoke through gritted teeth. 'Read the rest of it, will you - in the bloody file.'

*

The motorway traffic was gradually increasing and it had started to rain hard, visibility dropping to little more than thirty metres. Kramer paid no attention to what was happening outside the Fiat hatchback; he was engrossed in the papers on his lap. He gathered, or inferred, several disjointed facts, if that's what they were, before throwing the file back on the rear seat. First, the men who'd given him a beating in Belmarsh were remnants of Malaparte's Party faction, as were the pair of interrogators. Second, that Kramer too had been destined for a special security court and directly on to the embrace of the hungry guillotine, immediately after Exeter. A copy of the court order, classified secret, was in the file. Second, the bitter in-fighting within Party ranks had resulted in a purge of the Exeter-Mostert-Malaparte line-up, with dozens of arrests, just in time to save Kramer's neck, apparently. Third, Arden had taken Kramer's job, moving up in rank.

'A night of the long knives?'

'Uh-huh.'

'Why did they give up Exeter?'

'Party bosses felt he was compromised, and if they protected him or exonerated him, it would look bad. They do worry about public opinion, you know, and especially the views of the Party rank-and-file. Once Exeter had been arrested and charged, they felt they had to go through with it. So he took the fall, right or wrong. Wrong in this instance.'

'And why was I rescued from the Machine? I would have thought it would have been easier to have me share Exeter's fate.'

'Malaparte certainly thought so. He was blamed for Exeter's arrest - after all, he did order us to go ahead and charge him. But what if it got out that the Met had killed one of its own? Or that its legendary detective was in fact the murderer of a Party leader and government minister, an assassin, and had framed Exeter by planting false evidence? That would have ripped the Party apart and broken whatever's left of the Met's lousy reputation. So they reached a compromise and after last night's purge, closing ranks as they always do when under threat. Exeter was the sacrifice, you might say, and they wanted it to end there.'

'They? Who is 'they'?'

'The people on the fifth floor. The folk who gave me my orders. They like Earl Grey and chocolate biscuits, too, incidentally. You'd love it.'

'And now?'

'I'm authorised to offer you a deal, Kramer.'

'I thought it must something of the kind.'

18

Arden wanted breakfast and she refused to say another word until she'd eaten. She chose the services stop at junction 39 of the M6 - at Burton-in-Kendall. The rain had stopped, the clouds had cleared away, revealing a northern sky of delicate blue, but the instant Kramer left the warmth of the Fiat and managed to stand somewhat shakily on his bruised legs, the wind sliced through his thin clothing and he regretted getting out. He fumbled with his jacket buttons, put up his collar, then buried his hands in his pockets. He couldn't help his teeth chattering and he almost ran - would have run if he still wasn't in pain - to the restaurant, staggering through the door and waiting just inside for Arden to catch up.

She strode right on past him, flinging words over her shoulder. 'It's on expenses, Kramer. Have whatever you want. I'm breaking my own rules and having a full English.'

'What's this about a deal?'

'We'll eat first.'

Kramer sat down opposite Arden, studied the greasy menu, or pretended to and when he spoke, he did so without looking at her. 'You've done pretty well out of all this, haven't you?'

'I suppose I have.' She didn't look at him.

'You've got my job, improved your career prospects and come out of it with your reputation enhanced.'

'It's a little premature - we've a way to go yet."

Kramer shrugged. 'Joined the Party, did you?'

'You noticed, then.'

Her fingers touched the small gold rose in her lapel.

'What does Beth think about it? I mean, living with a card-carrying copper?'

'It's got nothing to do with Beth - or with you for that matter.'

'You were always practical, and collaboration has paid off in your case.'

Arden ignored that last remark. She ploughed through two fried eggs, fried bread, grilled tomato, two rashers of bacon and a mug of strong and sugared Ceylon tea. While this was going on, Kramer took a look round while appearing not do so. He got up and went over to the cigarette machine, gave it a good kick to get his change, then spent a couple of minutes in the men's, and stood at the big restaurant window and stared out at the motorway and drifting rain. He drank bad coffee and ate a slice of buttered toast during these peregrinations and then went out and leaned against the wall, shivering in the doorway, struggling to light up a Lucky Strike. He took three deep inhalations of his beloved nicotine and flicked the cigarette into a puddle.

There were only a dozen other people in the place, and half of them he had marked down as their minders. A man in a cheap anorak and his female companion in glasses and with pigtail and wearing grey jogging pants, apparently very much involved in each other, were the first pair. Kramer noted that although they were leaning forward on their elbows over their coffees, heads close and whispering, they weren't actually looking at each other. The woman was watching the reflections of other people in the window, and the man was watching the door - and Kramer. Neither was playing with a smartphone - a sure giveaway. Kramer thought they were probably 22 or 23 and probably junior Special Branch detectives. Then there was the middle aged, bald man in a leather jacket, check shirt, blue jeans and black work boots reading a red top and sitting by himself, perfectly still, his broad, muscular back turned to Arden. Kramer had him down as the team leader. He didn't turn the sports pages of his paper once, but then again he could have been a slow reader. Then two men in their thirties or early forties - one with a blond moustache and the other with a black beard - sat opposite one another, not speaking and both in dark suits, drinking the coffee or tea, or pretending to do so. They seemed too much on edge to be playing the role of watchers. Maybe they weren't, but they had a certain stiff, military aspect to them. A different agency? The Security Service? Last was a well preserved woman in her fifties sitting on her own who toyed with her grey hair and argued with someone on her cell, but to Kramer it seemed far too exaggerated and stagey to be genuine.

Kramer come back in and sat down again. He rubbed his chin with his right hand, felt the return of stubble and found it reassuring for some reason.

'Big team you've got today.' His tone was conversational, almost friendly.

Arden had wiped her plate clean of egg and tomato sauce, using the remains of her toast. She looked up.

'Yeah?'

'Same bunch all along or do you ring the changes?'

'This is the last of three.'

'They weren't behind us.'

'They weren't, no.'

So the teams were slipped in ahead of them, Kramer decided, using the service stations, allowing them to change their cars and clothing. Neatly performed if needlessly complicated and costly, requiring considerable coordination.

'What for? Why bother?'

'They're waiting for you to make up your mind.'

'You haven't told me about the deal.'

'It's simple, Kramer, okay? We let you slip away over the border. You take the job that's been lined up for you. You keep your mouth shut at all times and in all circumstances, and you don't even *think* about coming back. All of this - it never happened.'

'And what do I get out of it?'

'Your life. And a livelihood. More than you fucking deserve.'

'So if I say no, these nice friends of yours will take me off into the border country and I'll be found decomposed in a ditch or on some remote track several weeks from now, having fed the crows and foxes my eyeballs and other extremities.'

'That's about it. They'll take me, too. I'll share your fate, whatever it is.'

'You leave me no choice.'

'Unless you're feeling especially suicidal.'

Kramer nodded, looked down at his hands resting on the table.

'You accept our terms?'

'I have to.'

'I'm so glad.' She didn't sound it.

Something was very wrong, though. Kramer saw it in her eyes. Arden had tensed. She stared past him, and Kramer saw, almost in slow motion, her right arm move, jerking back, the elbow bend, crooked, the hand dropping down and reaching for the pistol. She shouted at him. He didn't recognise the words or understand the sense of them, but he turned to see whatever it was, just as she stood up, raised the Walther, both her arms locked, rigid, looking along the barrel, not aiming, both eyes open in the classic combat shooter's pose. Whatever it was, the target was moving, it was male, it was dressed in dark clothing and had almost reached their table.

Arden fired first. The crash of the explosion deafened Kramer because the weapon was only inches away. He had dived off his chair when she fired again.

Something struck him on the head just before he hit the vinyl and started to roll. It was like an explosion in his brain and he had only one thought: I'm hit and I'm going to die. It's my turn now.

David Mostert, big as a charging buffalo, roared at Kramer, a bellow of rage, a black revolver in his fist, one of those old .45 service pistols, a bloody cannon. He fired as Kramer squirmed away, kicking with his legs to find cover, such as it was, under the table. Arden fired again. And again. She fired continuously. Mostert went down as if he'd lost his balance, thrown back and skidding, taking much furniture and crockery with him.

Arden had emptied her weapon into the target.

So this is what it was like. Dying. Kramer couldn't see straight and in a moment he couldn't see at all. Everything faded, out of focus, became a kind of greenish-grey cloud.

The only sound was tomato sauce gloop-glooping steadily out of its bottle and dripping to the floor. The 'minders' seemed to have melted away before the first shot.

Arden stood over Mostert, pale and shaken, reloading her semi-auto with trembling fingers.

Kramer found to his surprise he was still alive. Despite excruciating pain, his eyesight was clearing and he managed to scramble up onto his knees, holding onto a bench. There was no blood; he wasn't even wounded. He'd hit his head was all.

'Poor bastard,' he heard her say. 'Come on. We've got to get out of here.'

Kramer gazed at her, transfixed by her coolness.

She grabbed her coat and glided towards the door. 'Move it, Kramer, for fuck's sake. We don't want to be here when the police arrive, do we?'

*

Arden decided she didn't hate Kramer; she wasn't even really that angry with him. It should have been him on that floor, though, not Mostert. She glanced over at him, slumped in the seat next to her, head against the door, asleep and, intermittently, issuing forth a loud, rasping snore. His mouth was half open and his eyes moved under their lids. So did his lips, sometimes a little smile formed, at other moments almost a snarl. He was still a mystery, only more so now. If she was irritated, she knew it was with herself for having agreed to this assignment. Kramer was right; she had benefited - from his murder of Chelsea Mostert, from the execution of an innocent man - innocent in the sense that Exeter, whatever other crimes he might have committed, had not been guilty as charged. She'd gone along with it because the rewards were obvious, and in the event of her refusing, the costs might include a lot more than loss of career and salary: it could have been as bad as a descent into the territory of the politically suspect and the status of a non-person, a hostile alien (God alone knew how many of them there were - thousands, tens of thousands, excluding foreigners), and that - Arden knew perfectly well - was a bottomless pit almost impossible to claw ones way out of once tossed into it by the power of the state. She had much to lose and much to gain and she'd done the sensible thing, but then Arden knew she had always been sensible, had always been willing to 'go along' with authority since she was a kid at school, whether that authority was parental, religious, educational, political or professional. She didn't have to believe in any of it and never had. It was just so much easier, tidier and above all, so much safer to please. Millions would agree with her - no doubt the majority. Most people just got along as best they could, she told herself, keeping their heads down, minding their own business and putting one foot in front of the other and praying, or at least hoping, that they'd never be faced with such a decision, that they could pass through life unnoticed, keep themselves and their families intact, deal with the overdraft and utility bills and ignore what everyone knew was going on. Of course; it was only human nature. Yes, okay, she was a conformist, one of the Little People - so what? Who cared? It was the only intelligent route to take. She didn't care what others thought. Beth didn't mind, in fact she seemed to approve. Beth saw it as a sign of Arden's mental health, the strength of her 'normal' personality holding it together in the face of adversity. She'd said as much. Now she'd killed for it. That was one hell of a price to pay. But what did that make Kramer? A psychopath? Crazy? Was there such a thing? Beth said there were mental difficulties, mental illnesses and disorders, psychological flaws, but no-one was truly, absolutely crazy. No such thing, she'd said. So Kramer was flawed. Deeply fucking flawed at that - but she couldn't bring herself to hate him any more than she could begin to understand him.

She still wanted to know why. Not the reason that others might come up with, but through Kramer's eyes. How he saw it, supposing he had some idea of what he'd done and why. Maybe he didn't. Maybe it was blind impulse. Rage. Fear.

'Wake up, we're nearly there.'

No response.

Arden nudged him with her left elbow and she wasn't gentle.

'Hey, Kramer you arsehole. Wake up.'

He jerked, emitting a loud snore. Her elbow had connected with his injured ribs.

'Where's here?' He asked the question without opening his eyes.

'We're on the A64. Scenic route. Five minutes more and we'll be at Carter's Bar. I'm told that at an elevation of more than 400 metres you'll have a fine view of your homeland.'

Kramer grunted, folded his arms.

'Thoughtful of you, Detective Inspector Arden.'

'I wasn't thinking of you, Kramer. It's the last major crossing that has yet to hardened, so there are no checks on vehicles or people and that's why we chose it. But this is going to be a hard border, all ninety-six miles of it, now that Scotland's in the European single market. Carter's Bar will be sorted within the next week, so the papers say. '

'I read the lies in the papers, too.' He pushed himself upright in the passenger seat and rubbed his face.

'Tell me,' he said. 'Was Mostert put up to it? Was it planned?'

'I don't know. Really I don't. Maybe it was Malaparte's last throw off the dice. He wanted you dead - who better than the vengeful brother, suitably primed, to pull the trigger?'

200

'And our minders?'

'They were there to make sure I deliver you. I'm in their sights too, you know. They still suspect that I might have been in this with you from the start. If I'd given any sign of not following orders to the letter, I would have shared your fate.'

'Maybe that was the idea all along - to use Mostert to take out the both of us. Did that occur to you? I don't know if you noticed, but our watchers did a great vanishing act precisely at the right moment. It was no accident.'

Arden shrugged.

She slowed, drew in to the side of the road and stopped. There were big stone markers to indicate the border on either side and a blue sign above with 'Welcome to Scotland' and the Gaelic 'Fàilte gu Alba' in white letters.

Beyond were the fields and hills of the Scottish borders.

'You'll need this.' She handed him an envelope. 'It's addressed to you from your contact at Police Scotland, a man named Macrae. He's expecting you. You'll probably have to accept a cut in rank and pay, but knowing you as I do, I'm sure it won't be long before you're made up to detective inspector again.'

'Do they know?'

'About you? About Mostert and Exeter? No, Kramer, not unless they have an informant on the fifth floor of the Met passing them sensitive information. Seems unlikely 'cause all the Scots of senior rank have been purged or transferred, yeah? Police Scotland have had an application from you plus a couple of glowing recommendations and they'll have seen a redacted version of your personal file. That's it. The letter you're holding is an offer of an interview for a vacancy on their investigative staff. They know they're lucky to have you with them, or they think so. You'll get the job, no worries. You see that silver grey Volvo ahead? They're expecting you. They'll probably buy you a nice liquid lunch.'

Without looking at the contents, Kramer folded the envelope in half and jammed it into a jacket pocket.

'May I ask something, Kramer? One last question.' Arden noted that her hands weren't shaking any more, but she could smell the cordite residue on her clothing.

'What?' It was said with great weariness.

'Why? Was it the politics? Was it some kind of political vengeance?'

He shook his head as if shaking her off.

'Nothing like that.'

'You thought you'd committed some heroic act of resistance, was that it?'

'No.'

'No? Then why? You're nothing but a terrorist, Kramer.'

'It was a gift.'

Arden sounded indignant. 'A gift? How do you mean - a gift? Fuck's sake, to whom, to what?'

'A present for someone I knew.'

He couldn't explain, he really couldn't.

'Did this person - this friend, whoever it was - *appreciate* the gift of two lives?'

'I don't know. She's dead. She died before - this.'

Arden digested the remark for a few moments. 'And if this friend - whoever - *had* been alive to receive your present, what do you think she'd have said to you when you told her what you'd done?'

Kramer turned his face to hers, looked into Arden's eyes with his disconcerting stare, so close it was startling. It occurred to Arden that he saw right through her and always had; maybe he wasn't entirely human, maybe some part of him was the Devil in human form, something like that, yeah. It was the look he'd given her as she'd passed him in the hall of the house in Fentiman Road. Wouldn't the Devil - if such a thing existed - always assume some form of human identity? But then he'd probably choose a creature better looking, wouldn't he - someone taller, gregarious, smarter, a charmer, maybe the head of some huge corporate entity, or the chief software designer at Apple or Google. Someone with real clout, smooth manners and a gold American Express card and thousands of workers at his command. Someone very like the recently deceased Ryan Exeter and not some lowly detective with a smashed-up face and peculiar eyes.

Kramer, she realised, was answering her question. '...Mebbe she would have laughed. Mebbe she would have been disgusted. Mebbe she would have cried or congratulated me. I really have no idea. I do wonder myself. She herself never failed to surprise me.'

'Who was she, this friend? Your late wife?'

Kramer offered Arden a crooked half smile that failed to affect the deep facial muscles. 'Now that's a question too far.'

Kramer released the safety belt and opened the door, pulling himself out and up with his hands. Aside from their breaks at service stations, they had been on the motorway for eight hours, and Arden imagined his bruised body must have been stiff with sitting still. He didn't say anything more to her and he didn't raise a hand or give any sign that he recognised that this was the end of their association. He turned away, shaky on his feet, and shambled slowly along the verge, pulling up his collar and pushing his hands back into his pockets because the wind up on the ridge was steady, strong and very cold.

Arden half expected him to turn at some point and look back at her, but he didn't. Bastard. What did he think he'd done? How could he justify it? Arden accepted she wasn't angry so much as frustrated by her failure to penetrate his homicidal weirdness and only furious with herself for taking her forty pieces of silver for letting him get away.

He knew nothing of how she felt. How could he? He didn't care. He might have said 'thank you' to her for having saved his lousy life and she had her reply all prepared, something along the lines of, 'well, that's what partners are for'. Conciliatory to the last. But Kramer kept going, favouring his right leg and limping past an elderly man taking pictures of a group of people stood shivering and smiling next to one of the stone markers carrying the word 'Scotland'. The old man's white hair seemed to have taken flight, hovering above his head in the gale as if trying to escape. Further along the road and on the other side of the frontier, no more than fifty metres away or so, someone emerged from the Volvo, a stranger in black waxed jacket and flat cap with a scarf around his neck, and stood there, waiting, holding the rear door open; maybe it was Commander Macrae himself or possibly his driver. Arden still waited for the shabby figure to turn; she wondered how Kramer would live with the burden of two murders, whether it already bothered him or would ever do so. Yes, of course it offended her sense of professional rectitude that she'd helped a murderer escape justice, but what justice was there, really, when one thought about it? The raise of a paltry twelve hundred extra quid a year that came with her new rank didn't matter one way or the other; at least half of it would be taken by the taxman. Her life with Beth in Camden was what did matter, and she knew she would do absolutely anything to protect it. She'd just killed a man - the wrong man - to keep it safe. As for Kramer, he was on her conscience too and she would have to live with it.

The wind gave the car a mighty shake as if trying to break in.

A terrible thought struck Arden, so ghastly that she moaned through clenched teeth as if in physical pain and leaned forward, forehead on the steering wheel, nails digging into the flesh of her palms. What if Mostert and Exeter hadn't been his first? What if there were more? What if Kramer's extraordinary performance at solving murders was due entirely to his having committed them in the first place, so as to ensure he could 'solve' them? Had she been his stalking horse all along, his dupe for 11 eventful months, his guarantee of professional integrity? Was she that stupid, that naive, that trusting? Jesus. She shuddered at the thought. If she went through the records of his investigations, all the way back, what would she find? That Hatton Garden watchmaker, battered to death in Euston, the wealthy woman designer shot at point blank range as she sat in the driver's seat of her Porsche in Kensington, the postal worker strangled in his Hackney council flat - surely not. Impossible! They had the evidence, the culprits, the convictions - hadn't they? Of course they did. What would Beth have to say if she were there, right at this moment? That Arden was paranoid, that it was all brought on by stress, by the shock of witnessing the execution, by her shooting the unfortunate Mostert? Yes, she was overwrought, upset, fragile. That was all there was to it. It was exhaustion. Of course it was. She was imagining things. And yet -

No, don't think it, she told herself. Don't go there. That way lies madness. Arden straightened up, wiped the tears from her face with the back of one hand and started the car, and as she released the handbrake she looked along the road and saw that Kramer had gone.

Thanks for reading my novel. I hope you enjoyed it. Please do let me know what you thought of it, either on Amazon Kindle, Goodreads or via my website: www.johnfullertonauthor.scot.

All reviews are welcome. You can also subscribe to my free newsletter.

Printed in Great Britain
by Amazon

50418379R00125